"I think a simple design would be best—white on navy blue," Dave suggested.

I agreed. "It would have to be one of our medium-sized pillows, like the cormorant ones. That many words wouldn't fit on our smaller pillows. Make it as simple as you can. If the design works, we could advertise in one of the yachting magazines. We've never done that. But for Christmas this year . . ."

We heard a heavy, repeated knock on the door.

Dave frowned. "I wasn't expecting anyone else today," he added as he went to the door.

Leo, the boy we'd seen with Ike Hamilton yesterday, was breathing hard, as if he'd just stopped running. His shirt and hands were covered with blood. "You're the one Ike said was a good man. You said you'd help me."

"Come in, Leo," said Dave.

Leo backed up when he saw me, then glanced over his shoulder. Was someone chasing him? He looked as though he was ready to run at any moment. What had happened to him?

"This is Angie Curtis, Leo. Remember? She was with me yesterday. You can talk in front of her. How badly are you hurt?"

"It's not me that's hurt." ___ ___ ed with emotion. "It's ___

Books by Lea Wait

TWISTED THREADS

THREADS OF EVIDENCE

THREAD AND GONE

DANGLING BY A THREAD

TIGHTENING THE THREADS

THREAD THE HALLS

THREAD HERRINGS

Published by Kensington Publishing Corporation

Thread on Arrival

Lea Wait

KENSINGTON BOOKS
www.kensingtonbooks.com

KENSINGTON BOOKS are published by

Kensington Publishing Corp.
119 West 40th Street
New York, NY 10018

All Kensington titles, imprints, and distributed lines are available at special quantity discounts for bulk purchases for sales promotion, premiums, fund-raising, educational, or institutional use.

Special book excerpts or customized printings can also be created to fit specific needs. For details, write or phone the office of the Kensington Sales Manager: Attn.: Sales Department. Kensington Publishing Corp., 119 West 40th Street, New York, NY 10018. Phone: 1-800-221-2647.

Kensington and the K logo Reg. U.S. Pat. & TM Off.

First Printing: May 2019

ISBN-13: 978-1-4967-1673-6
ISBN-10: 1-4967-1673-6

ISBN-13: 978-1-4967-1674-3 (ebooks)
ISBN-10: 1-4967-1674-4 (ebook)

10 9 8 7 6 5 4 3 2 1

Printed in the United States of America

To my husband and love, Bob Thomas (1945-2018), my most faithful supporter, who, despite his illness during the last three years of his life, continued to cheer me on and encourage me to write and edit. He made it all possible. And thank you to the doctors, especially Rob Hunold, who were always available to talk when Bob or I had a question or concern, and to everyone at hospice who helped make the hardest days easier.

Chapter One

Ornamental Accomplishments will but indifferently qualify a woman to perform the duties of life, though it is highly proper she should possess them for amusement.
—Hannah More (1745–1833), *The Ladies Pocket Library*, Philadelphia, Pennsylvania, 1792

"How many from Haven Harbor died?"

Patrick held my hand as we joined the crowd of Haven Harbor residents walking toward the waterfront.

The bright sunshine of a late April day would have warmed us, even here on the coast of Maine, if a stiff sea breeze hadn't been blowing from around the Three Sisters, islands that protected our harbor from the full brunt of the ocean.

"One hundred and twenty-three. The first, a twelve-year-old boy who fell from the rigging, and the most recent, Arwin Fraser's father. His ankle caught in a trap rope and pulled him overboard two years ago. Gram wrote to me about it when I was in Arizona." I shivered, despite the heavy sweatshirt I was wearing. Five of my ancestors' names were carved on the large granite memorial near the town wharf.

"But Arwin lobsters," Patrick pointed out. "His father's death didn't discourage him."

"Men in his family have always fished or lobstered. He inherited his father's boat." Those who worked the waters knew the risks. Arwin had probably never considered another profession.

The words Lost At Sea Not Forgotten were carved at the top of the granite memorial above the outline of a three-masted schooner and the list of names and years. The memorial had been raised in 1890, with ample space left to be filled in the future. So far all the names were of Haven Harbor men and boys, but more women fished and lobstered every year. Inevitably, some of their names would be added. The sea was an equal opportunity killer.

Like most Harbor residents, I'd attended the annual reading of the names and Blessing of the Fleet since I was a child, walking down from our house on the Green with Mama and Gram. Walking from the same home two of those men hadn't returned to.

Gram always reminded me that Blessing of the Fleet day was both a time to remember and a time to pray for the safety of those who still tempted nature's power every day by making their living from the sea. I remembered imagining the lives of those who'd been lost, many of them not much older than I was, but also enjoying the Blessing ceremony and knowing that our small community was praying together.

At a Blessing Day one hundred years ago the islands and the harbor and the streets of Haven Harbor would have been the same. But women gathering at the waterfront would have worn ankle-length skirts and their long hair would have been pinned under big hats decorated with the feathers of now-extinct birds. Men would have been somber in their best suits with high collars, or perhaps in their World War I uniforms. They'd be remembering comrades who'd fallen during the war, as well as those lost at sea.

Clothing might have changed over the years, but the parade of mourners hoping their prayers and the Blessing of the Fleet would protect our men from the sea's power was the same. As long as men and women made a living from the waters, mourning and re-membering would continue, and names would con-tinue to be carved on the monument.

No wonder the Greeks and Romans prayed to gods of the sea. Waters were unpredictable.

I shook my head, chasing pictures of the past away, and smiled at Patrick. Because of my ten years in Ari-zona I hadn't attended a Blessing since my senior year in high school. Certainly the reading of the names was one of the more somber yearly occasions in Haven Harbor, but the prayers that followed were joyful, hoping for fair winds and following seas, a good catch, and safe harbors for all those who made their living from cold Maine waters.

"Will Reverend Tom be reading the names and conducting the Blessing?" asked Patrick.

This was Patrick's first spring in Haven Harbor; his first Blessing.

"Local pastors, priests, rabbis, and imams take turns. They'll all be on the wharf today, but it's Reverend Tom's year. He and Gram went down to the town wharf a couple of hours ago to talk with the captains of the boats to be blessed and arrange the parade."

"The parade?"

"The order of the boats to sail by and be blessed," I explained.

"Looks like everyone in town is here."

I nodded. Ed Campbell, head of the Chamber of Commerce, and his wife, Diane, were talking to Reverend Tom, while Gram was chatting with Sandra and Jim Lewis, who lived near me. I'd seen them around town and in church but didn't know them well. I'd admired their yard, though, filled with bright daffodils, late-blooming crocuses, and wide patches of lilies of the valley. Sandra must be a hard worker. She managed to take care of Jim, who was in a wheelchair, and garden too.

Across Main Street, Dave Percy and Sarah Byrne were walking slowly next to Ruth Hopkins. I waved as the crowd parted for Ruth and her walker. Dave and Sarah and Ruth were Mainely Needlepointers, along with Gram and me and Captain Ob and his wife, Anna, who were undoubtedly out on their fishing boat in the harbor now, waiting for the ceremony to begin.

Mary Clough and Cos Curran, who'd graduate from Haven Harbor High in June, were chatting with several of their classmates near Gus Gleason's Book Nook, where Cos has been working part-time this spring. Gus and his wife, Nancy, were talking to Henri and Nicole Thibodeau, owners of the local patisserie. Their hot cross buns had been even more spectacular than usual this year. I wished they made them all year round. Cindy Bouchard, the home health aide who took care of Henri's mother, who had Alzheimer's, was wheeling Madame Thibodeau.

Sergeant Pete Lambert was trying to direct traffic so a few cars could make their way through the crowd now filling the streets leading to the waterfront.

"Let's join Sarah and Dave and Ruth," I suggested, and Patrick and I maneuvered our way through the crowd to where our friends had stopped.

"Haven't seen you in a while," Patrick said to Dave as I hugged Sarah and Ruth.

"Seven weeks to go before school's over. Then I can see people other than teachers and students," Dave agreed. He taught biology at Haven Harbor High. "I don't know who's more ready for summer vacation, the kids or me."

"Good to see you out and about," I said to Ruth.

"Glad to be here," she agreed. "My arthritis is much better in summer, so I'm looking forward to warmer days. But this past winter you and Sarah and Dave were wonderful about making sure I got out of my house, even in snow and ice."

"Everyone needs to breathe fresh air sometimes," I agreed, looking around. "It looks as though everyone in town is here."

I held up my phone and snapped pictures of all the Mainely Needlepointers.

"Don't take pictures of me," said Ruth, trying to duck. "I'm too old. I don't want anyone to see what I look like now."

"We see you, and we love you," Sarah assured her. "But why the pictures, Angie?"

I shrugged. "Some of our website's out-of-state customers have said they're curious about us and our lives here. Someday I may come up with a newsletter, or put some pictures on our website. Or start a Facebook page."

"I suspect they're more interested in how our custom needlepoint will fit into their homes," Sarah answered, making a face as I clicked my phone. It was going to be harder than I'd thought to get relaxed, candid photos of the needlepointers.

"Probably a dozen students reminded me about the Blessing and told me to look for them," said Dave, looking over our heads toward the harbor. "Most will be with their families on working boats in the harbor today, but I was surprised at the number who said they'd be in their own."

"Kids planning to be lobstermen often start with their own skiffs when they're eleven or twelve," said Ruth. "Or they could be having sailboats or kayaks blessed. Used to be just fishermen and lobstermen who came for the Blessing. But every year more people in town get their recreational boats in the water in April and join the ceremony."

We'd found a spot near the wharf where we could hear Reverend Tom and see the growing line of boats. Fewer men lobstered now than when I was a child, so fewer lobster boats were in the line than I remembered, but Ruth was right. Their places had been taken by other, usually smaller, crafts. Most were normally anchored here in the harbor, but a few were moored at or near private piers outside the harbor. No one wanted to miss the Blessing.

"Look!" I pointed to the water. "Male eider ducks with the females!"

Patrick looked and then looked back at me. "So?"

"The males are the ones with the dramatic black and white coloring. Females are brown. We see males this close to land only during mating season, when they're courting."

"What happens after that?"

"The males go back out to sea. The females lay eggs and take care of their nests. When their ducklings are born, the females band together, like an extended family. In the summer you see maybe half a dozen females with forty or fifty ducklings. The group is called a raft of eiders."

"So the male eiders are handsome cads?" said Patrick, nudging me suggestively as he looked out at the ducks. "Like some human males?"

"Maybe. But today it's spring, and both sexes are together, and courting." I loved seeing the ducks together, even if it was for a short time, and then seeing the ducklings that followed.

Patrick was more interested in people than in ducks. He nodded toward a gray-haired man who was bent over and dressed in layers of torn and stained sweatshirts. "I've seen that man walking around town, and I keep forgetting to ask you who he is."

"That's Ike Hamilton," I said quietly. Ike had been around town since I'd been a child. I'd taken his presence for granted.

"I've seen him forage for empty bottles and cans," Patrick added. "See? He has a garbage bag, as usual, in that old grocery cart he pushes."

"That's one of the ways Ike supports himself," Dave put in. "He redeems the bottles. A good number of people in town save their wine, soda, beer, and liquor bottles and cans for him, and he makes rounds to pick them up. Five cents a bottle isn't much to most people, but it adds to Ike's Social Security disability income."

"Do you save bottles for him?" I asked.

Dave nodded. "I leave mine in a corner of my barn. He knows where they are and stops in every week or two to collect them. Saves me the pain of having to take them to the redemption center, and it helps him out."

"How does he get to the redemption center?" I asked out of curiosity. "Does he have a car?"

"Pax Henry, the postmaster, takes him and his bottles there every Saturday at noon, after the post office closes. I'm surprised you didn't know that."

"Guess I just never paid attention," I admitted. "Maybe I should be saving bottles for Ike too."

"It's a good deed," Ruth agreed. "When he stops to pick up my bottles, we chat a little. He always has a story to tell, or a bit of gossip he's collected along with his bottles. I suspect he stops at my house about lunchtime because I always invite him in to have a sandwich with me."

"Who's the boy with him?" Patrick asked. We all turned toward the end of the wharf parking lot, where Ike was standing.

A skinny teenager with long, straggly hair dropped a couple of bottles in Ike's bag. I assumed he'd then move on, but he didn't. He stayed with Ike. I took a couple of pictures of them together.

"I know all the kids in the high school," said Dave. "I've never seen that boy before."

He looked sixteen or seventeen and was wearing grungy jeans and a Windbreaker with a tear on the side. He and Ike talked a little, and then the pair moved on, together, toward the blue barrels Haven Harbor set out to collect recyclable bottles and cans on the wharf.

People moved aside to let the pair look inside the barrels, and the boy reached in, pulled out the empties, and tossed them into the bag Ike held toward him. After he'd emptied the barrel, they moved on through the crowd.

"That's Ike's young friend," said Ruth. "I've known that man for twenty years and never saw anyone helping him like that boy does. Some of us in town keep an eye on Ike, but I couldn't say he ever had any real friends except Jim Lewis."

"I don't know the boy," Sarah agreed. "But I've seen him around town with Ike the past couple of weeks. And you're right, Ruth. Before that, Ike was always alone. But that Ike sure can talk! Once I commented to him about the weather and he talked my ear off for fifteen minutes."

Dave frowned a bit. "That boy should be in school. I wonder where he's from, and how he hooked up with Ike." Dave turned to Ruth. "You know Ike's story. Does he have any relatives?"

She shook her head. "All gone now. He was an only child. He was slow, and for years his mother kept him close to home so he wouldn't be teased by other kids in town. I don't ever remember him having friends his own age, except Jim. They lived close to each other and spent a lot of time together as boys. But Jim's disabled now, of course. Ike's father died maybe ten or twelve years ago, and his mother a year or two later. He's always collected bottles, but until his parents died it was almost a hobby with him. It gave him something to do. Now the bottles are his job. He needs the money. After his folks died, Ike stayed on in the home where he'd always lived, but six winters back a nor'easter tore up an old tree in their yard and it fell through his roof. Ike stayed there a couple of years after that, using an old wood stove, but the house just fell down around him. The Chamber of Commerce convinced the town to condemn it. It wasn't safe for anyone to live in, and I'll admit it was an eyesore. Ed Campbell had just become head of the Chamber then. He thought Ike was an eyesore too. Ed wanted to move Ike to a home up near Augusta, but Ike refused. Instead, he moved into the garage at the back of the lot where his house had been. So far's I know, he's been living there ever since. Doesn't bother anyone. Has a toilet and sink in there his father put in next to his workbench, and a space heater for cold days. Folks at the Y let him shower there when he feels the need."

"Is he on welfare?" I asked.

"Don't know. But I remember talking with his mother, years ago, about his getting Social Security disability payments."

"I'm going to find out who that boy is," said Dave. "He may need help. Angie, come with me. If there are two of us, he may not feel threatened. Ike knows who I am."

I squeezed Patrick's hand as he nodded agreement, then followed Dave as he wove through the crowd. Reverend Tom's voice rose over the attendees, welcoming people to the Blessing of the Fleet and then beginning to read the names on the memorial.

"Davy Thompson, twelve years old, died at sea, May 14, 1697."

Chapter Two

Friendships a name to few confirmed
The offspring of a noble mind
A generous warmth which fills the breast
And better felt than e'er exprest
— Anna Braddock, Evesham Township,
   Pennsylvania, stitched when she was four-
   teen years old. The verse is circled by flow-
   ered vines above the Westtown School
   building, a horse and rider, sheep, ducks,
   other birds, and assorted plants.

"Ike," said Dave, putting a hand on the man's arm.
"Good to see you."

Ike pulled his arm back but nodded. "Good pick-
ings today. Always is at the Blessing."

Reverend Tom's voice continued. "Brothers Ethan
and Aaron Thompson, ages sixteen and eighteen,
died at sea, March 4, 1746."

"Who's your friend?"

Ike turned toward the boy, who was trying to blend
into the crowd. Up close I could see the fear in his eyes
as he looked quickly from Ike to Dave to me. "Leo's my
friend."

"Leo," said Dave, stretching out his hand. "Pleased to meet you. I'm Dave Percy. I teach over at Haven Harbor High."

"I ain't going to school," said Leo, backing up farther and not taking Dave's hand. "I'm old enough not to."

Dave smiled. "Seventeen, then?"

Leo hesitated, and then nodded. Seventeen was the age Maine set for being old enough to drop out of school. Leo looked younger than that, but he was scrawny and nervous. He could be seventeen.

"No school," Leo said, looking from Ike to Dave and back again. "No school."

"I understand," said Dave calmly. "But if you should change your mind, or if you need help for any reason, come and see me. I live in the yellow house on Union Street. Ike knows where it is. Where're you from?"

Leo shook his head, pushed his way back into the crowd, and disappeared.

"Boy's wicked shy," said Ike.

"Is he staying with you, Ike?"

"Helps me with the bottles." Ike put his hand on his lower back. "Back's been bothering me something awful these days. Leo's young. Back doesn't hurt."

"He must be a help then," Dave nodded. "But if the boy needs anything, you let me know."

"He don't need nothing," said Ike. "I look out for him."

"I'm glad, Ike. You're a good man."

"I am," Ike agreed.

Reverend Tom's voice continued. "Abraham Winslow, age twenty-seven, lost at sea, August 31, 1847."

"Shh!" said Ike, listening. "Honor the dead."

Dave nodded as Reverend Tom continued reading, and Ike pushed his shopping cart away from us, through the crowd, in the same direction Leo had fled.

"Why do you think Leo is here? Where did he come from?" I said to Dave quietly, as we headed back to where Patrick and the others were listening to the reading of the names.

"No way to know." Dave shrugged. "He sounded like a Mainer. And if he's helping Ike, he's a good kid. Could've run away from home, or his family might've thrown him out. It happens. He looked afraid. I'd guess, for whatever reason, he doesn't want to be found."

"You offered to help him, though."

Dave half grinned. "Least I could do. The kid's been in trouble of some sort, I'm pretty sure. He probably won't come to see me. But, on the other hand, someday he might. Ike's a kind man, but he's not equipped to help a frightened seventeen-year-old boy."

"And you are?"

Dave hesitated and looked directly into my eyes just before we reached the others. "I've been a frightened seventeen-year-old boy."

Before I could ask him any questions, we got back to where the others were standing.

"You've missed some of the names," Patrick whispered to me. There were tears in his eyes, which were focused on Reverend Tom. "What a special service this is."

I nodded and squeezed his hand. He wasn't the only one moved by the reading of the names. Others near us had bowed their heads, and not far away I saw tears streaming down Cindy Bouchard's face. She spoke both French and English, which was important because Madame Victoria Thibodeau didn't speak English. Cindy wasn't from Haven Harbor, but maybe she had family members who'd been lost at sea. Today's reading of the list was certainly affecting her. Gus Gleason leaned over and said something to her, and she nodded and managed to smile.

When Arwin's father's name was read, the last on the list, I looked over at the lobster and fishing boats idling in the harbor. Arwin was there on his *Little Lady*, the boat that had been his father's; that his dad had fallen from. Today Arwin's wife and infant son, and Rob Trask, his sternman, were with him. Arwin's dad would be proud that his son was carrying on the Fraser family's lobstering tradition.

Reverend Tom then announced the official Blessing of the Fleet. His words rang over the crowd, where attention was now on the living, not the dead. When he'd finished the overall blessing, Tom turned to the harbor and gave the signal for the parade of boats to begin slowly passing the town wharf. As each went by, he and the other religious leaders said special blessings.

I'd heard a few people in town call the Blessing of the Fleet a superstition, but I'd never heard that from anyone who worked the waters. The Blessing was a dearly held tradition. And who had the right to question a custom or belief?

After all the boats had been blessed, Reverend Tom said a short benediction and the crowd dispersed, some heading for Harbor Haunts, the only restaurant in town open in April, and others gathering in homes and businesses to continue the celebration.

"Will you be home tomorrow?" I asked Dave before we started heading in different directions. "I'd like to pick up those cushion covers you finished for Mrs. Rose."

"See you then," he agreed. "I'll be home all day. Papers to grade."

Patrick and I held hands as we headed back to my house. We'd planned a quiet evening, cooking spaghetti and watching a movie. I was looking forward to getting warmed up; the chill breezes were getting stronger.

Mud season was over. Gardens were still empty except for early tulips and late daffodils. Bright yellow forsythia in some yards were the only sign that the long winter was over. Above us, a canopy of bare branches etched dark lines across the gray sky. Maine's slow spring wouldn't turn to summer for a few weeks, but birds were mating, days were longer, and the sounds of spring peepers filled the night air.

Maine's springs were brief. By June, summer would return.

I could hardly wait. I'd come back to Maine last May, thinking it would be a short visit. Now I had friends, family, a house, a business, and even a special man in my life.

I squeezed Patrick's hand for no reason other than I was glad we were together.

He grinned and squeezed back.

Life was good.

And I promised myself to start saving bottles for Ike Hamilton. Not everyone in Haven Harbor was as lucky as Patrick and me.

Chapter Three

Adam and Eve while Innocent
In Paradise were Placed.
But soon the Serpent by his wiles
The happy pair disgraced.
HE's come let every Knee be bent
All hearts new joy resume
Let Nations sing with one Consent
The COMFORTER is come.
  —Rachel Geiger, age twenty-one, Mrs. Leah
    Meguier's School in Harrisburg,
    Pennsylvania, 1806. Rachel was born in
    Mifflin County, Waynetownship,
    Pennsylvania, in 1785. Rachel's sampler is
    unusual because it includes scenes of
    Adam and Eve and the snake, and Mary
    nursing her son Jesus, in addition to
    hearts and flowers and birds.

Later that night, after Patrick had left and I was in
bed, cozily wrapped in my blue flannel nightgown
with my black cat, Trixi, curled up near my feet, I
thought back to what Dave had said.

He'd been a frightened seventeen-year-old boy.

What had Dave's childhood been like? He'd never mentioned his parents, or anyone else in his family. He hadn't been born in Maine, I knew. He'd been in the navy for about ten years and worked on submarines, where he learned to needlepoint, and now was a Mainely Needlepointer. He'd spent time in a VA hospital after he'd hurt his leg in an accident. He'd gotten his degree after he left the service and now taught biology. He organized activities at the high school and had watched out for a fellow veteran he'd met in the VA hospital. He had a poison garden. He was an excellent cook and kept his home neater than I kept mine. He'd been seeing Dr. Karen Mercer on and off for the past few months. I suspected he hoped someday they'd be more than friends.

That was all I knew about the facts of Dave's life.

But he'd been a good friend to me since I'd returned to Haven Harbor. He'd befriended other people too, including Gram and others who stitched for Mainely Needlepoint, the business I ran now that Gram was married to Reverend Tom.

Those facts were more important than where Dave had come from.

I wasn't surprised he'd offered to help Leo.

But I still wondered about his remark. What had happened to him when he'd been Leo's age?

I fell asleep wondering.

Sunday morning meant church. When I lived in Arizona I hadn't been a regular churchgoer, but now that Gram and Reverend Tom were married I tried to make it to our front pew most weeks. I'd planned

a busy day, so I slid in next to Gram for the early service. "Do you and Patrick want to come for dinner
this afternoon?" she whispered.

I shook my head as the organ music changed.
"Can't today. I have Mainely Needlepoint work to do,
and Patrick will be at his gallery all afternoon setting
up a new exhibit. Maybe later in the week."

Gram nodded and opened her hymnal to the first
psalm listed on the front wall of the church.

After church I'll check to see if anyone else has completed
pieces of needlepoint I can pick up and then stop to get
Dave's, I thought, as our voices rose in enthusiastic, if
slightly off-key, praise.

Now that I was part of the reverend's family, I
couldn't escape the after-service coffee hour, either.

I glanced around the room of parishioners sipping coffee or tea and nibbling on scones, brownies,
and cookies provided by the women of the church.
Cindy Bouchard was standing in a corner next to
Madame Thibodeau's chair. "It's kind of you to bring
Madame Thibodeau to the service," I said. Henri
had brought his mother to Maine from Quebec so he
could care for her. But his long hours at the patisserie meant that he and his wife, Nicole, had needed
additional help.

"Part of my job," Cindy answered, handing Madame
a molasses cookie, which she held but didn't eat. "The
patisserie is open Sunday morning, so Henri and
Nicole don't get to church, but Henri insists I bring
his mother. He says she always attended in Quebec,
and even if she doesn't understand the service, it
may bring her peace."

"Do you think it does?" I asked, looking down at
Madame Thibodeau in her wheelchair. Her hair was
combed and she was dressed simply, but nicely, but

her face was blank. The cookie Cindy had given her now rested, uneaten, in her lap.

"I can't always tell. It makes Sunday an easy day for me, though. I get Madame dressed, we attend church and then stay for the coffee hour, and by the time I get her home it's noon. Henri and Nicole are home from the patisserie then, and they take over."

"Is she always in her own world, as she is now?"

"Not always. Sometimes she talks. Rambles, really. Her thoughts are mixed up, and they usually don't have anything to do with what's happening anywhere but in her mind."

"Sad. And that must make it difficult for you, to try to figure out what she's trying to say."

Cindy nodded. "It's part of the job."

"How many hours a week do you work?" I asked, out of curiosity.

"Tuesday through Saturdays I work from four in the morning until two in the afternoon. Then Henri or Nicole come home, and I'm free to leave. Sunday mornings, four until noon. I have Mondays off."

"It sounds like a hard schedule."

"Long hours." She nodded. "But I live in the Thibodeaus' apartment over their garage, so I don't have to pay rent. I'm saving to buy a car. If I had one, I could go back to school and become an RN, like Nancy Gleason. I don't have any friends in town, so I don't mind working. In the afternoons I go for walks or stop at the bookstore. I'm looking forward to the summer. Everyone says more people are here then and there are more things to do."

"So you're a big reader?"

"Maybe not so big. But I like some stories." She smiled a little self-consciously. "Romances, mostly."

Madame Thibodeau started drooling, and Cindy pulled a tissue out of the bag on the back of the wheelchair and dabbed Madame's face. "It's probably time for us to leave. It's a nice enough day, so I can take her home the long way."

Gus Gleason held open the heavy church door so Cindy could wheel Madame Thibodeau out. I didn't see Nancy, his wife, but as I glanced out the door after Cindy I saw a car pulling out of the church parking lot. Maybe Nancy was heading for her shift at the hospital.

One other person in a wheelchair was in the church hall: Jim Lewis.

"Hello. I'm Angie Curtis, Reverend Tom's stepgranddaughter." That was a mouthful, but it did identify me. Jim looked up at me and nodded pleasantly. "I think you and your wife live near me."

"We do, dear," said Sandra Lewis, joining us and handing Jim a cranberry scone. "We live down on Oak Way, about two blocks from the Green and your house." She leaned over. "I used to visit your grandmother there before she got married last year."

"Oak Way. I know where that is," I agreed. "Is yours the large, white colonial with the widow's walk?"

Widow's walks weren't common in Maine, but I loved them.

"Exactly, dear. And you took over Charlotte's Mainely Needlepoint business."

I nodded. "I'm so glad I finally got a chance to meet you both. I've seen you here in church, of course."

"Can't miss us. I think everyone in town knows Jim and his chair. It's a struggle to get him into it and out into the world, but I do what I can."

"Did you enjoy the church service this morning?" I asked Jim.

He smiled but didn't reply.

"Oh, Jim doesn't talk anymore. His MS has been getting worse, and he can just make sounds now. See? I have to tie him into the wheelchair to keep him from falling." She pointed at a strip of fabric I hadn't noticed until then because most of it was concealed by Jim's jacket. His left hand, in his lap, was badly bruised.

"I see you're looking at poor Jim's hand. A few days ago he tried to get out of bed by himself and fell, didn't you, dear? Of course, I had a dreadful time getting him off the floor. He must have bruised his hand when he fell. If I hadn't taken care of my mother for so many years, and learned how to care for invalids, I could never cope with all the problems we have. But he's my world, aren't you, Jim?" She reached down and patted Jim's head, almost as someone would pet a dog.

Jim didn't say anything, but his face showed emotions, and he was clearly listening to all we said, unlike Madame Thibodeau, who might not even have known she was in church.

"I love the daffodils in your yard," I said. "And the lilies of the valley. They look like spring."

"You must come and pick a few to take home," said Sandra Lewis. "Daffodils are my very favorite flower. I'd always dreamed of being able to see them from every room in my house, and finally that dream has come true. We do love living here in Haven Harbor, don't we, Jim?"

Jim was silent, but he did close his eyes for a moment. Did that mean something? Or was he just tired.

"Thank you for the offer," I said. "If I'm near your home, I might take you up on it." People were beginning to leave the room. I glanced at the clock above the refreshments table. "The eleven o'clock service is about to begin, and I have to get home. It was lovely meeting you both."

It was almost eleven-thirty by the time I returned home, changed into my usual jeans and sweatshirt, fed Trixi, and scanned my record of projects and who they'd been assigned to. We were on track to deliver balsam sachets with needlepoint lighthouses and fir trees to six gift shops we stocked for the summer and an assortment of the "Save the Cormorants" ornaments and pillows we'd started making last fall. They'd proved more popular than we'd imagined. A lot of Mainers and visitors to Maine were environmentalists and loved the idea of helping to protect an endangered species. We donated profits from those items to the Maine Audubon Society to help protect great cormorant nesting sites.

Today was warmer than yesterday. The air was still, with no breeze.

I decided to walk to Dave's house. His yellow Cape with green shutters and a white picket fence wouldn't have looked out of place anywhere along the New England coast, although it was smaller than my home and the other large, white nineteenth-century captains' homes surrounding Haven Harbor's Green. Patrick's backyard included a barn, a shed, and his tightly fenced-in poison garden. This time of year he'd be looking forward to working back there.

I dropped the brass lobster-shaped knocker on his front door, and he answered almost immediately.

"Good to see you, Angie," he said, running his

hand through his wavy, graying hair. "I'm ready for a break. Grading multiple choice and fill-in-the-blank test questions isn't hard. But I made the mistake of putting three essay questions on the last test I gave. I have to keep reminding myself that English is the first language of most of my students. You can't tell it by some of their answers."

I laughed and walked in. Dave's house was always immaculate, but today he'd been working in his living room. His couch and coffee table were covered with students' papers.

"Coffee? I could use a cup," he offered.

"Sounds good," I said, following him to his kitchen. "I won't disturb you for long. I just wanted to pick up the needlework you finished."

"It's ready to go," he said, pouring us each large mugs of black coffee, just the way I liked it. "I wrapped them in tissue paper this morning and put them in a bag for you. I would have brought them over myself if I hadn't had so much schoolwork to catch up with."

"Not a problem. It gives me an excuse to get out of the house. I walked over."

"The Blessing yesterday was moving, wasn't it?" Dave added, as we headed back to the living room. "I've been every year since I've lived in Haven Harbor. It never gets old."

I nodded. "It brings the past to life."

"And melds it with the present and future. Arwin Fraser was one of my students when his dad was lost."

"Gram wrote me a long letter about it."

"The whole town mourned," Dave said. "I think it helped Arwin and his family accept what had happened. After his dad's name was carved on the memo-

rial, people put fresh flowers there almost every day for
the rest of the summer. His death at sea was treated as
the town's loss, not just his family's."

"So many of the old families in town have lost men
or boys at sea," I agreed. "It's part of the fabric of the
town."

"After the Blessing, last night I was wondering,"
said Dave. "What would you think about embroidering one of our pillows for the gift shops with the
phrase 'Fair winds and following seas'?"

"That's a great idea! Perhaps with a small outline
of a two or three master beneath it?"

"Good! I'll design one. In the navy we used that
phrase as a kind of blessing. 'May you have fair winds
and following seas.' "

"I've heard it all my life. Of course, it means a safe
journey, with the seas and winds taking you with
them, not fighting against you. But the sentiment
could be true of many parts of life." Fair winds had
brought me home to Haven Harbor, and following
seas had made it clear I was going to stay in the town
where I was born. At least for now.

"I think a simple design would be best—white on
navy blue," Dave suggested.

I agreed. "It would have to be one of our medium-
sized pillows, like the cormorant ones. That many
words wouldn't fit on our smaller pillows."

"True. But I think anyone who'd been in the navy,
or was into boating at all, would like one. And a lot of
summer people decorate their cottages with nautical
themes."

"Make it as simple as you can," I suggested. "If the
design works, we could advertise in one of the yachting magazines. We've never done that. But for Christmas this year . . ."

Someone knocked loudly and repeatedly on Dave's front door.

"I wasn't expecting anyone else today. Just a minute."

Leo, the boy we'd seen with Ike Hamilton yesterday, was in the doorway. He was breathing hard, as if he'd just stopped running, and his shirt and hands were covered with blood. "You're the one Ike said was a good man. You said you'd help me."

"Come in, Leo," said Dave.

Leo backed up when he saw me, then glanced over his shoulder. Was someone chasing him? He looked as though he was ready to run at any moment. What had happened to him?

"This is Angie Curtis, Leo. Remember? She was with me yesterday. You can talk in front of her. How badly are you hurt?"

"It's not me that's hurt," Leo's voice cracked with emotion. "It's Ike. He's dead."

Chapter Four

I would not live life over again
With all its joys. To share its pain, tho
Life's spring and pastimes tempt me,
To wish its cares again are my own
Our pleasures to the world are known
Our silent griefs are all our own.

> —Rachel James (1802–1825), Philadelphia,
> Pennsylvania, 1811. She stitched this
> sampler at the North School, a Quaker
> school. Rachel married William Yardley
> three months before her death.

My first impulse was to get a wet cloth and clean the blood off Leo's hands before it dripped onto Dave's carpet.

Had Ike been hit by a car? If so, why would Leo come here? Why wouldn't an ambulance and police have been involved immediately?

I'd helped solve several murders. I didn't know what had happened to Ike, or to Leo, but the blood said a crime might be involved. If so, the police wouldn't want Leo to have cleaned up.

I don't know if Dave had thought of murder as immediately as I had, but he had glanced at his beige carpet. "Come out into the kitchen, Leo. Let me get you something to drink—some cola? And tell me what happened." He glanced over at me. "Angie, join us. You might be able to help."

I followed the two of them. Dave wasn't a tall man—maybe five foot ten—and he kept in shape. He was a little taller, and definitely sturdier, than Leo. Today the boy wasn't wearing the sweatshirt or jacket he'd had on yesterday, and his slight body was shaking. With cold? Fear? Anger? Where had he walked from?

What had happened to Ike?

Dave stayed amazingly calm as he filled a glass with ice and poured soda for Leo.

Leo took several gulps, then put the glass down and took a deep breath. His bloody fingerprints stayed on the glass. "I don't know what to do. But yesterday you said to come here if I needed help."

"Sit, take a deep breath, and tell us what happened. I'll do what I can."

"I went to the Y." Leo took another gulp of soda and then perched on the edge of one of Dave's kitchen chairs. "There's no shower at Ike's place, and the Y people let us shower there. I wasn't gone long, maybe half an hour. When I got back, Ike was on the floor. His head and face were all cut up, and bottles and blood were everywhere. I looked at him to see if I could help. But he was dead. Dead!" The boy was pale. He looked down at his bloody hands, wiped them on his jeans, and repeated, "Blood everywhere. Broken bottles. And a knife. Someone killed him."

"How did the blood get on you?" I asked.

"I tried to move him. To see if I could feel a pulse. In school we had to take a CPR course. I thought maybe I could help."

So he'd been in school somewhere, at some time.

"Did you touch anything else?"

Leo shook his head. "I don't think so. It all happened so fast. When I knew Ike was dead, I just wanted to get out of there as fast as I could. I didn't know where to go or what to do. I walked a few blocks. Then I thought of coming here. I remembered you'd said your house was yellow."

"Did you call the police?" Dave asked.

He shook his head. "No police. I don't want police. And I don't have a cell."

"We're going to have to call the police, Leo," said Dave.

Leo jumped up and headed for the door. "No police! I don't want police!"

Dave grabbed him by the shoulder and turned him back toward us. Leo looked very young and paralyzed with fright. His dark blue eyes were like the north Atlantic in a winter storm. Dave looked straight at him. "Leo, did you kill Ike? Did you hurt him in any way?"

"No! He was my friend! I told you, I found him when I got back from the Y."

"Understand me. If you didn't hurt Ike, you won't be in trouble. But you have to tell the police exactly what you know. The whole truth, so they can figure out what happened."

Leo nodded slightly, but that was all.

"Angie and I will stay with you as long as we can," Dave continued. "But if you don't tell the police, they'll think you have something to hide."

"They'll think I killed him, right?" Leo glanced at the door, as though checking to see if bolting was still an option.

"Not if you tell them the truth," said Dave.

I hoped Dave was right. But a teenager they didn't know, covered with blood, who'd just come from a murder scene? The police would definitely have a lot of questions, and I wouldn't blame them. But why would Leo have killed Ike? And, if he had, why hadn't he cleaned himself up and gotten out of town? Why ask Dave for help?

Leo looked at the floor and didn't say anything. He probably had something to hide. But did it have to do with Ike?

"Did anyone see you at the Y?" Dave asked.

"The lady at the reception desk. And two men were in the locker room when I was showering."

"Okay. Just take it easy. We know a good local policeman. We'll talk to him before you have to explain anything."

Leo nodded again, but hesitantly.

He could have just taken off when he'd seen what happened to Ike. Instead, he'd come to Dave. He might not trust Dave or me entirely—I suspected there'd been people who'd betrayed him before—but no matter what had happened in the past, today he was a kid, probably an innocent kid, caught in a horrible situation.

He relaxed a little as Dave took charge. "Angie, would you call Pete? Tell him we need him to come here. Now."

Chapter Five

Make an unguarded youth
The object of thy care,
Help me to choose the way of truth
And fly from every snare.
   —Margaret Hall, Delaware, 1823. Verse on
      elaborate sampler stitched with wide
      colorful border of flowers, a large alpha-
      bet, grapes, a weeping willow, and butter-
      flies. Margaret may have been an orphan.

Sergeant Pete Lambert's private number was on my phone, but I went into the living room and called the Haven Harbor Police Department directly.

Pete might or might not be in his office, but I wanted to go through official channels. If Ike had been murdered, the local police would have to call in the state police, who handled Maine homicides outside of Bangor or Portland. I didn't want anyone to think that because Pete was dating my friend Sarah, I was going around regulations.

Luckily, Pete was at work.

"Pete, I'm at Dave Percy's house, and we need your help."

"Trouble, Angie? You sound serious."

"I am. A young man who's been staying with Ike Hamilton came here a few minutes ago. He says he went to the Y to shower and when he got back, Ike was dead." I hesitated. "We haven't asked him details, but it doesn't sound as though Ike died of natural causes."

Pete paused. "Ike's still at that place, that garage, where he lives?"

"Right."

"Why did that kid—what's his name?"

"Leo. I don't know his last name."

"Why'd he go to Dave's house? What has Dave got to do with this?"

"Dave hasn't anything to do with it. He and I saw Ike and Leo down at the Blessing yesterday, and Dave was concerned about the boy. He told Leo he could come here if he ever needed help." I paused and lowered my voice even further. "Pete, the boy's covered with blood."

Pete's voice faded as he covered his phone and spoke to someone in his office. Then he was back. "Angie, do you think this kid—Leo—killed Ike?"

"I don't know. I don't think so. But he's afraid of the police."

Pete sighed. "I asked someone to call an ambulance and to meet the medics over at Ike's to check the situation there. I'm heading to Dave's now. Keep that kid with you."

"Will do."

Dave and Leo were now sitting at the kitchen

table. Dave had refilled Leo's glass of soda, and a plate of brownies had appeared in the center of the table. Neither of them were talking, but the brownies were steadily disappearing.

"Pete's coming here. He also sent someone to check on Ike."

"Check on Ike? You mean, see if he's dead? He's really dead. I told you." Leo's body was tense, and his knuckles were white as he clutched his glass. The wrong word would send him out the door.

"I believe you. But the police have to check everything. If Ike was killed, his place is now a crime scene," I pointed out, trying to remain calm. I didn't know this boy. Neither did Dave. What if he *had* killed Ike and was pulling Dave and me in to help him? Dave seemed to trust Leo, and he'd worked with a lot of teenagers. Leo's story sounded credible. Almost too credible. But I wasn't convinced.

Why would anyone kill Ike Hamilton?

"He was killed. I'm sure."

I nodded. "When Pete—Sergeant Lambert—gets here, he'll ask you questions about what happened. Try to take it easy, even if he asks the same question twice. And tell the absolute truth. That's the most important thing."

"That's what I've been doing!" Leo's words exploded. "You may think this cop is a nice guy, but I don't know him." He looked from Dave to me and back again. "I don't even know you people." He started to get up. "I don't need you. I can take care of myself. I sure don't need any cops!" Despite his bravado, Leo's hands were still shaking, and his eyes were beginning to fill.

Dave put his hand on Leo's shoulder. "You're right. You don't know us. We don't know you either. But we believe you." He glanced at me for confirmation. I nodded slightly. "Ike was your friend, right?"

Leo slumped down and nodded.

"We need to know who hurt him. And that's the job of the police."

A few minutes later, Pete arrived.

I answered the door and spoke quietly. "Leo's in the kitchen with Dave. He's really upset, Pete. Take it easy on him."

Pete nodded. "Who is this kid, anyway?"

"I don't know," I admitted. "He says he's been living with Ike for a few weeks. All I know is he was with Ike down at the Blessing."

Pete shook his head. "I'll talk to him. But if Ike is dead . . ."

I took Pete's arm as he started back for the kitchen. "If Ike's dead, the boy's had a major scare. Don't scare him any more." For the moment, I wanted to give Leo the benefit of the doubt, although I knew Pete's job was to find out what had happened, not be sympathetic.

Pete blinked and hesitated briefly when he saw Leo's shirt and hands. Then he joined Dave and Leo at the kitchen table. I stood in the doorway and listened. Without thinking, I reached up and held the small gold angel on the necklace Mama had given me for luck the day I'd been confirmed.

Leo could use some luck today. Where were his mother or father? If ever a boy needed parents, it was Leo, today.

"Angie Curtis tells me you've been living with Ike

Hamilton," Pete said, getting out his notebook. "That true?"

Leo nodded. "For a couple of weeks. Maybe three."

"And your name?"

Leo hesitated. "Leo Smith."

"Where're you from, Leo?"

"Dexter."

"That's a distance," Pete pointed out. "How'd you get here?"

"Hitched," said Leo, almost defiantly.

Pete nodded. "You know Ike before you got here?"

Leo shook his head. "I started collecting bottles so I could buy something to eat. I ran into Ike doing that too. He said I could stay with him if we collected together, if I helped him." Leo hesitated. "I needed a place to stay. And Ike couldn't carry as many bottles as I could, or bend as well to pick 'em up. He was pretty old and his back hurt him. He said we could be partners."

Pete nodded. "So you stayed with him."

Leo shrugged. "It was a place."

"Why'd you come to Haven Harbor?"

"I wanted to see the ocean. I'd never been to the coast."

"And what happened this morning?"

"It's Sunday. Ike didn't collect on Sunday. He said it was a day to rest. When I woke up he was still sleeping. I ate some cereal we'd bought yesterday and then decided to shower, so I went to the Y."

"You walked there?"

"It's only a few blocks from Ike's place."

"And what did you do there?"

Leo looked at Pete as though these were crazy

questions. "I took a shower. The lady at the desk lets Ike and me get cleaned up there once a week or so. She gave me a towel and soap, and I went to the men's locker room and took a hot shower."

"What was the name of this lady at the desk?"

Leo shrugged. "I don't know. She had gray curly hair and long earrings."

It wouldn't be hard to find out which volunteer was on duty at the Y desk this morning. Pete didn't push the point.

"Anyone else in the locker room?"

"Two guys. One old fellow, maybe in his fifties. He'd been in the pool. Dripped all over the place. The other guy was younger. Maybe thirties?"

"No names?"

Leo shrugged. "I didn't talk to anyone. No one talked to me."

"And then what happened?"

"I walked back to Ike's. The door was open a little. I'd closed it when I left—it's still cold outside. I figured Ike was up and maybe he'd gone out for a walk too. He likes to walk around town, even when he's not collecting."

"And?"

"He was on the floor, near his mattress. He'd been cut, bad, on his face and head and neck. There was blood all around him." Leo started shaking again. "The bottles we'd collected yesterday were all over the floor. Some were broken. And there was a knife."

"What did you do?"

"I went over to him, to see if he was still alive. I was going to do that CPR stuff, or maybe try to stop the bleeding."

"Did you do that?"

Leo shook his head. "He was dead. I was sure he was dead."

"How'd you know?" asked Pete.

"I've seen dead people before," Leo said simply.

Pete looked at him. "Is there anyone you'd like to call? Parents? Brother or sister?"

"No one," said Leo. "I have no one."

Chapter Six

Oh virtue! thou daughter of grace
Come dwell in my bosom for guest.
And banish foul vice from that place
In which thou intendest to rest.
Oh come thou delight of my heart
Deny not thy visit to me.
I'll supplicate GOD on my part
To increase my attention to thee.

    —Julia Ann Croley, "Washington City"
       (Washington, DC), April 14, 1813. Center
       of delicate embroidery by Julia Ann, who
       stitched her words above a church and
       steeple and surrounded her work with a
       floral border. Her work is now owned by
       the DAR Museum in Washington, DC.

I was pouring Dave another mug of black coffee when Pete's cell rang.

"Yeah. That's what I heard. Okay." He paused. "Go ahead and call Ethan. He'll make the arrangements." He ended the call and turned to Leo. "Well, Leo, you were right. Your friend Ike is dead. I need

you to go with me to the police station to answer
some more questions."

"No!" said Leo, starting to get up.

Pete was faster. He grabbed Leo's arm to restrain
him. "The faster we get answers to some of our questions, the better for you."

Leo glanced from me to Dave. His eyes pleaded.

"Okay if Angie and I go along with you, Pete?
Leo's had a rough morning. He'll talk to you"—Dave
glanced at Leo, his expression sending the message
that cooperation was the best strategy now—"but he
needs a friend or two nearby."

Pete hesitated. "How old are you, Leo?"

"Eighteen," said Leo softly.

Yesterday he'd nodded when Dave asked if he was
seventeen. How old was the boy, really?

"Eighteen's an adult. I can question him alone."

"Legally," Dave agreed. "But is it necessary? Is he
being arrested?"

Leo's hands were shaking and his head jerked at
the word *arrested*. He suddenly bent over and held his
stomach.

"Bathroom?" he asked.

Pete let go of him as Dave pointed to a door in the
hallway. Leo disappeared behind it.

I followed him, in case he made a break for the
front door, but he had other problems. I heard retch-
ing sounds from inside the bathroom.

"Right now he's just a person of interest," Pete was
saying to Dave.

"Then there's no reason he has to be questioned
alone."

Pete hesitated and then shrugged. "You and Angie
come along, then. But the boy has to go with me in

the police car. I don't want him to disappear. You can follow us."

"We'll do that," Dave assured Pete.

Leo, looking paler than he had before, came out of the bathroom.

"You go along with Pete," Dave said. "Don't worry. We'll meet you at the station."

As Pete hustled him out the front door, Leo looked back at us. His eyes were big and fearful, like those of a cow being herded to slaughter.

Dave sighed and reached for a jacket hanging on a peg in the hallway. "Guess not all my students' tests will be graded today. Angie, you just walked into this but you've had more experience with the cops here in town than I have. Are you okay coming with me? We can take my car."

"I'm okay," I agreed, picking up the bag holding Dave's needlepoint.

Were Dave and I doing the right thing? We didn't even know Leo. What was going to happen to him? Should Dave and I even be involved?

Fastening my seat belt in Dave's car a minute later, I asked the major question on my mind: "Are you sure he's innocent?"

"I don't know, Angie. But he's a scared kid who came to me for help. That's enough reason to stick with him until the police figure this all out."

I nodded. "All we know is he's Leo Smith and he comes from Dexter. He could be a runaway; his family might be looking for him."

"It's possible," Dave agreed. "I suspect your friend Pete will be checking that out. And he said he was going to call Ethan. That was important, right?"

I nodded. "Ethan Trask's the homicide detective

with the Maine State Police who handles murders in this area of Maine." I'd known Ethan most of my life; we'd both grown up in Haven Harbor. When I was in eighth grade I'd had a real crush on him. He was a high school football star, and usually he'd ignored me. Now he was married and a father, and I was dating Patrick West. We might have history . . . maybe more history than either of us acknowledged . . . but now we were adults. The past was past.

Ethan was a good detective, but I'd seen him all too often in the past year. Historically quiet Haven Harbor had seemed to attract violence recently. "Ethan will call in a crime scene unit to study the place Ike and Leo were living, and the medical examiner's office in Augusta will take care of the autopsy and determine the official cause of death. Pete will work with him, but Ethan's office will be in charge of Ike's death if it was a homicide."

Dave nodded. He was clearly more focused on Leo's situation than on how the case would be handled.

"Unless Pete comes up with Leo's parents, and assuming he isn't arrested, Leo will be homeless again in a few hours," Dave pointed out.

"The police know the local shelters," I assured him. "Isn't there one near here for adolescents?"

"It's usually full to overflowing. And Leo's eighteen. Just on the legal line between being a teenager and an adult." Dave pulled into the parking lot of our local police station. "Not a good place to be from a support services point of view."

"What do you think he meant when he said he'd 'seen dead people' before?" I asked as we headed inside.

"I don't know. But I suspect we'll find out," Dave said, frowning. "For right now, we'll let Pete ask the questions. And—do you know a lawyer, in case he needs one?"

I shook my head. "No. If he needs a lawyer, won't the court appoint one for him?"

"He looks like a good kid. I think he should talk to a lawyer before much more happens. If not today, then soon," said Dave. "I'll pay for one."

"Are you sure?"

"I'm sure," Dave said grimly. "That boy needs all the help he can get, and you and I aren't lawyers."

"I'll bet Reverend Tom knows someone," I suggested. "I'll ask him."

Chapter Seven

O may I seize the transient hour
Improve each moment as it flies
Life's a short summer . . . man a flower
He dies. Alas, how soon he dies.
   —"Wrought" by Clarinda Parker, 13 years
      old, August 31, 1824. Clarinda
      surrounded her words, and a house and
      trees, with elaborate, medieval-styled
      flowers in satin stitch.

Leo was sitting on a bench in the small reception area of the Haven Harbor Police Department. Stacy, the department's clerk, was the only other person in the room. Pete must have decided Leo wouldn't run.

The boy looked relieved when Dave and I walked in. "Remember," Dave told him, "just answer the questions. Don't elaborate. And tell the absolute truth."

Leo looked askance. "Will that policeman believe me?"

"Why shouldn't he?" Dave answered.

Leo looked as though he wanted to say something else, but he just nodded. About a minute later, Pete joined us. "The room is small for four of us, but we'll make do. Angie, I have to ask you and Dave not to say anything when I'm questioning Leo."

"We won't interfere," I assured him.

"And, Leo, I'm going to record our conversation. You don't need to worry about that. It's to save me the trouble of taking notes."

Right, I thought. And so he'd have Leo on record if the boy said anything that would be incriminating. Did Leo understand that? But I'd promised not to say anything.

Pete took us into a room that was, as he'd indicated, small. Four chairs just fit cozily around a table on which he'd put a small recorder. Leo glanced at the mirror on one wall as he sat opposite Pete, his shoulders hunched over. Did he know the mirror was one-way glass? The way he glanced at it occasionally, I suspected he did.

"I already told you all I know," he said as Pete adjusted the recorder. Dave and I sat on opposite sides of the table. The room was already stuffy.

"For the record," said Pete, clicking the "on" button. He looked and sounded more official than I'd ever seen him. He was a friend. In the past he'd let me know a little more than he should have, unofficially, about cases involving people I knew. He'd confided in me when his wife left him, and I'd been happy for him when he'd started seeing Sarah.

Today my friend Pete was on the job. He was Sergeant Lambert.

"Your name is?"

Leo swallowed hard. I hoped his stomach was more settled. "Leo Smith."

"Address?"

"I don't know the address. I've been living with Ike Hamilton, over at his garage."

"For how long?"

"Maybe three weeks."

"And before that?"

"Here and there."

"Where, 'here and there'? Where does your family live?"

"Got no family. Used to, but they're gone now. Lived up to Dexter."

Pete nodded. I felt Dave tightening next to me. His hands were clenched in his lap.

"And you're how old?"

"Eighteen. Told you that already."

"Where did you meet Ike Hamilton?"

"We were both looking for bottles, down at the wharf. He said we should work together, and he'd give me a place to sleep."

"And what did you do for Ike?"

"Like I told you. Helped him collect bottles. Ike's back wasn't good. He'd wheel the cart, and I'd fill it with bottles. Then, Saturdays, we'd take them to the guy at the post office. He'd drive us and the bottles to the redemption center out on Route 1."

"And that's all?" Pete paused. "Did Ike make sexual advances to you? Expect you to do anything other than collect bottles?"

Leo recoiled. "No! Nothing like that. He was just a nice old man who said I could sleep on his floor in my sleeping bag. That's all! We got some food from Ike's friends, and sometimes we went over to the soup kitchen at the Baptist church. Ike showed me where everything was. He had a whole setup."

"Did you and he argue?"

"I didn't kill Ike!" Leo said, leaning over the table toward Pete. "I told you that. Ike was my friend."

Pete didn't react. "Tell me about this morning."

Leo repeated the story he'd told us earlier: He'd woken up before Ike and gone to the Y to shower. When he came back, he'd found Ike's body.

"You said the door was open when you came back."

"It was. I'd left it closed when I went out. Ike had a heater, but it got pretty cold in there, anyway."

"Do you have a key to the garage?"

"No key. Ike didn't have no key either. He said he didn't have anything worth taking."

"Where did he keep the money he got from the bottles?"

"In his pocket, sometimes. Or under his mattress."

Pete looked at his phone. "Ike slept on a mattress on the floor?"

"Right."

"Where did you sleep?"

"Near the heater."

"On the floor?"

"In a sleeping bag."

"And you didn't hurt Ike?"

"I didn't! I keep telling you that! Why would I hurt an old man who was nice to me?"

"You ever hear Ike talking about someone else who might hurt him?"

"He talked a lot. He knew everyone in town, seemed like. Told me all about 'em when we went on his route. He never said anyone was angry with him or nothing. He did say some folks were nicer than others. We didn't stop at every house."

I winced a bit. Mine was one of the houses they skipped; I hadn't saved bottles for Ike.

"His route?"

"He had houses and shops he stopped at. Places people kept their empties for him. Some people gave him sandwiches, too, or other stuff. He liked those places. He always said 'Thanks' and told me I should do that too." Leo smiled a little. "He said being polite was why people saved bottles for him."

"So you don't know of anyone who would want to hurt Ike?"

Leo shook his head. Then he added, "But some folks didn't like him around. He told me that."

"Like?"

"Some people, he called them the Chambers, wanted him to leave his garage. They said he was a nuisance and an embarrassment and tourists wouldn't like seeing him around town."

"Do you know who those people were?"

"No. I never saw 'em. But Ike was always watching for them. He said they came to see him pretty regular, and if they came when I was there I should disappear, or they might want to ship me up to Augusta too."

"Augusta?"

"That's where they wanted Ike to go, he said."

I glanced at Dave. There was a psychiatric hospital in Augusta. Ike might have been a little slow, but he didn't seem crazy. What other facilities were there? Or did those "Chambers" people just want Ike out of Haven Harbor? I'd had a few confrontations with Ed Campbell, head of the local Chamber of Commerce. He might well have thought Haven Harbor would have been better off without Ike. But kill him?

"And you never met these people?"

"Nah. Ike just warned me about 'em. He was wicked worried about 'em. He wanted to stay in his home."

Despite the recorder, Pete had made a few notes. Now he pushed his chair away from the table. "You know Ike Hamilton's dead. The medical examiner will have to rule, but it looks as though he was murdered."

Leo nodded.

"You have blood all over your clothes."

"It's Ike's blood. I got it on me when I bent down to see if I could help him."

"The crime scene folks from Augusta are going to want to take your clothes and test the blood on your hands."

Leo nodded. He didn't seem surprised. "I don't have other clothes," he said.

Pete sighed. "I want you to stay here for a few minutes until the crime scene folks arrive. I'll find you something to wear." Pete stood and looked at Dave and me. "Could you come with me for a few minutes?"

Leo looked startled. "They're leaving?"

"Just for a few minutes," Pete assured him as he gestured for Dave and me to follow him. The three of us stood in the narrow corridor. Pete was direct. "Okay. His story's a little shaky. And I'd feel better if he'd given us the name of someone we could call."

"You think he killed Ike?" asked Dave.

"It's too soon to know anything," said Pete.

We were interrupted by the arrival of two young men. "Sergeant Lambert?" the taller of the two asked Pete.

"That's me," Pete responded.

"Detective Trask said you have a possible suspect to be checked?"

"He's in the conference room." Pete pointed. "You'll need his clothes. I'm going to find him some others."

The men nodded and went into the room where Leo was waiting.

"What are you going to do with him now?" Dave asked.

"He's the only suspect we have, but I don't have enough evidence to arrest him. While Ethan's investigating, we need to find a place for him to stay," Pete said. "Somewhere close by, in case we need to talk with him again. If he isn't guilty, he's at least an important witness. I need to be sure he doesn't take off on us."

Dave glanced at me and then said, "He can stay with me. I have a couple of extra bedrooms, and I can find him clothes that fit."

"That's a generous offer, but I don't think it'll work. You teach. You're not home all the time. I need someone to keep an eye on him," Pete explained.

"I'll take him to school with me," Dave said.

"You think he'll go with you?" Pete asked skeptically.

"I'll tell him that's his only option."

Pete still looked doubtful.

"The boy needs a friend right now, Pete."

"Maybe if he had one, he'd be more forthcoming," Pete agreed. "Okay. I'll buy it. But you're responsible for him. If he runs, I'll hold you accountable."

"Agreed," said Dave.

"Let me get the kid something to wear for now," Pete added. "We keep a few boxes of clothing in the station for emergencies." He headed back into the depth of the building.

"Dave, are you sure?" I asked. "Leo may need a friend, but do you need the responsibility? What if he refuses to go to school with you?"

"I'll tell him he stays with me or the police will come after him. That's the truth," said Dave. "And in the meantime I'll see if he'll tell me anything more about his family. He must have relatives somewhere."

"Sounds as though he's been on his own for a while."

"An eighteen-year-old . . . if he is eighteen . . . can get in a lot of trouble on his own. If he didn't know that before, he knows it now." Dave shook his head and looked off into the distance, as though seeing a different time, a different place.

"He's the only suspect in Ike's murder," I pointed out, bringing Dave back to today.

"Exactly. We can't let him face that alone."

"I'll talk to Reverend Tom about a lawyer," I promised.

Chapter Eight

Indulgence soon takes with a noble mind
Who can be harsh that sees another kind
Mildness in Temper have a force Divine
To make even passion with their nature joined.
      —Hannah Trample, 1752. She bracketed
         these embroidered words with two deer,
         and surrounded them with wild flowers.

Leo, dressed in an old flannel shirt and a loose pair
of jeans that only the belt held on his skinny hips,
didn't say anything on our way back to Dave's little
yellow Cape, his front yard surrounded by a white
picket fence and a gated metal fence protecting the
poison garden in his backyard.

Two areas of his life—his personal and his work—
neatly separated and contained. Low stone walls
weren't unusual in Haven Harbor; one separated my
house from my neighbor's. But Dave was the only
one in town who had a picket fence. Maybe he'd
been overly influenced by Tom Sawyer, or perhaps
he remembered a picture from a book he'd had as a
child and was re-creating a safe and cozy place.

Today I hoped it would be safe and cozy for both him and his guest. Leo hadn't even said "Thanks" when Pete had told him he could leave; that Dave had volunteered to host him, but he needed to stay close.

How would I have felt if I'd been homeless at eighteen and found the body of someone who'd befriended me?

Mama had disappeared when I was ten, but I'd never doubted Gram would be there for me, waiting to welcome me home from school with milk and cookies and understanding when I needed to talk.

When I was eighteen I left Haven Harbor, determined to get far away from the town I both loved and hated. I ended up in Arizona and, still searching for my own future, got a job working for a private investigator. From him I learned to shoot a gun; to "follow and photo," usually in divorce cases; and to keep the books for his two-person business. Not a bad set of skills.

What skills would Leo need? Where would his life lead him?

Leaving Dave and Leo at the yellow house, I headed for the rectory. Reverend Tom might be there, and I could ask him about a lawyer. Or maybe that was an excuse. Maybe after spending time with Leo, I needed the reassurance that, even though I was almost twenty-eight, Gram was still there for me.

Both of their cars were in the driveway.

Gram answered the door. "Angie! I'm glad you stopped in. I've made a pot of chowder for supper. It's much too much for Tom and me."

I gave her a hug and realized I was hungry. "That sounds wonderful." I sniffed the lobster broth, haddock, bacon and onions. And bread. "And smells even better than that!" I hung my jacket in the hall. "But I didn't drop in to eat."

"That doesn't mean you can't," Gram pronounced. "Come on into the kitchen and join me. Bread is about ready to come out of the oven."

"I don't know how you do it. All the church work you're doing, and the house, and you still have time to make chowder and bake bread," I said appreciatively as Gram removed two loaves of wheat bread from the oven.

"She's a miracle worker," said Reverend Tom, joining us in the kitchen and putting his arms around Gram. "Loaves and fishes, right here."

Gram giggled a bit. She'd seemed younger than her sixty-plus years since she'd married Tom last summer. He was ten years younger than she was, and maybe his enthusiasm and love made the difference.

"Speaking of loaves and fishes and such, have you decided what you want for your birthday dinner?" Gram asked, filling her brass kettle with water for tea and joining me at the kitchen table.

"I haven't even thought about it," I admitted. "You don't have to make a special dinner for me. I'm going to be twenty-eight, not ten." I'd hoped Patrick would take me out for dinner that night, but he hadn't mentioned it, although he knew my birthday was at the end of the week. I'd seen a note on his appointment calendar.

"You can invite Patrick," said Gram, almost reading my mind, as she often did. "Maybe lobster bisque? That's one of your favorites."

I smiled. "And a daffodil cake. You always made one for my birthday. I missed it in Arizona."

"One daffodil cake, I promise," she agreed. "I

haven't made one of those in years. I always made one for your mother's birthday too. It was her favorite."

We were both silent a few seconds. Mama was gone, but sometimes it felt as though she hadn't gone far. She was still in Gram's and my heart and mind.

"So what brings you to visit us today?" asked Tom. "It doesn't happen to be anything about Ike Hamilton, does it?"

"You've heard?"

"Ministers are always among the first to hear what's going on in town." He nodded. "Sandra Lewis lives down the street from that garage he's been living in. She saw police cars and an ambulance there this morning and called me. And I know you, Angie. I don't know your connection to Ike, but I suspect you have one."

I nodded. "It's funny, isn't it? I've been home almost a year and I seem to have gotten involved with a murder just about every month. I never remember Haven Harbor being this violent."

"It isn't, usually," said Tom dryly. "So, tell us what happened today. Sandra's a great gossip, but she's stuck at home most of the time taking care of Jim."

"It's a pity he's been so ill so many years," put in Gram. "If it isn't one problem, it's another with him."

"If it were up to Sandra, she would have been out questioning the police herself, I'm sure," said Tom. "But as it was, she called to find out if I knew anything. Of course, officially she called to find out if there was anything she could do for Ike's family."

"I didn't think he had any family left," I said, sniffing the bread. It was too warm to slice, but I wished it would cool quickly. In the meantime Gram poured us each a mug of tea and added a plate of molasses oatmeal cookies to the center of the table. I didn't hesitate to indulge.

"He doesn't have family. Sandra Lewis knows that as well as anyone in town. She was just hoping to hear gossip. I thanked her for letting me know about Ike and got her off the phone. Then I called Pete, and he filled me in." Tom reached for his second cookie. "He also mentioned you were involved in some way. I didn't quite understand, but I had a feeling I'd find out."

"Angie, you need to take care of yourself, and the Mainely Needlepoint business, and maybe your relationship with Patrick, if you want that to last," Gram advised. "I don't know what happened today, but you may be getting in over your head again."

"Whoa!" I said. "Both of you relax. It's very simple. Yesterday at the Blessing of the Fleet, Dave and I saw Ike Hamilton with a teenage boy. Dave was concerned about the boy—he didn't recognize him as one of the Haven Harbor kids. So he introduced himself and told the boy he was a teacher and he could come to him if he ever needed help. The boy's name is Leo Smith. He comes from Dexter, and he was living with Ike."

"That's concerning," said Tom. "Ike's lifestyle wasn't exactly mainstream, and I've never known him to host a guest or have a roommate. On the other hand, I've never heard a bad word about him, even from those who didn't appreciate his eccentricities. He's a good man—or he was. I'm guessing he's dead?"

I nodded. "Leo went to the Y to shower this morning, and when he got back to the garage he found Ike's body. He was scared, and he thought of Dave." I turned to Gram. "I was at Dave's house, picking up some finished needlepoint, when Leo got there. We called the police, and Pete took Leo back to the police station to question him."

"Where's the boy now?" asked Tom.

"With Dave. Dave's volunteered to give him a place to stay, at least until the police figure out who killed Ike."

"Is that safe? I mean, for Dave?" Gram asked. "Is he sure this teenager didn't kill Ike?"

"He's sure. And I agree. Leo looked scared to death this morning. He's sort of a lost soul. I think it's great that Dave's offering him a place to stay. And Tom"—I turned to him—"Leo should have a lawyer. He's being asked a lot of questions. I don't think he's guilty of anything, but he needs someone on his side who knows the law. I thought you might suggest someone."

"I assume the boy has no money."

"No. But Dave said he'd help out. He doesn't want Leo to depend on a court-appointed attorney. Maybe you know someone with a special interest in young people? If Leo didn't kill Ike, it shouldn't be a complicated situation."

Reverend Tom nodded. "I agree the boy should have a lawyer. Charlotte, what about that young woman who came to services for the first time last week? Willow Sinclair. Didn't she say she was a lawyer?"

"She did. She seemed bright, and caring. But she's just passed the bar. If Leo's case gets serious, wouldn't he need someone with more experience in criminal law than an attorney that young?"

"For now, maybe she'd be willing just to talk with him," I suggested. "If she's young, maybe he'd relate to her. And as long as he isn't charged with anything, he shouldn't need anyone with criminal law experience, should he?"

"You may be right, Angie. Tell you what. Willow Sinclair wrote her telephone number and e-mail address on the visitor card in her pew and dropped it in the collection basket. I don't think she has a local address yet, but I'll try to reach her and see if she'd be interested in helping this boy. Leo Smith, you said his name was?"

"Right."

"What about his family?"

"He said he didn't have a family."

Tom frowned. "A teenager without a family? Unfortunate. Although some families kick kids out, or they age out of the foster care system. I've got a couple of friends in social services. I'll see what I can find out. If he's a runaway, maybe we can get his family back in the picture. Sounds like he needs all the help we can get him."

"Thanks, Tom." I finished my tea and stood. "Gram, your chowder is one of my favorites. But I need to get home and check messages."

"Let me give you some to take with you, then," said Gram. "We've got more than enough."

Gram's cat, Juno (the queen of her household), stood up with her paws on Gram's lap. "Sorry, Juno. This fish is for people, not cats."

"Then none for Trixi, either?" I asked.

"What happens at your house stays at your house," said Gram. "But I put cream and butter in the chowder. A little rich for a cat."

"Meeeeooooow!" Juno responded as though in protest.

Gram laughed as she ladled chowder into a bowl with a tight top. "Juno, I'll get you some cat food in a few minutes. This is for Angie."

"I'll let you know when I get in touch with Willow Sinclair," Tom said as he headed for his study. "Tell Dave we'll do what we can for the boy." Then he turned around. "I assume the garage is a closed crime scene. Does Leo need any clothes, toiletries, whatever?"

"He hasn't got anything, so far as I could see," I answered. "The police even took his bloody clothes."

"His clothes were bloody?" Gram asked, frowning.

"He was trying to help Ike," I explained.

"Let's hope that's what the police decide too," said Tom. "I'll call Dave and find out what size the boy wears. Maybe I can find a parishioner who has teenagers who've outgrown their clothes and would like to help out."

"Thanks, Tom," I said, meaning it. "He just seems like a lost kid who was at the wrong place at the wrong time."

"I hope so, Angie. For his sake, and for Dave's."

Chapter Nine

Curriculum: "English, Natural Philosophy, English and French Languages, The Mathematical Sciences, Botany, Needlework, Drawing. Boarding and Tuition, $30. Washing, 36 cents a dozen. Reading books are kept for the use of students. Other books, stationery, etc., at the usual prices. The school is well supplied with philosophical apparatus."

—*American Republican* newspaper advertisement, Downington, Pennsylvania, January 22, 1827. This ad was for the Downingtown Boarding School for Girls, which opened August 27, 1827.

Trixi greeted me at my door. She clearly sniffed Gram's chowder and led me directly to her dish in the kitchen, sitting there in silent petition until I gave her half a can of cat food. While she gobbled it, I put the bowl of chowder in the refrigerator to heat later for my own supper.

In the meantime, I put Dave's embroidery away and checked the Mainely Needlepoint website. Three orders had come in during the past two days. I'd been paying more attention to Haven Harbor events than to my business.

Gram had started Mainely Needlepoint while I was in Arizona. She'd gathered a group of local Mainers who enjoyed doing needlepoint and were looking to add a little to their incomes. A varied group, from Dave to Captain Ob and his wife, Anna; to my friend Sarah, who was a dealer in antiques; to Ruth, my seventy-nine-year-old neighbor who wrote erotica. They produced high-end needlepoint for gift shops and, increasingly, did custom-designed needlepoint for interior decorators or individuals. I was the least experienced of the group, and most of my time was spent managing the website, contacting our customers, and being the public face of the business. That was fine with me. Sitting still wasn't my favorite activity, even when I had needlepoint in my hands.

I'd almost answered all the e-mails we'd received and prepared the orders to send tomorrow morning when Tom called.

"Angie? I just talked to Dave, to check on what Leo might need. I'm concerned, though. That boy was nearby—I could sense Dave couldn't really talk—so I didn't say anything. But he mentioned again that Leo was from Dexter."

"That's what he told us," I agreed.

"Well, I called my friend who's in social services and asked her whether she knew of a boy named Leo Smith, from Dexter. A lot of children and teens are in the Maine system, and she has access to computer files of the cases. She couldn't give me any private information, but I thought she could tell me whether Leo was listed, and whether he had a family."

"What did she say?"

"She was very gracious. Told me she couldn't help me. She had no record of a Leo Smith."

"So he wasn't 'in the system,' as you said. Not every kid in Maine who isn't living in a family household is."

"True enough. But I keep wondering how Leo ended up in Haven Harbor, living with Ike."

"He said he wanted to see the ocean."

"Not that amazing. You'd be surprised at the number of young people in Maine who haven't seen the ocean. Or who live on the shore and have never been to the mountains, when we have both right here in the state."

"So do you think you'll be able to find some clothes for Leo?"

"Probably. I'll check with a couple of families, and we keep a closet full of emergency clothing at the church for families whose houses have burned, or who've come into hard times. I'll pull together some things for the boy. But I keep wondering what kind of a family he came from and if anyone is looking for him."

"He could use a family, that's for sure. The police will probably check into his past, too, so they may find something. Although Leo said he didn't have anyone, so they may not find much."

"Unless he has relatives he doesn't want to see, or who don't want to see him. That happens, especially with runaways. Or throwaways. I just wanted you to know what I'd found out so far. If you see Dave when Leo's not around, you tell him. I don't want the boy knowing we're investigating him."

"Investigating is a strong word, Tom. You were just trying to find out whether he had people somewhere who cared about him."

"True. And I know there are all sorts of families. But I hate thinking of an eighteen-year-old boy without ties to anyone."

"That's the way Dave felt. That's why he's taking an interest in Leo."

"Dave's a good man. Leo's lucky to have him."

"I agree. But I'll let Dave know you tried to find out whether he'd been in foster care, or had some other official connection."

I put down my cell. If Leo had family problems . . . well, a lot of people had family problems while they were growing up. Some problems were more serious than others, true, but Leo would have to live with whatever had happened in his life.

Right now it was more important for him to have a safe place to stay. And for Pete and Ethan to find out who'd killed poor Ike Hamilton, collector of bottles and stories. What possible motive would there be to hurt someone like Ike? He was just trying to make his way in a world that hadn't always been kind to him.

No wonder Ike had offered Leo a place to stay. They'd had more in common than might appear at first glance.

My cell rang again. "Sarah! How is your world?"

"I'm fine. Pete stopped in for a cup of coffee. He and Ethan are working on a new case, and he hinted you might be involved. What's happening?"

I filled her in. "So Leo's staying with Dave, Tom's trying to gather some clothes for him, and I assume Pete and Ethan are trying to figure out who killed Ike."

"That dear little man! I always left my bottles in back of the store for him," said Sarah. "He stopped every Tuesday afternoon. I think he had a regular route, because although I saw him around town sometimes, he came for my bottles only on Tuesdays. Sometimes I saved cookies or muffins for him, when I'd baked too many. 'Undue significance a starving man attaches to food. . . .' "

"What?"

"Emily Dickinson, of course."

"Of course. I should have guessed." Sarah often quoted Emily at odd moments. "Guess you'll have to start making trips to the redemption place yourself," I said. I headed there every two or three weeks, or whenever I'd accumulated enough bottles to make the trip worthwhile. I could have saved myself the hassle and helped Ike if I'd known he'd depended on empty bottles for income.

"Pete said you and Dave were looking out for that skinny boy we saw with Ike."

"He came to Dave to ask for help, and I was there picking up needlepoint Dave had finished."

"I wonder where he came from."

"He's from Dexter, and he's eighteen."

"He didn't look eighteen. But maybe he's just small, or underfed. Where's Dexter?"

"It's a rural town in the center of Maine. Used to be mills and shoe factories there, but they've closed down. We have a customer who lives in that area. She saw our cormorant pillows in Betty's Gift Shop last summer, loved them, and then ordered several other pillows with birds on them for a window seat overlooking her bird feeders. And I agree, Leo is skinny. But Dave's a good cook; he'll be well fed there."

"What's Dave going to do with him when school's in session? You said he didn't want to go to school."

"Dave will figure out something," I said. "This all happened suddenly. I suspect Dave and Leo are talking tonight about how they'll manage. Pete made it clear he wants Leo available and under some sort of supervision."

"Do you think he killed Ike?" Sarah asked the question everyone had.

"I don't see any reason he would have. Unless he's a great actor, he seemed genuinely upset and scared when he came to Dave's house today. I just hope Pete and Ethan figure out who did kill Ike, and figure it out soon. That poor boy ended up in the middle of a real mess."

"Sounds that way. But they'll figure out what happened. They always do."

They did. Although sometimes they needed a little help. "Leo said the men in the Chamber wanted Ike out of town. You've owned a business here longer than I have. Do you know anything about that?"

"Ed Campbell's been on a tear in the past year or so. Reverend Tom would know more about that than I do. He's on the Chamber. Ed's been trying to make the families that use the soup kitchen invisible, especially in the summer months, when tourists are here. Last fall he asked me to sign a petition saying only nonprofit organizations could collect bottles in Haven Harbor."

"Ike's the only individual who did that, right?"

"So far as I know. Except for the school's bottle drive once a year. I didn't consider Ike a nuisance. Actually, he performed a service."

"So I assume you didn't sign the petition."

"I didn't. But a list of people already had. I don't know how many signatures he needed, but I didn't hear anything more about bottles after that."

"I know Ed's trying to attract more people to town."

"And to his car dealership, don't forget," Sarah put in.

"I haven't forgotten. But I can't see the use in trying to get Ike out of town. He's always lived here."

"He lived in that grungy garage, and maybe he wasn't as clean as he might have been, but he was always cheerful and friendly when I talked with him. He always had a tale or two to share about something going on around town." I could hear the smile in Sarah's voice.

"Like what?"

"A couple of weeks ago he was indignant because Gus Gleason had been flirting with Cos Curran—you know she works at Gus's bookstore after school and weekends—and Cos was upset."

"Gus is a bit of a flirt," I agreed. "But he and his wife live above the store, the way you live over your store. I wouldn't think he'd do anything inappropriate when Nancy was nearby."

"I wouldn't think so either. But Nancy's a nurse. She works different shifts, and isn't always home. And Cos is only seventeen or eighteen. She may have misinterpreted something Gus said."

"Could be. But she's not naïve. Remember, her sister is in jail. Last time I talked with Cos she was excited about graduating this year and hoping to go to U Maine in Farmington. She's not the sort who'd get upset at a little innocent flirting. And after all that's been in the news, I don't think Gus would try to get away with anything more than flirting."

"Who knows? And maybe Ike was exaggerating. In any case, it doesn't have anything to do with his death, which is the important thing now."

"True. I have to finish up some more work. Maybe we could have supper later this week?"

"Sounds good. Shall we include Patrick and Pete?"

"If Pete can get away from his investigation."

"I'll check. Talk soon!"

The chowder Gram had given me was delicious. She was right: It was one of my favorites. But I didn't often take the time to make it for myself. A pot of chowder seemed a lot for one person, or even two, if Patrick was joining me. And I wasn't as organized as Gram, who made stock out of lobster shells whenever she had them. Lobster stock was the secret to a great haddock chowder.

Talking with Sarah had reminded me of those bird pillow covers the woman in Dexter had ordered. Captain Ob and Anna were making them, and I'd planned to stop and pick them up today after I saw Dave.

I called them. Yes, the covers were finished. I could pick them up in the morning.

Good.

In fact, maybe I'd deliver them to Dexter myself. It wouldn't do any harm to check out Leo's hometown.

I looked at my phone. I'd taken a lot of pictures at the Blessing. I was sure I had one of Leo and Ike.

I smiled to myself as I printed the photo out. It reminded me of my days in Arizona, when I'd learned to investigate people. It might be fun to use those skills again. If Leo hadn't been in the foster care system, and he was from Dexter, someone there should know about him and his family. And maybe I could find out why he'd left there and was essentially homeless in Haven Harbor.

There might be secrets behind closed doors in small towns, but no one was invisible.

Someone in Dexter would know Leo.

Chapter Ten

United States! Your banner wears
Two emblems—one of fame;
Alas! the other that it bears
Reminds us of your shame.
The white man's liberty in types
Stands blazoned by your stars;
But what's the meaning of your stripes?
They mean your negro's scars.

    —Embroidered on a satin pillow and presented by her students to Betsy Mix Cowles, who'd taught in Ohio schools for forty years. An active abolitionist, Cowles traveled throughout the state giving anti-slavery lectures. In 1864, when Abraham Lincoln issued his Emancipation Proclamation, she read it and said, "The two great tasks of my life are ended together. My teaching is done, and the slaves are free."

Anna Winslow greeted me at her kitchen door the next morning. "Glad you called, Angie! We just finished those pillow covers Sunday. Fun project! Ob and I liked working on them together. I loved stitching the chickadees and cardinals, and Ob did the junco and downy woodpecker. They're his favorites in the winter. Coffee?"

"Coffee sounds great," I agreed, sitting at her kitchen table. "Is Ob around?"

"He's down working on the boat today. Weather's nice, and the deck needs sprucing up before we open for the season. Our first party of fishermen booked the second weekend in May."

"That's early, isn't it?"

"It is. But the men were planning to attend a conference in Portland that week and decided they'd 'bond over fishing' on the weekend."

I shook my head. "Bonding over fish?"

"They'll pay well, and Ob'll do his best to make sure they come home with some fish. Although sounds as though they don't want the fish for eating; they 'want an experience,' as one of them said to me over the phone."

One day of deep sea fishing was enough for many of Ob's customers from away. They looked forward to a day on the water, bragging rights if they caught anything, and a martini with the seafood dinner they'd order at a restaurant that night.

"So you might end up with some good eating, as well as paying customers."

"Hope so. Ob's polishing brass and painting and such. We got the boat out of dry dock for the Blessing, but it needs looking after."

"Understood." Anna's coffee was strong and dark, the way I liked it.

"So, what's been happening with you? Haven't seen that new car of yours over to Patrick's very often lately."

"Patrick's gallery is open for the season, so he's in town most days. And I've been making sure all our orders from the gift shops are finished and ready to deliver. Some of the shops are already open, and others will be opening in May."

"Well, I'm glad we have the bird pillows ready for you. What will we be doing next?"

"We're pretty much up-to-date, but we could always use more little balsam sachets stitched with pine trees or lighthouses. We never seem to have enough of those. You and Ob could work on a few when you have the time."

"Lots of time right now. Ob won't have many fishing parties until June, and it's early to put in the garden. Spinach and early peas are about all that'll survive being planted this early. A few needlepoint projects would fit right into our schedule."

"Good! Once summer starts, everyone is pulled in all directions," I agreed. "Whatever you could do now will be a help."

"We'll do what we can. It's something we both enjoy, and we can watch movies on the TV at the same time we're creating something fun." Anna smiled. "And bringing in a little extra money too."

"A win-win," I agreed, standing and picking up the bag containing the pillow covers. "I'll take these up to Dexter and get you a check."

"Good for everyone." Anna smiled, walking me to the back door. "Tell Patrick we watch for his lights at the carriage house every night. All winter, they've added a cheerful glow. For too many years we were the only folks in the area. Nice to have a neighbor, even if we don't see him often."

"I'll tell him," I promised.

Back in my car I kept thinking about the order that needed to get to Dexter. Leo's hometown. Was it providential that the Winslows had finished Mrs. Whitman's cushions now? I checked my phone and called her. "Mrs. Whitman? This is Angie Curtis at Mainely Needlepoint. I have your bird cushions, and I have another errand near Dexter. Any chance you'll be in today? I could deliver the cushions in person and save you the shipping cost."

Mrs. Whitman agreed immediately. I confirmed her address and entered it in the car's GPS. I'd heard of Dexter, but I'd never been there. Growing up in Haven Harbor, I'd known only my hometown well and occasionally visited other coastal villages. Since I'd been home, and run Mainely Needlepoint, I'd been back and forth to Portland and Bangor and Augusta and a number of coastal towns, visiting gift shops and interior designers and picking up needlepointing supplies. I'd attended auctions and visited the sampler collection at the Saco Museum. But this was my first trip to Dexter.

On my way up the peninsula to the turnpike I stopped at Dunkin' Donuts for my third cup of coffee of the day and a blueberry doughnut sticky with sugar that would sustain me until I got back to town.

Heading north on the turnpike, and then west into the countryside, where trees and bushes were just beginning to bud, I planned what I'd do when I got to Dexter.

I'd check with the local high school first. I had the picture of Leo I'd taken at the Blessing. He might have dropped out, but any high school in Maine would know their students, past and present, and should be able to point me to Leo's family.

I'd been trained as an investigator. Finding out where Leo came from and why he'd left his hometown and headed for the coast would be a piece of cake.

Or at the very least, a blueberry doughnut.

Chapter Eleven

*How many young ladies, who waste their time over
novels and small embroideries, would, by aiding
their mothers in the dress-making and tailoring of the
family, fit themselves to become excellent wives, and,
by their ingenuity and skill, make the fifteen hundred or two thousand a year which may constitute a
young man's income, easily and pleasantly cover the
expenses of two instead of one!*
    —Lyman, Joseph B., and Laura E. Lyman.
    *The Philosophy of Housekeeping: A Scientific
    and Practical Manual.* Hartford, CT:
    S. M. Betts & Company, 1869, p. 303.

Mrs. Whitman was delighted with her needlepointed
cushion covers and had foam pillow forms ready to
slide inside them. She showed me the window seat
where they were to go, and together we put the pillows together and stood them up under the window.
Outside, chickadees, cardinals, and goldfinches flit-
ted through a dense forsythia bush bright with yellow, then perched on her bird feeders and selected a
sunflower seed or a thistle seed or two.

"The pillows look great, just as you'd planned. And

I love that you can sit here and see the birds," I said. "Would you mind if I took a picture of your window seat with the pillows? I'd like to share it on the Mainely Needlepoint website, to show some of our custom work."

"Go right ahead. Just don't mention my name or where I live," Mrs. Whitman decided. "Security and all that."

"Of course," I said, taking out my phone and snapping several pictures.

"They do look wonderful, don't they?" she said, handing me a check for the work, minus the deposit she'd given me in January. "I'm so glad I took the name of your company when I saw your Save the Cormorant pillows. We don't have cormorants here in Dexter, but we certainly have more than our share of inland birds."

I tucked the check into the canvas bag I always carried when I was working. "This is my first trip to Dexter. I didn't realize Lake Wassookeag was so large. It's a beautiful area."

"Yes. And the river runs right through the town. That's why so many mills used to be here. Of course, they're closed now. Been hard on the local economy."

"I met someone from Dexter the other day," I said, deciding I might as well start asking about Leo.

"Who was that?" she answered easily.

"Leo Smith," I said.

She frowned and shook her head. "Sorry. I don't know any Smiths in town. Thought I knew everyone around."

I fished into my bag and pulled out the picture I'd printed. "This is Leo," I said, pointing at him.

She looked closely. "He looks a little familiar. But,

no. I don't know any young men named Leo. I'm sure of that."

"Well, thank you. You have a lovely home, and it was a pleasure doing business with you."

"I'll be sure to tell all my friends about Mainely Needlepoint when they admire my cushions. And I'm sure they will," she answered as she showed me to her front door.

A chipmunk chased another across the slate path to the road. How many generations of chipmunks had lived here? Maine's rocky shore and hills suited them. They'd even solved the challenge of surviving frigid winters: long naps and underground storage rooms for January and February snacks. If only life for humans was that simple. "Avoid hawks, cats, and automobiles, and stock up on nuts, seeds, and grains." Chipmunks had life figured out.

Back in my car I checked directions to Dexter Regional High School. It wasn't far.

At the office I signed in and asked to speak with the principal.

"She'll be back in a few minutes. She's meeting with a group of parents right now," I was told.

No one asked why I wanted to speak with her, which was just as well. I still had the picture identification card saying I worked for the Combs Investigation Service, but the address of Wally's company (which consisted of Wally and me) was in Mesa, Arizona. We weren't licensed in Maine.

"Ms. Curtis?" asked the woman sitting outside the principal's office. "Mrs. Basinski can see you now." She pointed to the door.

Mrs. Basinski must have two doors to her office. I hadn't seen her come in.

The woman behind the wide desk could have been intimidating, I suspected. She was tall and broad, and her salt-and-pepper hair was trimmed severely, although her fuchsia jacket made a bright spring statement.

"How can I help you?" she asked.

I came right to the point. "I'm Angela Curtis, from Haven Harbor. A young man—a teenager—came to our town about three weeks ago. The man he was staying with has been murdered, and he's a suspect. He told me he was from Dexter. I wondered if you could tell me anything about him, or about any family he might have in the area."

She frowned. "Are you with the police?"

"No. I'm trying to help the boy."

"Is he violent?"

"I don't think so. But he's definitely scared of what might happen to him."

"His name?" asked Mrs. Basinski.

"Leo Smith. He might have attended here and then dropped out."

She thought for a moment and then shook her head. "I don't believe I know him. You're sure he's from Dexter? Our high school is regional, so we get students from several towns. But I pride myself in knowing all our students."

"I have a picture of him," I said, handing her the photo I'd taken Sunday afternoon.

She peered at it closely. "No. I don't recognize him. I don't think he's been one of our students, at least not recently. But let me ask our school secretary. She keeps track of all the students, and if this young man has been absent—which he must have been if he's been in your town for three weeks or if he dropped out earlier—she would know." She pushed a button on her phone. "Sheila? Could you come into my office for a moment?"

Sheila was older and looked as though keeping track of all the high school students in Dexter was a wearying job. "Yes, Mrs. Basinski?"

"This young woman is trying to find out about a boy who said he was from Dexter. I thought you might know him." She handed Sheila the picture. "His name is Leo Smith."

Sheila looked at the picture carefully and then at me. "I do know him. I'm almost positive. But his name isn't Leo Smith, and he's not from Dexter. Has he gotten himself into trouble again?"

Chapter Twelve

Tell me ye knowing and discerning few
Where I may find a friend both firm and true
Who dare stand by me when in deep distress
And then his love and friendship most express.
Friends are like leaves which on the trees do grow
In Summers Prosperous state much leaf they show
But art thou in Adversity then they
Like leaves from trees do fall away
Happy is He who hath a friend indeed
But He more happy is who none doth need

    —Ann Willet, age nine, England, 1860. She
       stitched these words using wool threads
       on linen, with lions on either side of a
       butterfly and flowers, and bordered her
       work with vines.

"Who is he, then?" I asked. "And how do you know him?"

"I work here in Dexter. Have for thirty-two years. But I've lived over to Corinth all my life. Grew up there. Anyway, this picture looks awfully like a young man who got himself in a kettle of fish a couple of years back. Name was Leon Blackwell. Haven't heard anything about him in a while, but I'm pretty sure this is him."

Leon Blackwell. "What happened to Leon?"

"Blew up his house, people said. Police never said yes or no. Parents were inside, so they didn't say anything."

"Blew up his house? Sheila, are you sure?" Mrs. Basinski looked aghast.

"Sure as I'm here in your office. You've only been in Dexter a year. If you'd been around longer, you'd have seen the stories. Must say, that boy's parents weren't pillars of society. Cooking up drugs in their kitchen, some folks said. But he was outside when it all went *boom*, and most people in town were sure he had something to do with it all."

"Was he arrested?" I asked.

"Don't remember exactly. He was only maybe fourteen, fifteen, when it happened. Skinny kid, all elbows and knees. Kept to himself. Too young to go to prison, even if he was to blame."

"Does he have other relatives in Corinth? Or anywhere nearby?"

Sheila shrugged. "Not that I've heard of. Course, with a family like that, can't see anyone bragging those Blackwells were relations." She looked at the picture again. "Yup. Pretty sure that's Leon. Wherever he's been, doesn't look like they put a lot of meat on him." She handed me back the picture. "Has he blown something else up?"

"No," I assured her. "But he is in the middle of a bit of a mess. Thank you for the information, both of you." I backed out of the office. "I really appreciate it."

Should I drive to Corinth? But, no. If the case was as widely known as Sheila had implied, there must be something about it online.

I headed back to Haven Harbor, full of questions.

Sheila was a bit of a character, but she'd seemed certain. Could Leo Smith really be—or have been—Leon Blackwell?

If so, had he really killed his parents—intentionally or unintentionally?

In either case, the police would no doubt find out, and it wouldn't help Leo/Leon look innocent now.

Leo's parents were dead. His former roommate was dead. Now he was living with Dave. What if Leo—Leon—*had* caused the death of his parents? Where had he been since then? What was he really doing in Haven Harbor?

And was Dave safe? Was his sympathy for an apparently homeless boy putting him in danger?

My foot pushed down on the gas pedal. I had to get back to Haven Harbor.

I had to talk to Dave, and maybe to Leo himself, before I told Pete. Somehow I couldn't believe that boy had killed his parents—or Ike Hamilton.

But there were too many unanswered questions to ignore.

And I'd been wrong before. Murderers didn't always look like killers.

I raced the speed limit to get home.

Chapter Thirteen

Of making many books there is no end.
My library was dukedom large enough.
　—Boxed words with Adam and Eve under
　　the tree of knowledge and a floral border,
　　stitched on a sampler presented to John
　　Shaw Billings (1838–1913) on his retire-
　　ment as the first director of the New York
　　Public Library, April 12, 1903. Dr. Billings
　　was an American surgeon who also oversaw
　　construction of the Surgeon General's
　　Library at Johns Hopkins Hospital and led
　　the first effort to eradicate yellow fever in
　　the United States.

By the time I'd gotten home, I'd taken a few deep
breaths and decided I should first see what the Internet had to say about Leo Smith—or Leon Blackwell.
Searching for "Leo Smith" didn't help at all. I was
pretty sure the Leo I'd met wasn't a trumpet player
in his seventies.

"Leon Blackwell" turned up a number of Blackwells from Maine. The Blackwell family had been in
the Pine Tree State for generations. I skimmed head-

ings. No "Leon Blackwell." Of course not. He'd been a minor when his parents had died, and newspapers didn't print the names of minors. But, yes, Serenity and Joshua Blackwell of Corinth, Maine, had died when their home violently exploded on the night of April 5, two years ago.

Serenity and Joshua had been in their late thirties. Serenity had a history of drug use and arrests, and Joshua had spent time in prison for larceny. The police had been summoned by a neighbor who said the couple's son had banged on their door at 3:38 in the morning. Both houses were in an isolated rural area, and that nearest neighbor had been a quarter mile away.

By the time the fire department and police arrived, Serenity, Joshua, and their house were gone. One other neighbor, interviewed by a reporter, said the Blackwells had always been "pleasant, quiet people."

The cause of the explosion was "being investigated." No mention of what happened to the son.

I sat back in my desk chair. Trixi, seeing that as an invitation, jumped up and settled herself in my lap, purring loudly. Somewhere I'd read that the sound of purring could reduce stress. If that was so, I should record Trixi so I could play her purr at moments like this when she wasn't at hand.

As though she sensed my thought, she stretched a paw up and tapped my cheek. One more purr and then she jumped down, stopping at the door from the living room (aka the Mainely Needlepoint office) to look back and ensure that I was following her.

Trixi had a one-track mind, and that track was "food." Sure enough, she led me straight to her food dish in the kitchen and sat behind it, staring at me imploringly. "Trixi, you're not starving," I informed her. "I fed you this morning, before I left."

She didn't blink. Clearly she had no recollection of such an event.

"Okay, okay. I give up. I'll give you some more dry food. But no more canned food until tonight," I scolded while filling her dish. She immediately buried her face in it.

For Trixi, food was a priority. Gram's cat, Juno, also liked to eat, but I hadn't remembered that she'd been as insistent on a constant supply of food. But, then, Gram had been the Giver of Food then.

Trixi was the only cat I'd ever had. She'd be a year old in August. She and her sisters and brother had been born in Dave's barn and now lived with Patrick, Dave, and me.

I hoped Leo/Leon liked cats, since Trixi's brother lived with Dave. Trixi was black, except for a few white hairs on her chest, like an old man who was beginning to gray. Dave's cat was almost the opposite: white, with a small patch of black on his chest. He was shy; I'd rarely seen him. Dave once told me he hid in an upstairs closet when strange voices were in the house.

Their feral mother had disappeared, and Dave hadn't been acquainted with their father. Trixi and I had a lot in common.

Which brought my mind back to disappearing parents. Assuming Leo was Leon, his parents were, indeed, dead. No other relatives were mentioned in the articles I'd found. Which could mean that whoever wrote them didn't know anything about his parents but their police records. Or it could mean that their son was truly alone in the world.

Where had he been? Why had Sheila thought he caused the explosion and fire? Local gossip? Inside information?

And how had he been able to escape and get to a neighbor's house? Shouldn't he have been asleep at home at three-thirty in the morning?

So many questions.

I had no idea what the answers were. Or even if Leon was still with Dave. How had they coped with Dave's having to be in school today?

I wanted to talk to Dave, to tell him what I'd found out. It was almost four in the afternoon. He should be home.

But I didn't want Leo to overhear.

I started to text, but then realized the text would be on Dave's phone. What if Leon borrowed the phone? Or was curious and picked it up?

So I just called. "Dave? Angie. I wanted to check and see how the last twenty-four hours have gone."

"Pretty well," Dave said, his tone guarded.

"Is Leo with you?" I asked.

"Yes, that's right," Dave agreed.

"Just listen, then. Today I delivered some cushion covers that Ob and Anna stitched for a client in Dexter. The town Leo said he came from."

"Correct," Dave said quietly.

"When I was there I went to the local high school to ask about him. The principal didn't know him, but another woman who worked in the office thought she recognized him. His name isn't Leo Smith, Dave. It's Leon Blackwell. He lived in Corinth, Maine, until two years ago, when his parents were killed. Their home exploded."

"That's very interesting," said Dave. "Are you sure of your sources?"

"Just the woman at the school, and then the search engine on my computer. But I think it fits."

"Have you talked with anyone else recently?"

"You mean have I called Pete or Ethan?"

"Exactly." Dave's voice was steady but concerned. "That's what I meant."

"No. You're the only one I've been in touch with. But the police will find out. I think we should talk to Leo—Leon—and hear his side of the story."

"I'm making lasagna for supper. We have plenty. You'd be welcome to come and share it with us," Dave said.

"Your lasagna is terrific. A good idea. Talk over supper. Or after."

"See you about six, then."

I started to turn my phone off when Patrick's name appeared on it.

"Patrick. Are you at the gallery?"

"Where else? It's dead down here, and I'm tempted to leave. I've read every art magazine I subscribe to and memorized the number of steps from the front door to the back, with a stop at my desk in between. Any chance you could join me at Harbor Haunts for dinner? I'm going crazy, but I want the gallery to be open. Now I understand why the previous owner hired someone to gallery sit for him. Maybe patrons of the arts will crowd this place in July, but clearly the end of April isn't peak season."

"Sorry you're bored. But I just agreed to have dinner at Dave's."

"Dave? Did I hear right, that the boy who was living with Ike is now with him?"

"That's right. Who told you?"

"Sarah ran across from her shop earlier today and

gave me some cookies she'd made last night. She was as bored as I was. No one was shopping for antiques or art in Haven Harbor today. She told me Dave had offered sanctuary to that kid. Is he sure the boy didn't kill Ike?"

"Dave doesn't think he did," I said, hoping I sounded more convincing than I felt right now. Should I tell Patrick what I'd learned today? No. Not before Dave and I talked to Leo/Leon, or before we told the police.

"Okay. So you believe him. But why would anyone kill Ike Hamilton?"

"Pete and Ethan are trying to figure that out."

"And, let me guess. Somehow you're involved."

"I was at Dave's, picking up some embroidery, when Leo came to his home, looking for help."

"So you're going back tonight," he said.

"Just to chat. Give Dave a little reinforcement."

"Should I be jealous?"

"Oh, Patrick. You're kidding. Dave's a friend. And colleague."

"And a darned nice guy. I know. I just hoped you and I could spend some time together tonight."

"Maybe later this week. Did Sarah mention that you and I should have dinner with her and Pete as soon as Pete can free himself from the investigation?"

"She did say something about 'see you later in the week.' Maybe that's what she meant. But I'd still like to see you—without Sarah or Pete or Dave or anyone else." Patrick sounded almost petulant. That wasn't usual. He must have had a very bad day.

"Tomorrow night? I haven't been to Harbor Haunts for a couple of weeks," I suggested.

"Whoops. Not tomorrow night. I'm going to close early and go to Portland to have dinner with Linda Zaharee."

"Her work is terrific. Do you think she'll show with you?"

"She showed here when Ted owned the gallery. Her minor work, of course. But she knew Mom years ago, and I'm going to wine and dine her and see if I can convince her to paint something special for Haven Harbor."

"Sounds interesting! And fun too." I teased, "Should I be jealous?"

Patrick's laugh filled the phone. "Touché. You've met Linda. She's older than Mom."

"Well, enjoy the dinner. Let me know how it goes. We'll get together later this week. I promise."

I put down the phone and looked over at Trixi, who'd emptied her dish and was prepared to request more. "Trixi, I'm weary, and I don't think tonight is going to be a lot of fun. I'm going upstairs to take a hot bubble bath. Sometimes a bubble bath is almost as good a stress reliever as a purr."

And I could use a little less stress. I had a feeling supper at Dave's wouldn't be relaxing.

Chapter Fourteen

May virtue be my never fading bloom,
For mental beauties do survive the tomb.
  —Irene Tolman, age fifteen, Camden,
    Maine, 1828. Irene included several
    alphabets on her sampler, but no elabo-
    rate decorations.

While I was sitting in my deep Victorian tub, focusing on relaxing and hoping Trixi, who was circling the tub's rounded edge and occasionally sticking a foot out to break bubbles, wouldn't fall in, I realized why Tom's friend had said Leo/Leon wasn't in "the system." Of course, Leo Smith wouldn't be.

Leon Blackwell was.

Dave and I had to convince Leo to tell the police who he really was. Lying to police conducting a murder investigation was not the way to convince anyone you were innocent.

Freshly dressed in jeans and a clean, plaid flannel shirt—my go-to outfit for all but the hottest summer days—I debated whether to bring a bottle of wine to contribute to the dinner. Under normal situations, I would. But considering Leon's age and the discussion I hoped would be part of the evening, maybe not tonight.

Dave's house wasn't far, and the short walk would be good. I'd get some fresh air into my lungs and a little exercise on the way.

As I passed Ruth Hopkins's house I remembered Ike would stop there to pick up bottles, and sometimes stayed for lunch. Maybe she'd remember something about him that would help the police. I should talk to her. I glanced at my phone. Almost six o'clock.

Maybe tomorrow. Right now Leo/Leon was the priority.

I passed the Thibodeaus' house and made another mental note to stop at their patisserie and buy some eclairs. Besides, I should stop in to see them more often. They were struggling to take care of Henri's mother. It was an exhausting schedule, since they were up before dawn baking every day. I wished I spoke French; if I did, maybe I could mom-sit for them occasionally.

Thinking of everyone else's challenges kept my mind occupied until I reached Dave's house.

He answered the door immediately. "Come on in, Angie. I'm glad you could join us tonight." He nodded toward the upstairs and called, "Leo? Angie's here. Dinner in five minutes."

Today Dave's usually immaculate living room looked comfortably lived in. A Windbreaker was draped over one chair, a backpack was on another, and the papers Dave had been grading yesterday were still on the coffee table.

He ran his hand through his thick hair and spoke

softly. "Leo came to school with me today, under protest. He sat in the back of every class I taught, crossed his arms, and looked as though there was no place on earth he hated more than my classroom. But I told him he'd have to stay near me, and he did. I don't know how many more days we'll be able to keep that going. Several of the kids in my classes tried to speak to him, and he scowled and ignored them all. And the principal wasn't thrilled when I explained that the police wanted me to keep Leo in sight."

"Take a deep breath," I said, touching his arm. "I'm amazed you found time to make lasagna with all this going on."

"Leo may be upset, but his appetite is fine. Even before you called I figured I'd make lasagna. Usually one pan lasts me almost a week. Right now I'm hoping I made enough for us tonight and for Leo and me tomorrow night. I forgot how much teenage boys eat."

"He looks pretty skinny, too," I added. "He could use good food."

"Probably so. I teach teenagers every day. But I've never lived with one. Every hour I have more sympathy for parents."

I laughed. "Well, I promise not to eat a week's supply of your lasagna tonight. But yours is the best I've had, so I'm looking forward to it."

Heavy clumping footsteps coming down from the second floor announced Leo's presence. "Hey. I thought you said it was time to eat." He turned and started back up the stairs.

"It is, Leo. Come back down. We'll eat in the

kitchen. The lasagna is ready, and there's a salad and garlic bread, plus ice cream for dessert."

"Sounds good," agreed Leo, leading the three of us into the kitchen.

Dave's lasagna was excellent, as always. He was right, though. The three of us (I was no slouch myself, despite what I'd told him before supper) finished half a large pan of the pasta, cheeses, spinach, and sausage combination. A loaf of French bread baked with butter and garlic also disappeared, along with a good part of Dave's salad.

Did all teenage boys eat that much? My experience with such creatures was less than Dave's. I would have thought years in the navy would have prepared him for anything. But, of course, then he hadn't been the cook.

Dave nodded at me when everyone's hunger pangs had subsided. Time to have that serious talk.

"I went to Dexter today, to deliver some needle-pointed items to a client," I said.

Leo stopped chewing and looked at me.

"While I was there, I talked with a few people."

Leo looked as though he was ready to run. But I had to keep going, and confront him. The truth was important—for his sake as well as for the police investigation. "Leo, you don't come from Dexter, do you?"

I'd caught him off guard.

"Not exactly," he muttered.

"And your name isn't Leo Smith. It's Leon Blackwell."

"It's none of your business!" he said, pushing his chair back from the table and starting to get up.

Dave stood and looked at him. "Sit down, Leon.

Or whatever your name is. Angie and I are on your side. But if we're going to help, you need to be straight with us."

Leon sat.

"What happened, Leon? Your parents died two years ago. What happened then? Where have you been?"

"If you're such a good detective, you figure it out," he said, slumping in his seat.

"I am a detective, actually," I said. "Or at least I used to work for one. So I could probably find out what's on the record. But records don't always tell the whole truth. We'd like to hear your story."

Leon took a deep breath. "Dad and Mom weren't exactly like parents you see on TV. Mom was into meth, and Dad drank. I was alone a lot of the time. And that was better than when they were home—or at least when Dad was there. He was a wicked mean drunk. No matter what I did, it wasn't what he wanted." Leon looked from Dave to me and back again. "People like you don't know what it's like."

"Maybe we do," said Dave, gently. "Try us."

"What happened the night of the explosion?" I asked.

"Dad was out with his friends. Late. And Mom was out of it, like she was a lot. When Dad got home, Mom hadn't made dinner. He was messed up and angry. He started hitting on her, but she was in no shape to stand up to him. I couldn't take seeing him do that to her, so I pushed her away and hit him, in the stomach. He grabbed me and shoved me out the door and locked it so I couldn't get back in. Said I had no respect, so I didn't live with him no more."

"Then what happened?"

"I figured he'd forget about me after a while, or pass out, and I'd climb back in one of the windows and go to bed. I'd done that before. So I sort of huddled down on the porch to stay warm, hoping it would get quiet soon so I could sneak back in."

I shook my head in disbelief.

"I wasn't inside, so I don't know for sure, but it sounded like Dad beat on Mom a little more and then decided to cook dinner himself. He wasn't too together at that point, if you know what I mean. The police said there was a gas explosion. My dad never could figure out how to use our stove. He probably turned on all the burners, and then passed out, or . . . I don't know. Anyway, I was trying to sleep outside on the porch when the whole place exploded. It threw me into the yard. I tried to go back into the house." Leo hesitated. "I saw Mom. Her body was all twisted, hanging in some bushes. Flames were everywhere. One of the trees I used to climb when I was a kid was burning. I didn't see Dad, and I didn't know what had happened. I ran like hell to get help." Leon looked from me to Dave and back again. "Only, it was too late."

"What happened to you?"

"I was bruised pretty bad, and my wrist was broken. I'd hardly noticed it until our neighbors called for help. A policeman took me to the emergency room, and the doctor said I must have landed on it when the explosion threw me off the porch. After he set it, the police took me to their station. They never left me alone. They kept asking me questions. They thought I'd blown up the house and Mom and Dad. Only I didn't! I'm not the smartest kid around, but I'm not stupid."

"And then?"

"After a day or two, some experts they'd called in figured out the stove had exploded. I was off the hook, but they said I wasn't old enough to take care of myself. I ended up in a group home up to Bangor."

"What was that like?"

"Worse than at home. They made you go to school and live with this dumb man who said he was watching out for us but who just wanted a paycheck. The boys I was with—there were five others—were older than I was." Leo glanced at Dave. "They knew how to take care of themselves better than I did. But I learned."

"I'll bet you did," said Dave. "I'm sorry you had to go through all of that. But now you're eighteen, right? You're out of the system?"

Leon didn't say anything.

"You're not eighteen, are you?" I asked.

"Almost seventeen," he said defiantly.

Dave's mouth tightened, but he ignored Leon's answer. "So how did you end up here?"

"Hitched, mostly, like I told you. Just headed away. Wanted to get somewhere new. Start over," Leon mumbled.

"And the new name?"

"I figured maybe someone would look for a kid named Leon Blackwell. Leon's a dumb name, anyway. I always wanted to be Leo, like that actor. Acting would be cool. I wish I were him."

"Leon—Leo—I'll call you whatever you want. You have that right. But Angie was right. The police aren't going to be happy you lied to them about who you were. You have to get straight with them."

"I don't want to go back to that place in Bangor!"

Dave hesitated. Then his voice was strong. "I promise you won't have to. If you promise you're not lying to us now, and that you haven't lied about anything that happened to Ike."

"I told the truth about that."

"If I can fix it so you can stay here, you'll have to go to school. Really attend classes and do homework. Not just sit in the back when I'm teaching."

Leo shrugged. "I guess." He looked at Dave. "You'd really let me stay here with you?"

"I'd have to talk to people at the state," Dave cautioned. "So I can't promise. But I think I could work it out. In the meantime, though, you'd have to do exactly what the police tell you to. And what I need you to do."

"You're not my dad. And police don't care about me."

"Your dad's gone, and the police just want to solve Ike's murder. If they see you as a problem, they'd just as soon put you in jail, so they'd know where you were. Or send you back to that group home."

To my surprise, Leon nodded. "Yeah. I figured that. That's why I gave them a fake name."

"Well, you can be Leo so far as I'm concerned, but you're going to have to be 'Blackwell' again, I'm afraid."

"Got it."

"Good. Now, the sooner we get this straightened out the better. Angie, call Pete or Ethan, please." He looked at Leo, who was clearly nervous. "They may want to see Leo again. But I'm hoping they'll be understanding, since now he's willing to tell them the truth."

I nodded, picked up my phone, and went into the living room to call.

"Why are you doing this for me?" I heard Leo ask. "What do you want from me?"

"I want you to finish high school and plan a future with some hope in it," said Dave. "I'm doing it because no one did that for me. Life is pretty lonely when you have no one to depend on."

Chapter Fifteen

No words, but seashells, deer, and sprigs of flowers on a beautiful darning sampler—a type of sampler seldom stitched in North America.

—Sarah Isabella Hunt, age eleven, Wyverstone School, East Anglia, England, 1806, stitched these pictures on a darning sample. Darning samplers were practical demonstrations of skills needed to mend fabrics. A teacher or parent would tear the cloth in an "L" shape or cut a hole in it. (L-shaped tears were called "winkle-hawks," and holes were called "barn doors.") The task was to mend the holes completely, copying the weave of the cloth. A subcategory of needlework samplers, darning samplers were most often required of Dutch and English girls.

"He gave us a fake name? What else has he lied about?"

I'd called Pete, but he was with Ethan and had handed his phone over. Ethan was head of the murder investigation. "He was scared, Ethan. He's just a kid."

Ethan sighed. "Okay. You and Dave bring him back over to the station and we'll talk with him again. Maybe he'll remember more this time. And we'll contact DHHS—Department of Health and Human Services—and let them know where he is."

"He won't have to go back to the group home, will he?"

"Not if he's eighteen and has aged out. But I want him to be somewhere we can get hold of him."

I hesitated. "He's not eighteen. But Dave Percy's offered him a place to stay."

"If he's not eighteen, DHHS has to be involved. But, between us, I don't want him shipped off to some place. Percy's really stepped up on this one. He's probably not certified for foster care, but he's a teacher, and a navy vet, with no criminal record. Maybe we could get some paperwork through fast, if he's sure he wants to do this. We really don't know this kid."

"Dave's serious, Ethan. Anything you could do to help would be great."

"Well, bring Leo, or Leon, or whatever his name is, into the station now, and I'll see what I can arrange. I'll call DHHS and let them know he's not missing."

Half an hour later we were at the Haven Harbor Police Department, in the small, bare room usually used for questioning suspects. When he was working on a local case, Ethan used it as his office. The walls were painted off-white, and what looked like dried coffee stains were splashed against one wall. The oak table in the center of the room was scarred and bolted to the floor.

I'd been there before, but not often.

I wasn't usually a suspect.

Leo (he wanted to be called Leo, and I saw no rea-

son why we shouldn't do that as long as he acknowledged that, legally, his name was Leon) was sitting at
one end of the table, his shoulders hunched over
and his hands shaking. Ethan sat opposite him, and
Dave and I were relegated to a corner. Pete hadn't
joined us. He'd waved from his office when we'd
come in but was on the telephone. Maybe with DHHS.
I hoped he'd be able to cut some of the paperwork required so Leo could stay with Dave.

"Before I waste more time talking to you, understand that lying is not a good idea. Especially lying to
the police. And this is a murder investigation!"

Leo's hands were shaking. He nodded.

"Speak to me. Out loud."

"Yes, sir," he managed to get out.

I was torn. I felt like lecturing Ethan and telling
him to be kinder, gentler. Leo had gone through
hard times. But Ethan was a good guy. Right now he
was playing a role. He had to be tough. And Leo had
lied about some basic facts. Like who he was. I clenched
my fists and felt my fingernails cutting into my palms. If
I were Ethan I'd be wicked angry. The most important time for a murder investigation was the first
forty-eight hours. No detective wanted to waste time
interviewing a witness or suspect more than once unless it was absolutely necessary.

Which it seemed to be now.

Leo hadn't had an easy life, and he didn't trust
easily. But this wasn't a time for excuses.

I'd had a rough adolescence after Mama disappeared. Kids in town had called me a slut, just as
they'd called her. I hadn't made life easy for myself,
or for Gram. But Gram had been my rock during
those years, although I hadn't always appreciated her
concern or taken her advice.

Being a teenager was never easy. But it was much harder when you weren't like everyone else in your town or school.

"So, your real name?" Ethan asked.

"Leon Michael Blackwell."

"And your birth date?"

Leon gave a date, hesitating at the year.

"Your real birth date," Ethan repeated impatiently. "I told you to tell the truth. Lying about your age isn't going to make this easier."

Dave leaned over as Leon gave another date. My mind calculated quickly. He'd admitted to Dave and me that he wasn't eighteen. But he was barely sixteen. Dave gritted his teeth. No wonder Leo was worried about being sent back to the group home.

"Thank you. I might add that you'd better not lie about anything else. I've already checked with DHHS and talked with the head of your group home."

"I'll bet that guy hardly noticed I was gone."

"He noticed," Ethan replied dryly. "But right now I'm more interested in what happened in Haven Harbor. Of all the places in the country you could have run to, why did you come here?"

"I just wanted to get away. The first guy who gave me a lift was from New Brunswick. He had a lumber truck and drove me south. I told him I wanted to see the ocean. He said he'd been in Haven Harbor, and it was a nice place. Kind of old-fashioned, he said, but friendly. Next truck I hitched with, I said that was where I was going."

"You didn't know anyone in town before you got here?"

Leon shook his head. "No, sir."

"How did you plan to support yourself?"

"I figured this place was popular with people from

away, so in summer some restaurant or motel might
hire me. I'm a hard worker."

"So you started picking up bottles."

"I'd done that before, places I'd lived. And then I
met Ike."

"Did you ever steal from Ike?"

"No!"

"Pax Henry told me he took you and Ike to the redemption center on Saturday and redeemed bottles
worth thirty-two dollars and fifty-five cents. What
happened to that money?"

I did some fast math. Most bottles and cans returned five cents. For some liquor bottles, you got as
much as fifteen cents. But you had to have a lot of
bottles and cans to get thirty-two dollars and fifty-five
cents back. A lot of work. And, on the other hand, certainly not enough money to live on. Why was Ethan
bothering about thirty-two dollars and change?

Leon shrugged. "Ike kept the money. He's the one
who bought us cereal and stuff."

"Where did he keep his money, Leon?"

Leo shifted in his chair. "Under the mattress he
slept on."

Ethan made a note.

"Can I stay with Mr. Percy?"

"For the time being. I checked with DHHS and,
bluntly, the head of your group house doesn't want
you back. But, Dave"—Ethan turned to Dave—"you
have to be officially approved as a foster parent, since
Leon is under eighteen. I can help push the paperwork forward. Pete's working on that right now. I
think we'll be able to get it through. Not many foster
families are interested in teenage boys. But you'll
need to file immediately."

Dave nodded. "I understand. Leo has agreed to attend school here, so I'll go ahead and register him there with my address. They know me; they'll let him attend and wait for paperwork."

"Go ahead, then," Ethan agreed. He turned back to Leo. "And I don't want to hear about any problems at school, or anywhere in Haven Harbor, from Mr. Percy or anyone else. You understand both he and I are going out on a limb for you. Don't mess it up."

Leo shook his head. "No, sir."

"Good. Now, there were a lot of broken bottles in the garage. Some of them were bloody. And a knife was next to Ike Hamilton's body. Did you put it there?"

"No!"

"Did you touch it?"

"Maybe. I guess. If it was one of Ike's knives. I didn't touch it yesterday."

"But you recognized it."

"Ike had a bunch of knives he used for cooking and stuff. It looked like one of those. I didn't go to the cabinet he kept things in and check! There was blood all over, and Ike was dead!" Leo sounded as though he was reliving the experience. "I told you yesterday. I checked to see if Ike was dead, and he was. And then I got out of there!"

"Where did you go?"

"I just ran. Then I remembered Mr. Percy said if I needed help I could go to his house. He told me his house was yellow. I remembered a yellow house from going with Ike on his rounds."

"So you went to Mr. Percy's house."

Leo nodded. "Yeah."

Ethan turned over one of the papers in front of him. "Did you always go with Ike when he collected bottles?"

"Pretty much. His back hurt. I helped him."

"Did he go to the same places, in the same order, all the time?"

"He had a schedule. He went to houses where people saved bottles for him once every two weeks. Businesses, he went to once or twice a week. He went to Harbor Haunts every day, because they had a lot of bottles." Leo smiled a little. "He knew everyone, and everyone knew him. He told me stories about people. He was really nice to me."

"So you didn't mind living with him."

"Mind? No! He was good to me. He showed me where we could get food for nothing, like at the church, and at the end of the day at the bake shop—the patisserie." Leo didn't pronounce the word right, but we all knew what he was talking about. "Ike needed me to help him." Leo's eyes filled. "I wouldn't have hurt him. He needed me."

I wondered if Leo had ever felt needed before.

Chapter Sixteen

Keep cleane your samplers, sleepe not as you sit,
For sluggishness doth spoile the rarest wit.
—William Barley. *A Booke of Curious and*
Strange Inventions, called the First Part of
Needleworkes. England, 1596. This was one
of the first English pattern books that
specifically mentioned samplers.

It was after nine when we left the police station. At least for now, Leo would be staying with Dave. They dropped me off at my house, and I realized how exhausted I was.

Trixi reminded me to fill her food dish with canned food, and then, after a quick snack, she followed me up the stairs to my bedroom.

Longingly I looked at my bed, but decided to call Gram and Reverend Tom first. After all, Tom had already called his DHHS friend about Leo, and I wanted him to know that, yes, Leo was in the system. Just under another name and birth date.

"Been thinking about you," Gram answered. "Have you invited Patrick to your birthday dinner on Friday?"

No way was I going to avoid celebrating my twenty-eighth birthday. The night I'd turned twenty-seven I'd been sitting surveillance in a twenty-four-hour diner in Mesa filled with college students taking study breaks. Most were younger than me, but not by much, and the textbook and laptop I used as props said I belonged. All my life I'd used props to look as though I fit in, whether the props were low-cut T-shirts or cameras or books or eyeglasses with plain glass, or hats that covered my long hair when I pinned it up. I suspected everyone used props at times. But was everyone as aware as I was of what they were doing? What roles they were playing? Leo had said being an actor would be "cool." Was he playing a role now?

"Angie? Are you still there?" Gram's voice was patient but concerned. "Everything all right?"

"Everything is fine," I assured her. "I was just distracted. I haven't checked with Patrick yet. But I will." I didn't want him to think I expected a gift. Expectations made me nervous. Too many times in my life I'd hoped and then been disappointed. It was easier not to have expectations.

But if Gram was going to make a big deal about my birthday, I'd have to ask Patrick to come for dinner. And tell him why.

"I'll check with him. I promise. Is Tom there? I wanted to tell him something."

"He's over at the church for a late meeting. Can I give him a message?"

I hesitated. "You remember that boy we talked about yesterday?"

"The one living with Ike, whom the police were investigating?"

"Exactly. Tom called a friend of his who worked at

DHHS to see if the boy was in the system. They had no record of him."

"Lucky boy," Gram said dryly.

"Well, actually, not." I decided not to mention my investigations in Dexter; Gram would only be worried, and I was home again. "We found out his name isn't Leo Smith. It's Leon Blackwell. And he lived in a group home in Bangor for a while after his parents died." All true. Just no details.

"So he lied to you and Dave."

"At first. But now he's told us the truth. Ethan's going to help Dave be approved as a foster parent so Leo—that's what he wants to be called—can stay with him, at least for now."

Gram was quiet. "I hope Dave knows what he's getting into. Opening your home to a boy who's suspected of murdering someone is above and beyond what most people would ask."

"He volunteered," I assured her. "He's convinced Leo's innocent. And Leo's agreed to attend school here in Haven Harbor."

"Did Tom call you about the lawyer you were asking about?"

"He left me a message." I glanced at the note I'd made after listening to my messages. "Willow Sinclair. I'll have Dave call her." I was already more involved than I'd planned to be. But Dave was the one taking the lead on this case.

"I'll tell Tom," said Gram. "And let me know about Friday, right?"

"I will," I agreed. "I promise."

Patrick had suggested we have dinner together sometime this week. He probably didn't intend it to be at a family birthday party at the rectory, but that was the way it looked now.

I yawned and decided I'd call Patrick in the morning. Trixi seemed to agree. She was already asleep on my pillow. Gently, I moved her over and crawled under the covers.

My mind swirled with needlepoint designs and country roads and Leo's face. Behind everything, I kept seeing Ike Hamilton, who'd been born with disadvantages his family hadn't been able to change but who'd done his best to support himself. He'd grown up in Haven Harbor and made a place for himself here. He'd had friends, or at least close acquaintances. And he'd welcomed a stranger to share his limited world.

Haven Harbor had always accepted people who were a little different. Not everyone in town had approved of my mother's behavior, or even of mine, but most people had accepted us for who we were.

Who would have killed Ike? The Chambers might not have been thrilled that he was in town, but I couldn't imagine them killing him. Killing was an act of passion, or desperation. Feelings I couldn't fit into what I knew of Ike Hamilton or his life.

But others knew him much better than I did. He "made rounds," Leo had said. He hadn't wandered randomly through town. He went to places where he was welcome. People saved bottles for him. Ruth had sometimes shared her lunch with him.

Tomorrow I'd talk to Ruth, I decided, as my thoughts finally slowed. I pushed my pillow down and cuddled with it, and with Trixi.

Tomorrow. Ruth would know something. Maybe something that would help solve Ike's murder.

Chapter Seventeen

Immortal made what Should We Mind
So Much as Immortality
Of beings for A Heaven Designed
What but A Heaven the Care should be.
  —Robert Henderson, 1762. Embroidered
    on a square, bordered sampler, signed in
    black silk.

Morning came too soon.

I buried my head under the covers, but Trixi's paw was gently tapping my left ear. "It's still dark," I muttered, but she wasn't deterred. Finally I opened my eyes. It was after eight. And, yes, it was still dark. With my head (and ears) free of quilts, I could hear rain pouring on the roof.

"April showers . . ." I muttered as I pulled myself out of bed and headed for the bathroom, Trixi happily leading the way. She knew my schedule. The pounding heat of the shower woke me up. Trixi waited patiently as I pulled clothes on before she led me downstairs, where she knew her food dish—and my coffeepot—were waiting.

While Trixi focused on the can of salmon pate cat

food I put in her dish, I made coffee and mixed together oatmeal, raisins, dried cranberries, and water,
then put the bowl of cereal in the microwave. Oatmeal was usually a winter breakfast, but this dark day
required comfort and warmth.

Thank goodness I'd driven to Dexter yesterday.
Today I'd just as soon stay home.

After breakfast I sorted through bills, checked the
Mainely Needlepoint website (no orders today), and
then called Patrick.

"Good morning!" His voice was much more cheerful than I felt. "What's happening in your life? How
was the dinner at Dave's?"

Briefly I told him about Leo/Leon and our trip to
the police department.

"Are you sure he's innocent?" Patrick asked.

Why did everyone ask that? "He's only sixteen,
and he's had a hard life. But I can't see any reason he
would have killed Ike," I answered. "Dave doesn't
think he did, either, and Dave works with a lot of
kids."

"Not kids who're murder suspects," Patrick pointed
out.

"No. But maybe this was just a case of 'wrong time,
wrong place,'" I assured him. "He found Ike's body,
and he told someone. Would a murderer have done
that?"

"That boy's lucky to have Dave stand up for him,"
said Patrick. "And you too. How involved are you?"

"I don't know," I said honestly. "But I want to help
when I can." *Help Pete, too,* I thought. If I could find
other suspects for Pete and Ethan to check out, then
maybe they'd ease up on Leo. I was definitely going
to call Ruth.

"So, did you decide when we could have our dinner?"

"What about Friday?" I asked.

"Friday's fine," Patrick agreed. "Would you like to go to Damariscotta, or even Camden? We're both too busy to cook this week, and I'm getting a little tired of the Harbor Haunts menu."

Tired of the Harbor Haunts? That was like saying "tired of Haven Harbor." Maine was full of great restaurants (most of which I'd never been to). But I was loyal to Harbor Haunts. Eating there was like being at home, with no cooking or cleaning up but with a check to pay.

"Actually, Gram and Tom have invited us to the rectory for dinner Friday," I told him, hesitantly.

"Oh. Well, that's fine. They don't usually invite us for Friday night. Anyone else coming?"

"Not that I know of," I told him.

"What shall we bring? I know they both enjoy wine."

"Wine would be great," I seconded. Patrick knew a lot more about wine than I did, but Tom was learning, and the two of them had spent several evenings talking grapes and vintages while Gram and I sipped and talked about the past, or the future. "And . . . not a big deal. But I should tell you there'll probably be a birthday cake. And candles."

"I haven't seen one of those in a while," Patrick said. "Who's the honoree?"

"Me," I admitted.

"It's your birthday? On Friday?"

"Guilty," I admitted. He'd written it on his calendar. Had he forgotten? The situation was definitely awkward.

"Why didn't you tell me?"

"I just did. And it's not important," I assured him. "It was Gram's idea to invite us that night. She's going to bake the same cake she used to make for my birthday years ago. I'm sure she's not going to make a big deal of it. I'm not a child anymore." Besides, Gram wouldn't do anything to embarrass me— would she?

"You most definitely are not a child." Patrick laughed. "But I'm glad you warned me. I would have felt pretty stupid going to a birthday party without a gift."

"No! You don't have to bring a gift. This is just family," I assured him. "No big deal."

"Except for the special cake and probably candles, right?"

"Right," I admitted. "Anyway, we'll talk before then. I have some work to do, and you have the gallery to set up."

"Which is where I am now," Patrick agreed. "I'm considering bringing an easel and some paints down here so I can work instead of twiddling my thumbs between customers. What do you think?"

"That's a great idea. Sort of a live demonstration—artist at work."

"When you put it that way, I'm not as sure." He laughed. "But I may try it. Be in touch?"

"Absolutely," I agreed, putting down my cell.

Trixi was sitting at a window, batting at raindrops dribbling down the outside of the pane. Definitely a dank day.

Puddles were everywhere. Mud season was technically over, but damp days weren't.

I'd planned to call Ruth. Despite the weather, I picked up my cell. "Good morning, Ruth! Hope I'm not bothering you."

"Angie, you never bother me. I could use a break. I was just editing the chapters I wrote yesterday. I already know how the story ends."

Most folks in town didn't know that seventy-nine-year-old Ruth, living with serious arthritis, was also the erotica authors Chastity Falls and S.M. Bond. I'd read one of her books, and her work wasn't my style, but I'd never underestimate someone her age again.

"Ruth, would you have a little time to talk? I'd like to know more about Ike Hamilton. Dave and I have been helping Leo, the boy who was living with him."

"Love to see you and get caught up. And I hate to ask, the weather's so awful, but since you're going out, could you pick up a couple of things for me at the grocery? Getting out is such a pain, and I don't need much."

"I can do that," I assured her, pulling a pencil and pen out of my desk drawer and not mentioning that I'd thought we could talk on the phone. "What do you need?"

"A half gallon of milk, a dozen of those eggs from organically fed chickens, a pound of salted butter, a pound of hamburger. Maybe some green beans or broccoli—whatever looks best. And I'd love a pint of chocolate ice cream. I've been longing for a chocolate milkshake."

"No problem. Sure there's nothing else?"

"Nothing else. That's plenty. I don't eat so much these days."

"I'll stop at the grocery, then. I could use some cat food and milk myself. See you in about an hour?"

"That sounds perfect. Shall I make us tuna sandwiches for lunch?"

"I hate for you to go to that bother."

"No bother. I was planning to make one for myself. Making two shouldn't be taxing. I'm not *that* old," Ruth assured me.

I checked that Trixi had dry food and fresh water (she'd finished her canned cat food) and put on my hooded Windbreaker. "I'll be back after lunch, Trixi," I assured her. "You take care of the house."

She meowed in response. The house was in good paws.

Chapter Eighteen

When I can read my title clear
To mansions in the skies
I bid farewell to every fear
And wipe my weeping eyes.
Let cares like a wild deluge come
And storms of sorrow fall
May I but safely reach my home
My God, my heav'n, my all.

    —Jannet Christie stitched this part of an
    Isaac Watts hymn at a mission school in
    Calcutta, India, December 8, 1796. Jannet
    also included a crown, two lines of trees,
    and a simple floral border on her sampler.

The grocery store wasn't as busy as usual. I suspected that potential shoppers, given the choice, had opted to wait until after the rain stopped to do their errands. I easily picked up the groceries Ruth needed, and the items I could use, and checked them out separately. Cashiers were used to people shopping for others. Maine boasted the oldest population in the country, and many people shopped for elderly neighbors for whom navigating long grocery aisles was a challenge.

Ruth's little house was (on a sunny day) in the shade of the Congregational church's steeple. She and her husband, Ben, had grown up in Haven Harbor. Ben had been seriously disabled in Vietnam and died some years ago. Ruth had supported them both, and now herself, by writing.

Her dining room was her study, and she'd recently added a stairlift so she'd feel safer getting to her bedroom on the second floor.

I knocked on her door and waited. A year ago Ruth had walked with a cane. In the past months her arthritis had worsened, maybe because of the damp winter cold, and she'd been using a pink walker. It took her a few minutes to get to the door.

"Angie! So good to see you again!" She nodded at the grocery bags I carried. "And thank you for saving me a trip out in this dreadful weather. Come in, and we'll head for the kitchen and put those things away. I've already made our sandwiches."

It was noon, but on this dark day Ruth's kitchen lights were on, and the room was bright and cozy. I put her grocery bags on the counter, then quickly unpacked her few items and put them in her refrigerator.

"I really appreciate your getting those things," she said again. "I was dreading going out. Now I have plenty of food for the next few days."

"Happy to do it. I go to the store several times a week. Just give me a call if I can ever pick up something for you," I assured her.

"Thank you for that. Sarah sometimes picks up items for me too. And Dave is so kind. When he cooks too much for himself, sometimes he brings me a portion. I wouldn't make spaghetti and meatballs or meatloaf just for myself, and he loves to cook, so that's good for both of us."

"Dave's a great cook. I had dinner with him last night. His lasagna is terrific," I agreed.

"It is indeed," said Ruth. "Can I pour you a cup of tea?"

"Thank you," I said, sitting at one of the places she'd set at her kitchen table. "It's lovely of you to invite me for lunch."

As she opened a box of tea bags and poured water from her electric kettle, Ruth shook her head. "I've lived alone a lot of years, and I don't mind my own company. But I do enjoy a good talk, and sharing lunch with a friend is a wonderful way to break the day."

"You're writing?"

"I try to write a few new pages every day. But now that I'm self-publishing I'm also formatting and working with cover artists and doing my own social media publicity."

Ruth always amazed me with her productivity, and how she'd kept up with the times. For years she'd been published traditionally, but, as she'd once explained, readers of erotica often prefer to read privately, so when e-readers became popular, Ruth's sales increased. Now her books were sold only in digital versions.

She put our cups of tea on the table and sat with a sigh. "All set. Now, you eat, and tell me what you wanted to know about Ike. I keep thinking of that poor, dear man. He didn't deserve a violent end."

"No one does," I agreed, taking a bite of my sandwich. "Mmm. This tuna is delicious! What did you add?"

"A little sweet pickle relish and onion. My Ben always liked it that way," said Ruth. "Ike did too."

"You said he stopped in for bottles and had lunch with you sometimes," I reminded her.

"True. For years, he came to pick up my bottles every other Thursday, and we got to know each other a little. Ike did love to talk! I'll admit, sometimes in the days when I had publisher deadlines I just left the bottles for him on my back stoop. But in the past few years I've had more time, and after his parents died he depended more on the bottles for income, and was lonely so I made a point of inviting him in."

"That was kind of you."

"Perhaps. But in his own way, Ike was good company. He certainly kept me informed about all the local gossip. Or, at least, what he'd heard or assumed."

"Like what?"

"Let's see. Well, when the Standishes over to Pine Point Road were having marital problems a few years back, he told me they'd probably get divorced, because he'd seen Mr. Standish with a young redheaded woman at that motel near the redemption center. I didn't think much about it. But, sure enough, it wasn't two months later that the Standishes broke up, and Mr. Standish married that other young woman. Ike might have been slow in some ways, but he could add up what was owed him for the bottles, and he kept his eyes open."

"Do you have any ideas about why someone would have killed him?" I asked, sipping my tea.

"I've racked my brain, but the only trouble he ever mentioned was with Ed Campbell and the Chamber of Commerce. Reverend Tom would know more about that. He's on the Chamber. Ed was convinced

Ike was an embarrassment to the town. He was probably right in getting Ike's family home condemned. It was falling apart, so Ike was living in a dangerous situation. But trying to get Ike to live in a group home for those with disabilities, which is what Ed wanted—a home far from Haven Harbor—was just cruel. Ike lived here all of his life and was never a bother to anyone. He kept himself as clean as he could, and his collecting bottles actually was helpful to people like me, who didn't get out much, and kept Haven Harbor a bit neater. The only complaint I ever heard about his collecting bottles was when one of the schools ran a bottle drive to raise money for baseball uniforms or a senior trip, and people had to decide whether to save their bottles for the students or give them to Ike."

"I'm guessing he lost some income then."

"Probably did. But he never complained. And, keep in mind, Ike's bottle collecting rounds were just in the commercial sections of Haven Harbor, and homes close to the downtown area."

I smiled. I understood what Ruth was saying, but "downtown" meant something very different to most people than the approximately ten square blocks and the Green in Haven Harbor that probably were Ike's territory.

"I'd heard Ike had trouble with the Chamber of Commerce—even Leo knew about that. But I'm trying to find out if anyone else had a grudge against him, or any other reason to kill him." Ike's death had been a messy one. Someone had been very angry.

"How is that boy, Leo? He was with Ike the past two times he stopped here. They both came in for sandwiches once, and Leo hardly opened his mouth.

I wondered where he'd come from, but he seemed like a nice young man, and he was definitely helping Ike. I liked that about him."

"Leo's a suspect in Ike's murder, Ruth. But he's staying with Dave, at least for now, and Dave's being very supportive. He's even said he'll get Leo a lawyer if one is needed, and Reverend Tom has found someone who'll represent the boy if necessary."

Ruth shook her head sadly. "It's horrible that boy's a suspect in a murder case."

"That's why I'm trying to find out who else the police should be looking at."

Ruth looked at me. "You seem to find yourself in the middle of situations like this, don't you, Angie? You're like Dave: You want the world to be a fair and peaceful place."

"That's the way it should be, isn't it?" I admitted. "I was with Dave when Leo came and told us about Ike, so I was involved, although when Dave invited Leo to stay with him, I was concerned. I want to believe Leo had nothing to do with Ike's death, but I'm not fully convinced he's innocent, and I don't want Dave to be hurt in any way."

"That makes perfect sense to me." Ruth leaned back in her chair, her sandwich finished.

"The last few times you talked with Ike, did he have any special stories to tell? Any gossip he'd picked up that might somehow have gotten him in trouble?"

Ruth chuckled. "Nothing that would get *him* in trouble. But some that might get a few other folks' knickers in a knot."

"Like?" I leaned forward.

"Now, before I say anything, understand Ike had his own way of seeing things, and figuring them out. Sometimes he was right on target, like with the Standishes. Other times . . . well, Ike's imagination got the better of him. So if he said he'd seen strange flying objects, and aliens might be looking for a place to land, well, I always figured the Portland Jetport changed flight patterns, or one of the smaller airports had been taking people on charter sightseeing flights."

I laughed. "Okay. Not the UFOs. But anything about folks in town?"

"Let me think. Ike didn't like that young woman who works for the Thibodeaus—Cindy Bouchard? He told me Cindy yelled at Madame Thibodeau when she knew Henri and Nicole were at the patisserie and wouldn't know. And he thought Cindy was taking some of the things Henri thought his mother lost because she couldn't remember where she'd put them."

"Hm. Anything else?"

"He didn't like Gus Gleason, either," Ruth thought out loud.

"Gus Gleason? Who owns the Book Nook?"

"Right. Gus saves bottles for Ike, which is good, but Ike thinks he's cheating on his wife. In the past he's said Gus can't be trusted with young women. About a month ago he told me Gus was driving that young woman who works for him now—Cos Curran—crazy. Pinching and flirting and such. He'd seen Cos crying, and she told him."

"I know Cos. I don't think she'd work for anyone who'd harass her. But she's a senior in high school saving for college. Maybe she thinks she can handle it, if Gus really does bother her. And flirting doesn't mean he's cheating on his wife."

"True. I'm just telling you what Ike said. Sometimes he sees or hears things but doesn't get the full picture. Like, he told me Sandy Lewis hurts her husband, Jim, and that's why Jim's in bed a lot."

"But Jim has MS, right? Gram once told me he'd been sick for years."

Ruth leaned toward me and smiled. "Ike also told me, in strict confidence, that our friend Sarah was in trouble with the law."

"Sarah! Where'd he get that idea?"

"He's seen one of the local policemen checking out her shop recently."

"Oh, Ruth! Sarah's dating Pete Lambert!" I laughed. "Wait until I tell Sarah what Ike thought!"

"See what I mean? You can't take as gospel what Ike said."

"Got it."

"If you really want to find out what he was saying, I'd talk with Leo. True or not, Ike's stories might lead somewhere. Leo'd been with Ike several weeks. He'd know what stories Ike was telling recently."

"And he'd know where Ike went on his rounds. You're right, Ruth. That's an excellent idea. If Leo would tell me what he knows."

"If I were that young man I'd be singing every note I'd ever heard Ike hum. I'd do anything I could to get myself off the suspect list, and other people on it."

Chapter Nineteen

Tell me ye knowing and discerning few
Where I may find a Friend both firm and true
Who dares stand by me when in deep distress
And then his Love and Friendship most express.
  —Mary Ann Richards, England, June 1,
     1800. Mary Ann's elaborate sampler also
     included a border of flowers and several
     trees outside a group of brick buildings.

I took my own groceries home and made chili for dinner but kept thinking about what Ruth had said.

She made sense. Ike talked a lot. He might well have said something to Leo that would lead to his killer. Would Leo talk to me? I knew he was at school, and Dave was in charge, so I texted Dave, asking if he and Leo would be willing to spend some time with me.

My phone rang in the middle of the afternoon. "What do you have in mind?" Dave asked.

"I don't know exactly what the police are doing, but I think they still consider Leo their primary suspect. If we could find other people who might have motives, maybe the police would go easier on Leo."

"That makes sense," Dave agreed.

"How's he doing?"

"He's in classes, but the end of April is a hard time of year for a student to start in a new school. He doesn't know anyone, and everyone else is focused on the end of school and their summer plans. Plus, this is the first day he's been in regular classes, but all his teachers have told me he's behind. Not just in their classes, but generally. By his age he should be in tenth grade. But his basic skills are very weak—more like those of a sixth grader."

"Ouch. Can you help him with that?"

"If he's willing, I can tutor him this summer and see how much we can make up. He's not a stupid kid, Angie. He's just had to focus on surviving, not on school. We have to get through this murder situation, and then he and I will have a serious talk about where we go from here."

Dave had said "we," not "he." And he was thinking about the future. He'd already made an emotional commitment to Leo.

"I had lunch with Ruth today. She knew Ike pretty well, over a lot of years. She told me he collected gossip—stories—about people in town, and often shared them."

"Leo said Ike talked a lot," Dave agreed.

"And according to Ruth, Ike made regular rounds. He picked up bottles at the same places on a pretty regular schedule. Since Leo was with him for several weeks, they probably made those rounds together."

"True."

"If Leo could retrace those routes and tell us what he remembers Ike saying about specific people in town, it could be helpful. He may have heard something he didn't pay attention to, but that would explain what happened to Ike."

"You don't think the Chamber of Commerce was to blame?"

"I'm going to talk to Tom—he's on the Chamber. But Ed Campbell's the president, and several people have mentioned he was concerned about Ike. Ed might have been embarrassed that Ike was in town, but I can't see him risking his reputation or his used car business because of one man who picked up bottles."

"We can't know everything about everyone in town."

"True. And we know the Chamber was an issue for Ike. But I'd like to know if anyone else had a complaint about him. A major complaint. Since he knew so many people, and collected so many stories, he might have embarrassed someone, or found out something that would make someone angry enough to kill him."

Dave hesitated. "It's a stretch, Angie. Even if Leo remembers Ike's ramblings, he may not be able to connect them. He was so new in town, he didn't know people. And he has to stay with me—that's the rule at this point. But I could ask him if we could drive around town and he could point out what he knew."

"That would be great, Dave, although I'd rather we walk. It will take longer—but Ike walked. Maybe retracing the routes he took will help Leo remember."

"Leo's down at the gym. He should be back here any minute. Why don't I talk with him and call you back?"

I put down my cell. I hoped Dave could talk Leo into telling us some of Ike's stories. Based on Ruth's comments, they might be more strange than helpful, but what else could we do to help?

I checked the Mainely Needlepoint website. One order, for a product we didn't have in stock. Then I called Ob and Anna Winslow.

"Angie, hi! Sorry I missed you at the Blessing," said Ob.

"I saw you and Anna out on your boat," I assured him. "All set for fishermen from away?"

"Pretty much set to go. A few early reservations have come in, and one for Memorial Day weekend, which usually fills up pretty fast. Hope the weather cooperates and we have a good summer."

"Hoping for you!" I agreed. "I just wanted to check in. Mainely Needlepoint got an order in today for a wall hanging of a great cormorant. The same design as on our Save the Cormorants pillows, but without the words. Any chance you or Anna could handle that in the next month? Anna and I talked about your stitching more sachets, but this order would pay more."

"Don't see why not. Neither of us are wicked busy this time of year. It's too soon for Anna to put in her garden, and I'm pretty much waiting for reservations. I'll check with Anna, but I'm pretty sure we could each do one. We were working on the extra sachets, but we can put those aside for the moment. If we do two larger pieces you'd have an extra in inventory in case anyone else is interested."

"Great idea," I said. "I'll write to the customer and explain all our work is custom, but we could have this for her by—shall I say Memorial Day?"

"Don't see why not. We know the pattern and stitches. It'll give us something to do while we're watching the Red Sox or the Weather Channel."

I grinned. Captain Ob wasn't the only mariner in town who was addicted to the Weather Channel. "Thanks, Ob. My best to Anna too."

"Happy to oblige."

I hurriedly wrote a note to the customer, explaining she could have the hanging by the end of May, but I'd need a fifty percent deposit now. Credit card or check.

Having the website was good in the winter months; summer customers remembered us for Christmas gifts and other occasions, like the wedding favors that convinced Gram to start the business six or seven years ago. But in the summer months most Needlepointers had other jobs, and custom work with a short turnaround time could be a challenge.

Ruth's writing, of course, was year-round, and her arthritis didn't allow her to do much stitching anymore. Sarah's antiques store was busier in the summer than in the winter, and Captain Ob's charter fishing was seasonal. Dave Percy was the only one of us who had a regular job in the winter but free time in the summer. In warm months he spent hours each day in his poison garden, but he was the only one who did more needlepoint in the summer than in the winter.

Which reminded me that I should start looking for another person or persons to join us. Ob was right: We should have a basic inventory of the items that customers asked for regularly.

I made a mental note to ask Gram if she knew anyone else in town who was a needlepointer and might be interested. I'd keep my eyes and ears open too. Anyone we added had to be reliable as well as accomplished at needlepointing.

Dave's return call came in just as I was about to take a tea break.

"Angie, Leo's willing. He's not sure he knows anything that would be helpful, but he'll go with us. He says Ike had about a dozen different routes. He stopped at some businesses every day, but private homes stops were more apt to be every two weeks. To cover all the routes would mean walking fast, and doing one or two every day after school for a week or so."

Ouch. "I didn't realize it would take that long."

"I suspected. But if I drive we can stop every block or so. Our retracing might not be as thorough, but we could cover a lot more distance. And, Angie, tonight I have to get supper, and both Leo and I have homework to do."

"Of course. I understand."

"Could we start tomorrow? Meet us at Haven Harbor High at three in the afternoon and we could take off from there."

"It's a deal," I agreed. "See you then."

In the meantime, I thought, I'll check with Tom about the Chamber of Commerce and maybe talk with Ed Campbell. My tea water was boiling when the phone rang again.

"Sarah! How's business?"

"Slow," she admitted. "I'm thinking of going to Harbor Haunts tonight. Pete's working overtime on the Ike Hamilton case, and I wondered if you'd join me?"

Patrick had wanted us to have dinner. But he was busy tonight, and I was going to see him Friday. He'd also said he was getting tired of Harbor Haunts. Plus, I could stop at the Book Nook and chat with Cos Curran. She'd be there after school, and she was one of the people whom Ruth mentioned Ike had talked about. "Perfect. Meet you there a little past five?"

"See you then."

April was an in-between season. It started with "mud season," when melting snow and ice combined with April showers, but now the ground was drying out. Businesses that closed for the winter were back open. Snowbirds who'd wintered in Florida or North Carolina or Arizona—or even in Vermont (a subgroup of Mainers wintered in Vermont and summered in Maine)—were back, or on their way. But the crowds of summer tourists weren't here yet. People were restless; in waiting. They'd been weathered in during the winter and were anxious to get outside, or get back to work. Mainers were waiting for customers, waiting for ground to be ready to plant, waiting for summer activities to start up, and waiting to refill bank accounts that bills for oil and propane and wood had emptied over the winter.

Dinner at Harbor Haunts was definitely a good idea.

I gave Trixi a bit of extra food, pulled on a hoodie, and headed downtown. I hoped the Book Nook wasn't too crowded so I could talk with Cos. And that her boss, Gus Gleason, would be busy somewhere else.

Chapter Twenty

One did commend me to a Wife both fair and young
That had French Spanish and Italian tongue
I thankd him kindly and told him I loved none such
For I thought one tongue For a Wife too much
What love Ye not The Learned Yes as my Life
A Learned Schollar but not a Learned Wife.
  —Ann Wing, age thirteen, Boston,
     Massachusetts, 1739.

The Book Nook was silent. At first I didn't think anyone was there, but then I saw Cos Curran. Her dark
hair was shorter, in a more sophisticated cut than I'd
remembered it. Last summer had been rough for
her, but as far as I knew her winter had been quiet.
She'd convinced her best friend, Mary Clough, to
finish high school before she married Rob Trask,
Ethan's younger brother, and both girls would be
graduating in a few weeks.

I was proud of both of them. They'd had to cope
with serious family issues, but they'd both survived
and were stronger for it. I hoped Leo could do the
same.

I pretended to be looking through the books on

the sale table. I'd been collecting books about needlepoint and had bought a couple of cookbooks in the past year, hoping they'd magically turn me into a competent, if not gourmet, cook.

So far my cooking had improved (it had nowhere to go but up), and my knowledge of needlepoint had increased, but I still had a lot to learn in both areas.

Cos was in the back corner of the store, near the door to the loading area, dusting shelves and book jackets. Every few minutes she'd take a book off a shelf and move it somewhere else. People must pick up books, decide not to buy them, and put them back on the wrong shelves. Not good for inventory control—or for finding the specific books people were looking for.

She turned around as I walked toward her. "Angie! Good to see you."

"And you. You'll have graduated and be out in the world soon."

She nodded, smiling. "I'm really excited. I've been accepted by U Maine Farmington, my first-choice school. I got a couple of small scholarships, and my parents are covering room and board. Now I'm trying to save enough for a good computer and stuff for my dorm room. The list of things people say I'll need is much longer than I'd thought! Bedding, and a microwave, and some new clothes. Not counting what I hear textbooks will cost once I get there."

"So that's why you're working here."

"After school and weekends." She shrugged. "I like working with books. And it's not as exhausting as waitressing or cleaning motel rooms, like some kids do."

"I steamed lobsters during my summers in high school," I agreed. "Hot, long hours, and the smell!" I held my nose, and we both laughed.

When I'd been Cos's age I'd been saving for a car and money to live on. College hadn't been for me. I'd planned to get out of town right after high school graduation, and I did, heading west with no particular destination in mind. I hadn't thought of decorating a dorm room, although I did scrounge at Goodwill and found sheets and a blanket for the convertible couch I'd had in my tiny apartment in Mesa. That seemed years ago.

"And what about Mary?"

Cos hesitated. "She and Rob are still together, but they haven't set a date. Rob's still sterning for Arwin Fraser and saving for a boat. Mary has her parents' home, of course, but it needs some work. She's decided to go to beautician school in Portland."

"Like your sister did," I couldn't help saying.

Cos nodded. "Jude did make pretty decent money."

"Hey, Cos, I was wondering . . ." I glanced around to make sure no one else was in the room. "What's it like working for Gus Gleason?"

"Why? You're looking for another job?"

"No, no," I assured her. "I'm just a bit worried about you. It may just be gossip, but Ike Hamilton told Ruth Hopkins that Gus was being a bit . . . forward . . . with you. And that he'd been that way with other girls who'd worked for him in the past."

Cos lowered her voice. "Ike has—had—a big imagination. I'll admit, one day he saw me when I was pretty upset. But I'm fine. Nothing to worry about."

"Why were you upset?"

Cos sighed. "I was shelving back-up books—books we haven't put out on the shelves yet—in the storeroom." She pointed at a door I hadn't noticed before. "The shelves are pretty high, so I was going up and down on the ladder. Gus came in and whistled and looked up the ladder at me—up the skirt I was wearing—and said he liked my thong. Then he reached up and stroked my leg." Cos shuddered. "I panicked. I've never gotten down from a ladder so fast."

"What did you say?"

"I didn't know what to say. I batted his hand away and said, 'Don't touch me!' He said he was just making sure I didn't fall off the ladder." Cos sniffed. "Sure he was. I was totally embarrassed. I must have turned red as a sunset. Gus just laughed, said he'd seen a lot worse." Cos shook her head. "I wasn't sure what he meant, but I was mortified. I went out back and started crying, and that's when Ike saw me. He told me Gus always liked the girls he hired 'more than he should' and that I should leave the job."

"What did you think?"

"At first I thought he was crazy. Gus was married, after all, and he and Nancy live right upstairs. But then I remembered the little things he'd said—flirting, I guess it was. I'd ignored them all. But I couldn't remember any boys who'd ever worked here. And I like Nancy. She's always been nice to me. But she's a nurse. She works long hours and isn't around a lot."

"You didn't quit."

"I need the job! And I do like working with the books. Now I make a point of staying as far away from Gus as I can. And I don't climb that ladder unless I have loose jeans on, and even then I try to be sure Gus is working somewhere else in the shop or talking to a customer."

"Are you afraid of Gus?" I asked seriously.

Cos shook her head. "He just makes me uncomfortable. Unless his behavior gets worse, I'll stay for the summer. More customers will be here then, so everyone will be busy. Gus said he was going to hire another high school girl after school is out. Whoever it is, I'm going to warn her before she takes the job. I'm embarrassed that Ike told Ruth, and Ruth told you . . . do you think everyone in town knows by now?"

"I hope not," I said. "But from what I understand, Ike did pass along gossip."

"Do they know yet who killed him?" Cos asked. "At school some kids say it was that weird boy who's staying with Mr. Percy."

"The police don't know yet, Cos. Mr. Percy and I are trying to help Leo, to find out whether anyone else would have had a reason to want Ike dead."

Cos thought for a minute. "I can't think of anyone. Although Gus was wicked mad when he found out I'd told Ike what he called 'our business.' He stopped leaving bottles for Ike and told him not to come back here."

"How did Gus know you'd told Ike?"

"I'd run outside, in back of the store. Ike was there, picking up bottles, so I blabbed to him. Gus came looking for me, and Ike yelled at him, told him he should leave good girls like me alone or he'd tell Nancy."

"Wow! Ike really yelled?"

"He did." Cos smiled. "He stood in front of me, as though he was going to protect me, even though I'm a little taller than he is . . . he was. It was kind of cool."

"What did Gus say?"

"He yelled back. Said Ike didn't know what he was talking about, and if he ever talked to Nancy, he'd kill him." Cos looked at me. "But, I mean, he just said that. I don't think he'd really do it. Then he told Ike not to come back for bottles anymore, and he ordered me to get back to work."

"And?"

"I did. He told me to keep my mouth shut, that nothing had happened." Cos grimaced. "Since then, you're the only person I've told about that afternoon. And Gus hasn't done anything weird since."

"If he does, you let me know. Or, better yet, tell Pete Lambert. Bosses aren't supposed to talk to their employees the way Gus did to you. And he certainly should never have touched you."

"I know, Angie. It's just that I really need this job. And it'll only be for a few more months. I'll leave for college in August."

"I understand. But I wish you were working somewhere else."

"There aren't that many jobs in Haven Harbor. Even summer jobs are filled months—sometimes a year—in advance."

"I know," I agreed. "But just do what you've been doing . . . stay away from Gus as much as you can."

"I will," Cos promised.

We both looked up as the bell on the front door rang and Sarah came in.

"I saw you through the front window, Angie," she said. "Hi, Cos. Has that book on English porcelain I ordered come in?"

"Not yet," Cos answered. "But it should be here any day. I'll call you when it arrives."

"Thanks. I'd like to confirm the years some trademarks were used before the summer folks get here."

"The snowbirds are arriving," Cos agreed. "A woman who lives outside of town had me order ten new thrillers for her the other day. She said this time of year is damp and chilly, and the perfect time to catch up on her reading."

"She's right," Sarah agreed. "I'd be reading thrillers too if I didn't have to update my inventory." She looked at me. "Ready for dinner?"

"I am." I turned to Cos. "Keep in touch. You know where I am."

"Don't worry, Angie. Thanks for checking up on me, though."

Sarah and I headed down the street toward the Harbor Haunts Café. It was a little early for supper but not too early for a drink.

"You were checking up on Cos?" Sarah asked. "Pete told me you were investigating again."

"Pete is doing his job. I'm just following up on some things I heard," I said. "Let's get our drinks and I'll fill you in."

"I have a feeling this might be the evening for a martini," said Sarah. "You sound serious."

"A martini isn't a bad idea," I agreed.

Chapter Twenty-one

It was in this cheery kitchen
She worked the sampler fair
You'll see it hanging on my wall,
I love its presence there.
When Grandma was a little girl
In days we'll never see,
She sat beside that roaring fire
And made it just for me.
   —Anne Campbell, Arkansas, mid-twentieth
      century. Sampler designed and hand-
      painted, the design to be covered by
      stitching.

Two martinis arrived at our table. Sarah and I grinned at each other like two kids and clicked our glasses.

"To spring!" she said.

"And to murders, solved," I added.

We both felt a bit risqué. We usually sipped wine, or maybe a draft. Tonight we were women drinking martinis. Who knew where the evening might end?

"How's Pete?" I asked.

"Too busy on that case to do much else," Sarah admitted. "Pete's a really good guy, and I enjoy being with him, but we're both still a little nervous about the relationship. And his divorce hasn't come through yet."

"That can take a while," I added with wisdom. I had no personal experience with divorce, but in Arizona providing evidence for divorce cases had been the bread and butter of my boss's agency. Divorces weren't always simple, even when both parties agreed.

"Pete's wife left him, but to make desertion the ground for divorce in Maine you have to wait three years."

"Whoa."

"Exactly. They're probably going for irreconcilable differences, but that requires counseling. That's not easy, given his work schedule. Her getting involved with another man and moving to Bangor hasn't helped, either."

"Adultery, then?" That was the ground I was most familiar with.

Sarah shrugged. "Maybe. Pete's a nice guy, though, and he doesn't want to accuse her. They've been separated only five months. Some days I think he really doesn't want a divorce, although I'm pretty sure his wife does. I feel funny going out with someone who's still legally married."

"Understood." The waitress stood over us, waiting for our orders. "I'll have the lobster club sandwich and sweet potato fries," I decided.

"Crab cakes for me, and a small Caesar salad," Sarah said. "And another martini."

I looked in surprise. Her glass was almost empty. Sarah wasn't usually a heavy drinker, unless you counted our girls' evenings in her apartment when

we'd had no problem finishing a bottle of wine between us when we were chatting or watching a movie.

She saw my expression. "'Of juleps, part are in the
jug and more are in the joy—Your connoisseur in
liquors consults the bumble bee—' Of course, it's a
little early for bumblebees."

"I assume that's one of your Emily quotes," I said
dryly. "If not, maybe you shouldn't drink that second
martini."

Sarah made a face at me. "I'm fine. Just enjoying
the evening. So, you're helping Dave prove his young
protégé is innocent of Ike Hamilton's murder,
right?"

"At first I had doubts about Leo myself, but now
I'm on Dave's side. Why would Leo kill a man who'd
befriended him and given him a place to stay?"

"A pretty crummy place, I've heard," said Sarah.

"Not terrific. But better than the streets. Or, I suspect, the group home he said he never wanted to go
back to."

"So why would anyone kill a man who didn't
bother anyone, who just collected bottles?"

Sarah's salad had arrived and she'd started eating.

"That's what I'm trying to find out. Ike talked a
lot. He knew most people in town, and came to his
own conclusions about them, based on what he saw
when he was making his bottle-collecting rounds.
Ruth told me several stories she'd heard from him—
one about you." I watched Sarah's face.

"Ike talked about me?"

"He told Ruth you must be in trouble with the law.
Pete Lambert was hanging around your store a lot."

Sarah started laughing, and then almost choked.
"Love that! I'll have to tell Pete. If that's an example

of Ike's stories, I wouldn't take them very seriously. He may have seen things, but he didn't know the full picture. Or certainly he didn't in my case."

I nodded. "That's why I'm trying to talk to people he knew and hear their side of the story. Tomorrow after school I'm going to trace Ike's walks with Leo and see if he remembers any other stories."

"Was that why you were talking with Cos?"

"Ike thought Gus was acting inappropriately with Cos and had with other young women he'd employed over the years."

"Gus? Gus Gleason? The guy with the paunch and the comb-over who runs the bookstore?"

"That Gus," I confirmed.

"He's my neighbor, so I see him often, usually when we're both putting out garbage, or we wave to each other in the parking lot. We're both tied to our stores. His wife, Nancy, comes into my shop sometimes. She collects presidential political memorabilia—buttons, ribbons, banners, postcards, magnets—all sorts of things. In the nineteenth century, tokens that looked like coins were often used to promote candidates. You know, 'Tippecanoe and Tyler Too' and so forth."

I had no clue. "What?"

Sarah grinned. "Election of 1840. William Henry Harrison had won the Battle of Tippecanoe against Native Americans and had John Tyler as his running mate. 'Tippecanoe and Tyler Too' was their campaign slogan. It was printed on round metal medallions with both of their faces."

"You clearly know more about American history than I do," I admitted. "I didn't know they taught stuff like that in Australia."

"They don't. I've learned a lot from Nancy Gleason. She's asked me to look for anything she collects when I'm at auctions or shows. She's a real political history buff. What about 'Blaine, Blaine, James G. Blaine, the continental liar from the state of Maine'?"

"Hey, I'm not ignorant! I know Maine history. Election of 1884. James Blaine, who had some shady railroad doings, versus Grover Cleveland, who won despite the campaign slogan Blaine's supporters chanted in retaliation."

"'Ma, Ma, Where's my pa? Gone to the White House, Ha, ha ha!'" Sarah and I recited together.

A couple at the next table looked over at us oddly.

"Okay, so you know Nancy Gleason. Has she ever said or implied anything about Gus's behavior toward the young women who work for him?"

Sarah shook her head slowly. "I can't think of anything, and I'd remember something like that. We usually talk politics of the past, or antiques."

"I'd think she'd talk about nursing."

Sarah shook her head. "She's not supposed to talk about her patients. Privacy. Only once do I remember her saying anything. Sandra Lewis was wheeling her husband past the shop and Nancy commented that it was amazing how sick he'd been for so long. 'Everything seems to happen to Jim,' I remember her saying. She added that Sandra was as patient as an angel."

"I've seen them in church, but I don't know them well."

"I heard once he had multiple sclerosis," said Sarah. "But whatever his primary medical condition is, he seems to get pneumonia often, and he fell and broke his leg a couple of years ago. Broke his jaw once, too, trying to get out of his wheelchair."

"People with MS don't have strong muscles. Caring for him must be very difficult for his wife."

Sarah nodded. "Sandra's very devoted. I've never heard of her being upset, or depressed, or complaining. Sometimes she asks for prayers in church, but that's all."

"I should pay closer attention to the Lewises," I said, picking up my sandwich. Lobster, bacon, and tomato was a terrific combination. "How're your crab cakes?"

"Delicious, as always," said Sarah. "I should learn to make them myself. I order them all the time when we're out." She took another bite. "So, what are you going to do next to help Pete—and Leo?"

"Tonight I'm going to check e-mails and maybe call Reverend Tom to ask why the Chamber of Commerce scared Ike Hamilton so much. Tomorrow I'll probably talk to Ed Campbell about that. I promised to meet Dave and Leo at three o'clock at the school."

"I'm still hoping you and Patrick and Pete and I can get together for dinner soon."

I winced a bit. "I'd like that too. But Patrick and I promised to have dinner with Gram and Tom Friday night. Maybe soon after that?"

"After you guys figure out who killed Ike, and why. Until that happens, Pete isn't going to be able to relax." Sarah looked at me and raised her martini glass. "And I suspect you won't be able to relax either."

"Probably not," I admitted. "I'll feel better when everyone officially rules Leo out as a suspect. His background is cloudy, and he made the mistake of lying to Pete and Ethan."

"Not good," agreed Sarah. "And I've heard he had

at least one bad experience with the police before. He was nervous."

"Being nervous isn't an excuse for lying," I stated firmly. "Especially in a murder investigation."

"Well, like you, I just want the case solved. I want to have time together with Pete to figure out whether our relationship is a serious one or whether it's just nice to have dinner together occasionally."

"Sarah, Pete's a police sergeant. His life is never going to be totally his own. If he's going to be the man in your life, you're going to have to share him with the rest of Haven Harbor."

"True. But I need to know how I feel about him before I deal with the rest of his life."

I raised my martini glass, now almost empty, to hers. "May you both make the best decision, for yourselves and each other."

Chapter Twenty-two

There is a calm for those who weep
A rest for weary Pilgrims found,
They softly lie and sweetly sleep
Low in the ground.

—Frances Whidden (1816–1855),
   Portsmouth, New Hampshire, 1828. This
   verse, stitched on a mourning sampler, is
   above two tombstones, one "In memory of
   Anne Seavey, who died November 14,
   1826, aged 76 years" and one "In memory
   of William Seavey, who died March 15,
   1820, aged 84 years." They were her ma-
   ternal grandparents. She also included
   small depictions of them, stitched in
   black. Without explanation, Frances also
   stitched a small giraffe under a tree near
   the gravestones.

Home again. It had been a long day, although the
dinner with Sarah was an excellent way to end it.
Sarah had questions about her new relationship with
Pete, but that wasn't surprising. She'd listened pa-

tiently over the months to my tales of the ups and downs of my friendship with Patrick. Sarah and I'd only known each other about a year, but we were solid friends.

We didn't hesitate to lean on the other when one of us was troubled. And we'd both had trials in the past year.

I hoped Sarah and Pete worked out their hesitations. I liked them both, and Sarah deserved a good man.

Meantime, I was glad to be home and quiet while Patrick enjoyed his business dinner in Portland. I'd see him Friday night.

It would be my first birthday with Gram, back in Maine, since I was a senior in high school. Like Cos, I'd been looking forward to going out into the world but nervous about doing it. My journey home had taken ten years. I hoped Cos's wouldn't take as long. Home was a place to start from, but I'd learned it could also be a place to return to.

I piled pillows on the back of my bed. Trixi was chasing one of her plastic balls around the room as though she were a Manchester United star.

I dialed Reverend Tom. He answered immediately. "Angie! Did you get my message about Willow Sinclair? She said she'd be happy to represent Leo if he needed a lawyer."

"Got it. I gave her name and number to Dave, since he's in the process of being named Leo's foster parent, or guardian, or whatever will work and can be done quickly."

"Leo's a lucky boy. Not every teenager with his history would find someone to welcome him."

"Sounds to me as though he was a victim of being

born to parents who shouldn't have had children," I said, not mincing words. "He's had a rough time of it so far through no fault of his own."

"And it sounds like he has a lot of work ahead of him if he's going to catch up with other boys his age."

"Academically. But maybe he knows more about the world than they do."

"Perhaps so."

"I called because I'm curious, Tom. You've been on the Haven Harbor Chamber of Commerce for several years, right?"

"Sure. Of course, the Chamber is for businesses in the area. But they usually include representatives of local churches and other nonprofits. I try to attend the regular meetings. It's a way of learning what's going on in town, and sometimes I can get support for a church project or help with a town initiative. Why? Are you interested in joining?"

"A few months back Ed officially invited me. But I don't feel I have much to contribute."

"You don't know, Angie. You've had experiences in another state. You might think of something that could help folks running businesses here. You should think about it."

"I will. I promise. But in the meantime, could you tell me what, if any, relationship there was between the Chamber of Commerce and Ike Hamilton?"

Tom was silent.

"I've heard from a couple of people that Ike was scared of the Chamber and that people there wanted him off the streets of Haven Harbor and out of town. Maybe even to an institutional setting up in Augusta."

"A few years back, Angie, when Ike was still living

alone in his parents' house, the Chamber was concerned. The house was falling down around him. He had no way to repair it or money to pay someone else to do it. Then a wicked nor'easter took down one of the big oaks in his yard and it smashed right through the roof. A lot of us were worried about Ike. We were afraid the water and snow in the house would take ceilings and floors down and he'd be hurt."

"Aren't there organizations that could have helped him fix the house?"

"Minor repairs, sure. But that house had serious structural defects from its chimneys to its basement. Load-bearing walls were crumbling. It was a disaster waiting to happen. Ike was against it, of course, and held out right until the end, but the Chamber did push the town to declare his house unsafe and take it down."

"So it wasn't just unsightly."

"No. It was dangerously unsafe. Ike didn't take the demolition well. He'd always lived in that house. Haven Harbor is a small place. We don't have a group home, or a place for adults to live who can't totally take care of themselves. So other places were mentioned as possibilities for Ike."

"But he stayed."

"He didn't want to leave, and when it came right down to it, no one wanted to force him. He moved into that garage where he's been living. He has a heater and running water in there. His father put all that in when the garage was his workshop. In the winter, when it's really cold, Ike usually ends up at one of the church shelters. With a little help from an assortment of people, he seemed able to support himself and live independently."

"I'd heard Ed Campbell wanted Ike off the streets.

That he thought Ike didn't fit into the tourist-ready working waterfront town."

"That may be right, Angie. But so far as I know, Ed never did anything but grouse about Ike. It was always clear Ike was here to stay."

"Until, of course, he wasn't."

"Until then. Until now."

Chapter Twenty-three

Learning improves what nature gives
Virtue from wisdom strength receives
May virtue mark our footsteps here
And point the way to heaven.

—Maria Fiducia Ridgway, Keene, New Hampshire, 1818. Maria was born April 16, 1809, in Groton, Massachusetts. Her father was a silversmith and jeweler. Maria, the fourth of the children, stitched her sampler when she was nine years old, after her family moved to Keene, New Hampshire. She surrounded her alphabets and verse with elaborate flowers. In 1836 Maria died, and her sampler was passed down to her younger sister, Harriet, who in turn passed it to her descendants.

I woke up earlier than usual the next morning. Glancing at my clock, I wondered why.

Then I saw smears of blood near the floor on the wall next to my bed.

I sat up and looked around. Bloodstains on the wall. Blood smears on the carpet, leading to the hall.

I swung my legs out from under the quilt and followed the blood, suddenly realizing I hadn't seen
Trixi, who was usually curled up on the bottom of my
bed or on my pillow.

My curiosity turned into fear. Had Trixi fallen, or
somehow hurt herself? I thought quickly. Beatrix
Turing, our local vet, had emergency hours.

"Trixi?" I called, seeing the trail of blood end near
the top of the stairs. "Trixi!"

If she was hurt, maybe she'd crawled off somewhere. I shouldn't encourage her to move.

I ran down the stairs. No sign of Trixi in the front
hallway or the living room.

I tried not to panic. Where could she be?

"Meow?" answered my question.

Trixi was in the kitchen, sitting next to her (empty,
of course) food bowl.

Next to her was a (definitely) dead mouse, which
clearly had been the source of the blood.

Relief flooded over me as Trixi proudly picked up
the mouse and dropped it at my feet.

How had she known my birthday was this week?

Any old house offered a haven to field mice in the
winter, but somehow any small tenants at my house
had escaped Trixi in the coldest months. Where
she'd found this one, I had no idea.

"You're a murderer, did you know that?" I said to
her.

Trixi purred in response and then walked back to
her empty food dish. Was she sending me a message
that her dish was empty and she'd had to hunt for
her own breakfast?

I didn't ask. I filled her dish (with cat food), then

picked the small, furry body up with a paper towel and deposited it in my metal-topped kitchen garbage can.

My feet were cold, and it was only six-thirty in the morning,

"I'm going back to bed," I announced to the killer in my house, and headed back upstairs.

The next time I woke up it was almost nine, and Trixi was innocently sleeping on the pillow next to me. If the blood stains hadn't been there, I might have thought the killing field had been a dream.

But, after all, I owned a cat. She was growing up. I could keep her inside, away from the birds and chipmunks I loved to see in the yard. But any mouse brave enough to enter her domain was on his (or her) own.

After my shower I cleaned up the blood and headed for coffee. This morning I needed it.

Trixi happily led me to the kitchen, where she posed in back of her (again empty) food dish.

"No," I informed her, feeling like a Tough Love parent. "You've already had your breakfast. Dry food is it for now." I changed her water and cleaned her litter box while my coffee was perking. "No rewards for killing."

I knew people in town who fed feral cats in their barns, hoping the cats would eliminate any rats or mice there. That was fine with me.

But I hadn't expected my bedroom to become a murder zone.

By the time I'd finished my breakfast (an onion omelet and toast) and checked e-mail, it was almost ten o'clock. Ed Campbell's used car dealership

("Whatever your wishes, we have your wheels") would be open.

I headed out of downtown Haven Harbor. Ed's car lot was out on Route 1. No one going to Haven Harbor could miss the enormous American flag flying above the football-field-sized lot filled with lines of used cars and trucks of all makes and models.

One winter Ed's business had made the national news when an ice storm broke most of the windshields in his lot and dented half the cars. I'd even seen the story in Arizona, Ed offering "special deals" on most of his cars and promising that insurance would cover the damage.

I wondered if it had.

I parked between an old yellow station wagon and a blue Ford pickup in one of the customer spaces next to his display room.

Inside, several men (no women?) were talking with prospective customers. Within a minute a heavyset man in a brown suit lumbered over to me. "Welcome to Campbell's Cars. I'm Bob Dolan. What can I show you today?"

"I don't need a car right now," I assured him. "I'd like to speak with Ed."

"Ed's busy right now," he said, glancing over his shoulder toward the door to what I assumed was an enclosed office. "I'm sure I can help you."

"I need to talk with Ed," I emphasized. "It's about Chamber of Commerce business."

He hesitated, but then nodded. "Who shall I say wants to see him?"

"Angie Curtis."

"Why don't you take a seat over there?" He pointed

to several chairs arranged around a low table covered with brochures I assumed were about cars. "I'll let him know you're here."

Turned out the brochures weren't about cars. They were advertising pamphlets and postcards and maps showing Haven Harbor attractions. This must be the Chamber of Commerce table. I glanced at a few and found one for Captain Ob's deep sea fishing charters. Maybe I should put together a brochure for Mainely Needlepoint.

"Angie!" Ed Campbell was a tall man; even when I stood up he towered above me. "Winter well? I've seen you in church, but I don't think we've talked since the Christmas Cheer Festival. And how is Patrick these days?"

Of course. Ed had spent most of the festival trying to convince Patrick's famous mother and her friend, a movie director, that Haven Harbor would be the perfect location for their next production.

"Patrick's fine," I assured him. "He opened his gallery at the beginning of April, so now he's there most days."

"And how is his beautiful mother?" Ed continued, gesturing that I should come with him back to his office.

"She's well, so far as I know. She's out at her home in Los Angeles," I explained. "I haven't seen her since Christmas."

"But she'll be coming back to Haven Harbor this summer?"

"I guess so. I haven't heard her schedule," I explained as we entered his office. The walls were covered with framed commendations of various sorts

and what I assumed were pictures of Ed with customers.

He gestured toward one of the green imitation
leather chairs set up for customers and sat behind his
wide desk.

"What can I do for you today? Bob said you wanted
to see me about Chamber of Commerce business.
Have you decided to join us?"

"I may, Ed. I haven't decided yet," I said. "I've been
back in the Harbor less than a year now, and I'm still
finding my way."

"Meeting with other local business owners might
help," he assured me. "And we'd love to have your
friend Patrick join us too. Local art and crafts are big
draws for visitors to Maine."

"I agree," I said. "But today I'm here on another
kind of business. I wanted to ask you about your relationship with Ike Hamilton."

Ed pushed back his chair. "Ike Hamilton? The
strange guy who wandered around with his cart, picking bottles out of the trash? I didn't have any 'relationship' with him!"

"I'm sure you heard—Ike was murdered a few days
ago."

"A shame, of course. But what does that have to do
with me? A man like that probably knew all sorts of
shady characters. Could even have been involved
with drugs. Or maybe stealing things. He wandered
in and out of people's barns and houses. Always said
he was picking up bottles, but you never really knew,
did you?" He leaned forward. "Truthfully, I don't
think his death was a loss to Haven Harbor. Maybe
just the opposite. But what does Ike Hamilton, or his
death, have to do with you? Or me?"

"Ike had a young friend living with him—Leo Blackwell. Leo's the one who found Ike's body, and the police suspect he may have killed Ike. I don't think he did. I'm helping the police." (Pete and Ethan wouldn't appreciate my saying that.) "Helping them think about other possibilities."

"Why are you asking me about Ike?"

"Because Ike told several people in town that he was afraid of the Chamber of Commerce. I understand you sponsored a petition designed to keep people like Ike off Haven Harbor's streets. It said only nonprofits could collect bottles in town."

"Here in Haven Harbor we believe in recycling and in keeping the streets clean. But people who wander about, taking bottles and cans out of the recyclables containers on the streets, don't help. They call attention to themselves. And the town loses the money from the bottles in those containers."

"So the petition wasn't designed to keep Ike Hamilton from making a living collecting and redeeming bottles?"

"Rubbish. Of course not. That petition wasn't aimed at any one person. It was for the good of the town. That man was a little confused, to put it nicely," said Ed. "We only wanted the best for him. The only time the Chamber of Commerce was involved with him was when that old house he lived in fell down around him. We did suggest he'd be more comfortable living somewhere with other people like him. Somewhere with a kitchen and a bathroom and someone to look after him. Somewhere he didn't have to wander the streets in all weather, picking up trash."

"Bottles. To take for redemption. Actually, what he did helped eliminate trash in Haven Harbor."

"Whatever." Ed stood up, clearly dismissing me. "I don't know what that man said about me or anyone else on the Chamber of Commerce. Certainly none of us had anything to do with his death. He probably picked up some strange fellow on the streets—you said one young man was already living with him. Maybe whoever he thought was his new best friend killed him. Wouldn't be the first time someone a little slow was taken advantage of. You read stuff like that on the Internet all the time."

"So you have no idea who might have wanted to harm Ike?" I remained sitting.

"I know people who weren't thrilled that Ike was part of our town. But he was here, and he didn't want to leave. I'm one of those who isn't sorry he's gone. But kill him?" Ed shook his head. "I don't know anyone crazy enough to do that."

"If you think of anything that might help the police, please let them know," I said, going to the door of his office. "Thank you for your time."

"Let me know when you decide about joining the Chamber, Angie. You and Patrick would be welcome, any time."

"I'll let him know," I agreed as I left the showroom.

Ed Campbell wasn't my favorite resident of Haven Harbor, but all he'd said made sense, and agreed with what I'd heard from other people. There was no logical reason for Ed, or anyone else on the Chamber of Commerce, to have killed Ike.

Although, when were there logical reasons for murder?

I decided to make one more stop. The Haven Harbor postmaster, Pax Henry, had befriended Ike. Probably Pete and Ethan had already talked with him, but it wouldn't do any harm to ask a few more questions. And I could always use extra stamps.

Chapter Twenty-four

In the resplendent morn of youth
How gaily Pass the hours
Warm'd in the sunshine of thy hopes
Each Path is strew'd with flowers.
  —Lucinda Gould (1807–1900), Henniker,
   New Hampshire. She stitched this sampler,
   which included two alphabets and a simple
   border of vines and flowers, when she was
   thirteen. Ten years later, she married Abel
   Willard Kent. They had two daughters,
   but her husband died a few years later. In
   1850 she married again and settled in
   Wilton, New Hampshire. When she died,
   in 1900, she was living alone.

If I were casting the postmaster of a small Maine
town for an episode of *Sesame Street*, Pax Henry would
be my first choice.

Tall, thin, with a bushy red beard matching his
Afro-like red hair tinged with white, Pax knew everyone in Haven Harbor by first and last name, address,
and most of their business. He'd been postmaster for

as long as I could remember, and, as Gram was going to remind me Friday night, I was almost twenty-eight.

"Angie!" he greeted me as I walked in. He'd been chatting with a man I didn't know (unlike Pax, I don't know everyone in town) who said, "Got to get back to work! Nice talking with you, Pax!" and left.

I was next in line for conversation. I reached over and snagged a hard candy from the bowl of treats Pax always kept filled on the corner of the counter.

"Stamps today, Angie? You haven't bought any recently."

I didn't dare mention I'd been paying some of my bills online. Most times I had post office business it was to mail a needlepointed item to a customer.

"A book of stamps would be great," I agreed, and chose American flags from the assortment Pax showed me. "Do you have a minute to talk?"

"Always." He nodded, handing me the stamps. "What's on your mind?"

"Ike Hamilton," I told him. "You and Ike were friends, right?"

"I'd say we were," Pax agreed. "I'd known him for years. He and his mom and dad—good folks, they were. After they died, Ike had to deal with a lot of challenges." Pax shook his head sadly. "Horrible, the way he died. Just horrible. How could anyone do that to a soul who'd never hurt anyone in his life?"

"That's what the police are trying to figure out," I said. "And I'm doing what I can too. It just doesn't make sense that someone went into that garage where he lived and stabbed him to death."

Pax nodded.

"Did he have many visitors there, do you know?"

"Nah. No one I ever heard him mention. Didn't

even get much mail. Electric bills and circulars were
about it. He was pretty lonely. Used to come and talk
with me sometimes, when he was having a dark day."

"And you took him to redeem his bottles on Saturdays, I heard."

"Every Saturday, right as rain, I'd close up here at
noon and go to Ike's. He'd have all his week's bottles
sorted and bagged up. Folks at the redemption center we went to, out on Route 1, trusted that he'd
counted right, so I guess he did. They'd pay him
without even counting what was in his bags. How he
managed was beyond me. Can't believe I won't be
picking him up this coming Saturday. Sad times."

"So he didn't have many friends, that you knew of."

"I was probably the closest to a friend he had. Me
and maybe Jim Lewis. Jim doesn't get around much
anymore, but Ike visited him. Now, a lot of folks knew
Ike, and saved bottles for him, and even looked out
for him. Pete Lambert, he used to check on him
when temperatures got low and give him a ride to
one of the shelters. And folks on his bottle route
sometimes gave him food." Pax leaned over the counter.
"He'd always take the food, you understand, but it
was an embarrassment to him. He'd rather go to the
food bank, he told me once. There everyone needed
food. He wasn't being singled out."

"Did you know his young friend, Leo?"

Pax shook his head. "Not really. That kid was only
with him a few weeks. Wondered about him, to tell
you the truth. Why would a kid like that be living
with Ike? Not that living with Ike was bad—he was a
good guy, for sure. But in all the years I'd known
him, no one had ever lived with him before."

"Why did you think Leo stayed there?"

"Ike said the boy had nowhere else to go. That he

was looking after him until Leo'd decided what he was going to do. Seemed reasonable. And Leo did help Ike out." Pax shook his head. "Ike was getting on a bit. The way he lived wasn't the best. He hurt his back a couple of months ago—twisted it reaching down into one of those trash barrels down on the wharf, he told me."

"You said Ike talked a lot. Did he ever mention having conflicts with anyone?"

"Conflicts? I don't remember any, other than what everyone knows: He and the Chamber of Commerce didn't see his lifestyle eye to eye. But he didn't talk about himself much. Used to tell me what he'd seen around town, or who was saving bottles for him, or not. He didn't like seeing people being mean to each other, or using bad language, like you hear sometimes in the streets. He was real sensitive to stuff like that. Used to tell me when someone had yelled at their child, or chained their dog to a tree so the dog couldn't run around much. Once in a while he'd happen on someone doing something they shouldn't. That would upset him, and he'd tell me all about it."

"Anything recent?"

Pax stroked his beard, which just made it stick out more. "Can't recall, exactly. He mentioned a couple of teenagers he'd seen down at the wharf, skipping school. Not even sure who they were. Didn't seem important. They were likely getting their boat ready for the Blessing. He always had something to say about Sandra Lewis too. Never could figure out why. She saved bottles for him, and takes care of Ike's friend, Jim, so well. But Ike did get carried away sometimes. Once he told me he thought Sandra was a devil." Pax grinned. "I told him, with my red hair, I had a better chance of being a devil than Mrs. Lewis.

But he didn't get the joke. That Cindy Bouchard, who works for the Thibodeaus—he didn't care for her, either. Said she couldn't be trusted. But I suspect he just didn't like that she wasn't saving bottles for him, the way the Thibodeaus had before. She borrowed the Thibodeaus' car and took their bottles to redemption herself."

"So Ike never mentioned being scared of anyone?"

"Nah. He hadn't even mentioned the Chamber of Commerce recently. What are you doing? Trying to solve his murder?"

"The police suspect Leo, just because he was living with Ike and found Ike's body. And no one in town knows much about Leo. It's easier to accuse someone from away than someone in town."

"True enough. Sorry I can't be of more help," Pax agreed. "If I think of anything else, I'll let you know."

"Thanks, Pax," I said. "Most times when someone's killed, there are several people who have motives—or at least would benefit from his or her death. I can't find anyone—including Leo—who'll benefit from Ike's death."

"A whole lot of folks in town will have to take their own bottles to redemption," Pax pointed out. "Ike's being here made a difference. Thing is, the difference was a good one."

"You're right," I agreed, as a little boy ran into the office, followed by his very pregnant mother.

"Candy?" the boy asked, looking up at Pax and the counter he couldn't reach.

"All right?" Pax checked with his mother.

She nodded. "A lollipop, if you have one."

"I think we could find one up here," agreed Pax, and he dug through the bowl until he came up with a red lollipop to hand to the boy. "What can I help you with today, Lily?"

I waved and headed out. Pax was more of a fan of Ike's than many people in town, but he'd been right. Haven Harbor would miss the man who collected bottles.

Who'd believed the town would be better off without him?

It was still a mystery.

Chapter Twenty-five

Bliss of celestial origin:
Restless mortals toil for nought
Bliss in vain from earth is sought
Bliss a native of the sky
Never wanders, mortals try
There you cannot seek in vain
For to seek her is to gain.
—Elizabeth Keister, Wooster, Ohio, 1826.
Elizabeth also stitched "American
Independence declared 4th July 1779."
(Maybe she stitched her 6 upside down?)
Elizabeth married Joseph Hunter in 1834.

At three that afternoon, as I'd promised, I was waiting outside Haven Harbor High School for Dave and Leo. Yellow buses were lined up in the loading zone waiting to take home the students who didn't have sports or club meetings, older friends (with licenses and cars) to drive them, or a parent who'd agreed to pick them up.

When I'd attended the school, I'd lived close enough to walk. On snowy or icy or rainy days, or just on general principle, I'd envied students who had transportation of some sort. On good days, I'd often taken advantage of my "walker" status to walk wherever I pleased . . . to the practice field to watch the student athletes, like Ethan Trask, or to Pocket Cove Beach, to search for sea glass instead of answers to homework assignments, or to another student's house, where there might or might not be supervision.

No matter where I'd been, or what excuse I'd given for arriving home later than expected, Gram would be there, patient and trying to be understanding. She always had warm molasses or oatmeal cookies ready, and a cup of hot tea or cocoa or a glass of milk, depending on my mood and preference.

What if I hadn't had Gram after Mama disappeared?

What welcome had Leo found at his house after school, even when his parents were still alive?

From what he'd described, his home had been in the country, so he would have taken the school bus, like most Maine kids. But it hadn't sounded like warm cookies had been waiting for him.

He hadn't wanted to go to school. Neither had I. But I'd met minimum requirements and graduated with my class, thank goodness. That high school diploma had been my entry to taking several courses at Arizona State when I was out west. And when I decided college wasn't for me, I found even small businesses, like the private investigator I'd worked for, expected his employees to have high school diplomas.

I hope Dave had at least tried to explain that to Leo. His parents hadn't sounded like the sort to give good career guidance.

I waved to Cos Curran, who waved back and kept walking. She lived downtown; she was probably a walker, too, and on her way to the bookstore. I silently wished her well.

The buses filled with chattering teenagers, most dressed in the unofficial school uniform: jeans and T-shirts and hoodies. Most were also equipped with backpacks.

By the time the buses had pulled out, I started wondering about Dave and Leo. I wasn't worried. Maybe Dave had some teacherly duty to perform and Leo was with him. I only hoped they hadn't forgotten our agreement to retrace Ike Hamilton's bottle routes.

I was tempted to check out the bio lab where Dave hung his hat and hosted a homeroom of students, when the two of them came out the front doors of the school, walking separately. Not everything was sunshine and daisies at Haven Harbor High this afternoon.

Today might not work out the way I'd planned.

I waved, and Dave waved back. Leo didn't.

"Angie! Sorry to keep you waiting," Dave said, standing outside my car window, his voice tense and his expression stern. Leo stood on the other side of the car, several feet away. "We have a complication. Leo and I are going to take my car down to the police station to talk to Pete right now. If we have time, I'd still like us to take that drive we talked about, but it'll be delayed. Okay if we come by your house when we can and leave from there? I'll get pizza for dinner tonight, and we'll try to fit everything in."

"It's okay," I agreed, adding softly, "What's wrong?"

"I noticed an odd shape in Leo's backpack and insisted on opening the bag. He had a pint of vodka."

"What?"

"He said someone else got it for him, which opens up a whole other set of questions. But he paid for it. Angie, Leo lied to the police again. He took the money Ike had hidden under his mattress. I don't know how this will affect the agreement I had with Pete and Ethan that Leo could stay with me, but I'm insisting he go to the police department and tell them what he did."

"And then?"

"No matter what they say, then I'll come by your place. With Leo, or alone."

Dave gestured to Leo, and the two of them headed for the teachers' parking lot. Leo, as before, walked separately and behind Dave.

I wasn't sure which of them looked more angry.

It didn't look as though we'd be taking our investigative drive this afternoon. At least not right away.

How could Leo be so stupid?

Didn't he realize that taking that money and lying about it, even if it wasn't a lot of cash, gave him a motive to murder Ike?

And using the money to buy vodka (who'd done *that* for him?) didn't help either.

"Good luck," I said under my breath to Dave. And to Leo.

Chapter Twenty-six

How blest the maid whom circling years improve
Her God the object of her warmest love
Whose useful hours successive as they glide
The hook the needle and the pen divide
Who sees her parents heart exult with joy
And the fond tear stands sparkling in their eye.

 —Olive Wallingford (1817–1887), age nine,
  Kennebunk, Maine, 1826. Olive's sampler
  includes four alphabets and a simple border. Olive never married. As an adult, she
  lived with her brother and his family for
  many years.

I couldn't focus on getting any work done, or even
on what to do next.

All I could think about was that Leo had lied—
again. Didn't he understand that Dave and I were the
two people who believed in him—and now even we
had reason to doubt? And why the liquor? Sure, I
knew a lot of kids thought it was smart to drink vodka
because it was harder to smell on someone. But Leo
had told us his father drank. Drank too much. Why
would Leo follow in his footsteps?

I paced my first floor. Living room. Dining room. Front hall. Kitchen. Repeat. Trixi followed me, clearly confused. This was not normal behavior, but if I was going somewhere, she wanted to go too.

I paused next to the sideboard in the dining room on one of my rounds. Maybe I should have a drink myself. I stared at the bottles, and then kept going. I'd learned to drink in Arizona, with many trials and errors, and when I was first home in Maine I'd continued that habit, pleased that in my absence Gram had added a small liquor and wine supply to the house. She hadn't had that when I was growing up. Probably intentionally.

I still enjoy a glass or two of wine with dinner, especially when I'm with Sarah or Patrick or Gram and Tom, but without thinking too much about it I'd cut back on heavier liquors. I'd enjoyed that martini yesterday, though. And today the bottle of vodka in my dining room was calling to me.

On my next walk through the dining room I gave in and poured myself a drink. Maybe it would help me relax and get my mind off whatever was happening at the police station.

I slowed my pace, sipping occasionally. So far I'd learned more about Leo than I had about Ike. And unless that thirty-two dollars and change had been too tempting for Leo to resist, I hadn't found anyone with a motive to kill Ike.

My mind filled with reasons Leo might have for taking the money. Maybe he didn't think anyone would know Ike had money. Or was it a spur-of-the-moment survival reaction when he saw Ike's body?

Despite his former experiences dealing with police, Leo wasn't sophisticated. He'd been petrified when he'd arrived at Dave's house. He'd been scared enough to go to someone he'd met only for a few minutes, and hope Dave would help him.

But, even accepting that, why would he use the only money he had to buy liquor?

Unless Leo had a problem with alcohol Dave and I hadn't guessed.

It happened. Some kids his age did drink.

Thinking back, I'd had a few when I was his age, too, although my drinking had been pretty much limited to a few beers on the beach or a little rum added to my soda can by a boy who thought that would smooth his next move.

But, like Leo, I'd had a parent who drank. Mama had never physically hurt me, but my memories of her stumbling up the stairs after a late night with one of her gentleman friends were still vivid.

That was one reason I'd moved away from alcohol once I was back in Haven Harbor. I didn't want to see myself repeating that pattern, stumbling up those same steps. Children sometimes learned from their parents and didn't take after them.

What about Leo?

Had the vodka been open? Had he been drinking?

Dave hadn't said.

I finally sat on the living room couch and finished the drink I'd poured. I didn't want any more, and was pleased about that. Trixi sniffed the empty glass I'd put on the coffee table, and I took it to the kitchen. Trixi shouldn't drink even a drop of vodka, and I didn't want her knocking my glass onto the floor.

Cleaning up broken glass was not a task I wanted to take on.

Dave was coping with Leo's broken promises. His lies.

I went back to the couch, thoughts of past and present whirling in my mind, no doubt unleashed by the drink. Trixi curled up on my lap, clearly pleased I'd settled somewhere she might get a few strokes.

"Trixi, I don't know what to do," I explained to her as I scratched between her ears. She listened seriously but had no suggestions. I suspected what she'd like me to do was continue scratching behind her ears.

Then, unexpectedly, she jumped up and headed for the front door. As she did, I heard a knock.

Dave was alone, standing on the porch. "Pete's locked the kid up," he said as he strode past me into the living room. "Probably only for the night. He says Leo needs to learn a lesson. He stole, he lied, he was a minor in possession of alcohol." Dave sat abruptly on my couch. "And, of course, he'd also run away from a group home and is still under suspicion of murdering Ike."

"Oh, Dave," was all I could think to say. "What are we going to do?"

"Do you have a beer? I could really use one."

"I do." I nodded and headed to the kitchen. Who was I to question Dave's request? I'd just had vodka. I hesitated, and then pulled out only one beer. I wanted to keep my head together.

I handed him one of the Sam Adams bottles Patrick preferred. I kept a few in the house in case he stopped in.

"Thanks, Angie," said Dave, opening the bottle and taking a long swig.

Questions swirled through my head, but I decided

to start with the most recent issue. "Did you find out why Leo bought the vodka? Had he been drinking in school?"

Dave sighed. "The bottle wasn't open. He said he didn't drink. It wasn't for him."

I frowned. "Then?"

"He started crying on the way to the police station. Said he'd been trying to make friends at school— and I think he has been. Said one of the kids—he wouldn't tell me who, which is just as well since I might lose my image as a calm, understanding teacher— said he'd be Leo's friend if Leo got him some booze. So Leo did. I don't know who bought it for him, but I suspect the school custodian. I'll deal with that later. Leo hadn't even had time to give the other kid the bottle when I found it. He kept repeating, 'I just wanted to have a friend.' "

I winced. "What did you say?"

"I told him that wasn't the way to make friends and that he'd gotten himself in big trouble instead. By the time we got to the police department I think he'd gotten the message. And then, of course, Pete was pretty hard on him—rightfully so—about taking Ike's money, messing up a crime scene, which I hadn't even thought about, and then lying to everyone about it. He told Leo that the paperwork wasn't complete for him to stay with me, and he wouldn't be surprised if I changed my mind."

"Were you there when that happened? How did Leo react?"

"I was there, all right. I didn't know what to say. Pete had already told me I should keep quiet, that he'd handled boys like this before. I just wanted to give Leo a hug and bring him home."

I noted the word *home*.

"But I couldn't do that, and when Pete read Leo the riot act and said he was going to spend a night in the Haven Harbor jail to teach him a lesson, my mind had to agree. But I hated to walk out of there without him."

"He'll only be there one night?"

"That's the plan."

"Did he say why he'd taken Ike's money, and lied about it?"

Dave shrugged. "He said he'd needed the money, and he'd helped earn it. Which was true. He'd helped Ike pick up those bottles. Then he said he was too scared to tell anyone what he'd done. I don't think he'd connected taking the money with Ike's death. In his mind, they were two separate events."

"And he still says he didn't hurt Ike."

"Absolutely. That's one point on which he's never wavered."

We sat quietly for a few minutes. Dave gulped his beer. I wasn't sure what to say. The whole situation was a mess. "What do you think we should do now?"

"Well, we're sure not going to drive around town with Leo today," Dave said. "One of the last things he said to me was, 'Sorry about everything. Maybe we can work with Angie tomorrow.'"

I grimaced. "Okay. So he knows he's getting out of jail tomorrow?"

"Not officially. But he's hoping. I don't think Pete gave him any details about what was going to happen. He told me 'tomorrow' when we were out in the lobby. He's trying to scare Leo a little."

"The Haven Harbor jail isn't an awful place. They

just have two or three holding cells for drunks or
people waiting to go to one of the county jails."

"Have you ever spent a night in jail? Any jail?"
Dave asked.

"No," I admitted.

"Well, they're not fun places. Even holding cells."

Chapter Twenty-seven

Happy the child whose green unpractis'd years
The guided hand of parent fondness rears
To rich instructions ample field removes
Prunes every fault and every worth improves
  —Sarah Jordan, Portland, Maine, about
    1814. Sarah stitched an elaborate sampler
    with three alphabets, one set of numbers,
    a wide border of flowers, a three-story
    house, other buildings, and trees, in addi-
    tion to this verse.

Dave gulped the rest of his beer. I replaced his empty with a second one.

"You've been in jail?" I asked quietly, unsure of how far I should go, how many questions I should ask. Dave had never said much about his background.

What I knew about him was how he lived today. He was a great cook and a neat housekeeper. He'd learned needlepoint to fill off-duty hours when he'd served on submarines. He had a poison garden and used it to teach his biology students about what and what not to touch in the wild. His knowledge had helped solve several local crimes.

But had Dave committed a crime himself? Been in jail?

He put his beer on the table. "Not me. I haven't been in jail. My dad was."

I didn't say anything.

"A lot. Jails, prisons. He wasn't a good guy, Angie. When I was younger than Leo my mom took me with her when she visited him. I saw what those places were like." He shook his head. "Horrible man. Horrible places."

"Is he still there?" I ventured. "In prison?"

Dave shook his head. "Died in prison years ago, when I was twelve. That time he was in for armed robbery. That was his great plan for supporting us. Hold up a liquor store."

"And your mom? Is she still alive?"

"Don't know. Don't care." He looked at me. "I know. Saying that is crass." I'd never heard Dave use that tone of voice. "Mom always said I looked like my father. Scared me to death. I wanted to be anything other than my father."

"But she supported you?"

"Minimally. Food was in the house, but she had better things to do than prepare it for me." Dave's smile was grim. "Maybe that's why I like cooking. It's a way to show you care about yourself, and about the others you're cooking for. My mom was too busy trying to find love, or money, or both, to worry about her son."

Mama hadn't been a perfect mother. I'd never known who my dad was. But, with Gram's support— more support than I'd understood at the time— Mama had been there for me.

"Did your mother find what she was looking for?"

Dave shrugged. "I don't know, or care. She married again after my dad died. The guy was a brute. Maybe he was nice to her. He gave her money for clothes and took her out to dinner once in a while. But he hadn't planned on being a parent. It's like she never told him about me. At first he acted as if I were invisible. But then he noticed."

"And?"

"He had a heavy belt, with a heavier buckle. Mom didn't do anything to stop him."

"I'm sorry, Dave."

"Not as sorry as I was. I wasn't dumb. I got out of there when I was about Leo's age. Figured I could take care of myself. Found out that wasn't easy. Lived on the streets for a while. That was a really educational experience." Dave paused, remembering, looking off into a place I couldn't see. "Ended up in a residential center for teenage boys. Runaways, like me, or boys who'd been thrown out of their homes. Kids too old for the foster care system but not prepared for the world. Schools wouldn't take us without permanent addresses and guardians, so all we had were the streets."

"You enlisted in the navy."

He nodded. "Luckily, a group of local women volunteered at that place and tried to get us to study. Most of the boys laughed at that idea, but I was smart enough to know it was my only way out of a life like my father's. I didn't want to end up in prison or on the streets. I'd seen those worlds. I was able to get my GED, and I enlisted as soon as I could."

"Dave, I wish . . ." I wasn't sure what I wished.

"No words necessary," he interrupted. "I survived. Learned a lot about myself. Met a lot of different people, from different places, when I was in the navy. Then, after I hurt my leg, when I was in the VA Hospital—you know about that—I had a lot of time to think. If those volunteers hadn't come into that house and helped me study for my GED, I might not have gotten off the streets. That's when I decided to go to college and become a teacher. Maybe I could give back a little by helping other kids who were having rough times."

"That's why you didn't hesitate to help Leo."

Dave had been seeing himself in that skinny kid from central Maine.

"Yeah. I figured this was my chance to make a difference to someone. When I found out he'd stolen that money from Ike, and used it to bribe one of the older boys to buy liquor, it really got to me. I wasn't looking for him to be angelic, or to thank me a lot, but I really hoped he was being straight with me. With us."

"He took that money because he was desperate," I said. "And then he was trying to buy friendship. I'm disappointed in him, Dave, but he hardly knows us. He's still trying to take care of himself."

"And he's gotten himself in a lot more trouble," Dave added. "I really don't think Pete believes Leo killed Ike, but they don't have any other suspects, and here's a kid who lies and steals and was there on the scene. The police can't ignore those facts."

"No," I agreed. "Which is why we have to help him figure out who else would have been angry enough with Ike to have killed him."

"I can't see that anyone would have benefitted from his death," said Dave. "I've thought of every angle I can. Sure, Ike wasn't a citizen the Chamber of Commerce was proud of, but he helped clean up the streets, and I never heard of him bothering anyone, or getting in trouble."

"He talked a lot," I put in.

"You don't kill someone for talking. Not even for gossiping. You just ignore someone like that. I figure he talked because he wanted to connect with people. As far as we know, he didn't have any close friends, but he had a lot of acquaintances, and some even went out of their way to help him—like Pax, who drove him to the redemption center, and the folks who made sure he knew when the food bank was open."

I nodded. "I've heard Jim Lewis was his friend. Ruth gave him lunch when he stopped to see her, and the Thibodeaus gave him leftover bread and pastries from their patisserie." I smiled at Dave. "I heard another guy in town gave him food too."

Dave smiled sheepishly. "Guess Ruth told on me. Yeah. Seemed a little thing to do under the circumstances."

"More than most people did. I didn't even save bottles for him. Now that I know more about him, I feel really guilty about that."

"Don't. You're doing what you can now, trying to help the same boy Ike was trying to help."

Dave put his empty bottle down on the coffee table. "I'm going to take tomorrow off and pick him up in the morning."

"The school won't appreciate that."

"No. But the police won't release him to anyone else."

"Then let's both take the day with him and do the drive around town we were going to start today. It will keep Leo busy, and maybe we'll hear something that leads to finding a motive for murder."

"Thanks, Angie. Maybe talking about Ike and their time together will convince him we're really interested in what he has to say. That he can trust us."

I glanced at the black marble clock on my mantel. "It's almost six. Shall I scare us up some supper? I don't have anything exciting, but I made macaroni and cheese the other day and there's enough left for both of us." Gram's recipe for mac and cheese had always been one of my favorites, and I'd almost mastered it.

"Sounds good, Angie, but"—Dave looked a little embarrassed—"Karen called when I was on my way here. I'm going to have dinner with her."

"Great," I said. "Is that getting to be a regular thing?" Dr. Karen Mercer worked at Haven Harbor Hospital. She and Dave had met late last summer when he'd been injured. They shared an interest in poisons and had seen each other a few times.

"Not really," said Dave, standing. "But word in Haven Harbor gets around fast. She'd heard Leo was staying with me and that we were looking for information about Ike. We just spoke briefly, but she said she'd taken care of Ike a few times. She wants to tell me about him."

"Something that will help Leo?"

"I'm not sure, but I like Karen. And I'm willing to listen. I'll call you in the morning when I know what time Leo will be released."

Chapter Twenty-eight

When youths soft seasons shall be o'er
And scenes of childhood charm no more
My riper years with joy may see
This youthful Proof of industry
As memory o'er this task shall wake
And retrospective Pleasure take
How shall I wish, but wish in vain
To enter youth's careless hours again.
　　—Frances Litchfield (1823–1845), age ten,
　　　Merrimack, New Hampshire, 1833.
　　　Frances stitched these words on a large
　　　sampler adorned with flowers and fruit,
　　　most in satin stitch. She'd been born in
　　　Kittery, Maine, where her family originally
　　　lived.

After Dave left, I heated the leftover mac and cheese. I almost had the right combination of cheeses and spices. I'd added more dry mustard this time, and it made a big difference.

After washing the dishes, I realized I hadn't seen Trixi for a while. I'd fed her before Dave arrived, and she usually stayed close by.

"Trixi!" I called as I walked through the downstairs rooms. "Trixi?" Her favorite spots—behind the couch, in back of the books on a partially empty bookshelf, and on the cushion on her favorite dining room chair—were empty. No small black cat came running.

I headed upstairs, hoping she hadn't gotten into any trouble.

I glanced into all the second-floor rooms and closets. No cat.

"Trixi!" I called, standing at the door of my bedroom.

A lump under the quilt on my bed moved. I gently pulled the quilt down. Sure enough, Trixi was fine, wedged cozily between my pillows and the top of my sheets. She either had been sleeping too deeply to hear my calls or wasn't in the mood to move.

She stretched and looked up at me as if to say, "Why are you bothering me?"

"I plan to get under that quilt too," I explained. I left her briefly as I showered and picked out which jeans and flannel shirt and sweatshirt I'd wear tomorrow, and then she allowed herself to be bumped slightly so I could join her in the bed. She'd warmed up a nice spot for me.

After catching up with the news (none of which was good) and weather (tomorrow would be sunny, and warmer than today) on television and watching part of a reality show that didn't look like any reality I'd ever seen, I curled up with a book on early American embroidery designs Sarah had lent me. One chapter and the warm bed ended a long day.

I thought. But I hadn't turned my phone off. I sleepily reached for it, wondering why it was ringing after midnight. Was Gram all right? Had something happened to Tom? What about my friends who lived alone—Sarah, Patrick, Dave. And Ruth. Horrible pictures of automobile accidents and falling down stairs and sudden heart attacks raced through my mind. By the time I swung my feet over the side of the bed and picked up the phone, I was wide awake. Trixi took my warm place in the bed.

"Yes?" My voice still sounded thick with sleep, even to me.

"Angie? Sorry to wake you."

"What is it, Dave? Are you all right? Did something happen to Leo?"

"We're fine. I hope Leo's sleeping in jail. I hoped you'd be watching a late movie or reading or surfing the net."

"Not exactly. But I'm okay. What is it?"

"I wanted to talk to you before I pick Leo up tomorrow morning. I told you I was having dinner with Karen, right?"

"You did. Have a nice evening?"

"Oh, dinner was fine. We went to the Harbor Haunts, of course. Pete and Ethan were there too."

"Did you talk with them?"

"Briefly. I asked how Leo was coping, and Pete said he was sulking—not talking to anyone. But he'd eaten whatever dinner they'd given him. He was okay."

"Good." That lawyer Tom had suggested—Willow Sinclair—would probably be glad Leo hadn't been talking.

"Anyway, after Karen and I sat down she started quizzing me about what you and I knew about Leo and about Ike."

"And?" I didn't want to rush Dave. Clearly something was on his mind. But it was almost twelve-thirty and so far he hadn't told me anything worthy of a late-night call.

"Karen's a good doctor. She wouldn't say much about why Ike saw her. 'Doctor–patient confidentiality' and all that. But it sounded as though he stopped in at the emergency room once or twice a month with small complaints. Most times he came in during her shift, so he almost always saw her." Dave took a breath. "Leo said Ike complained about his back, so I asked her about that. She said it wasn't anything serious by itself."

" 'By itself'?" I asked.

"That's what I said," Dave agreed. "Karen hesitated, but then she said Ike had a lot of bruises on his back."

"Bruises? You mean, he fell?"

"She said his lower back looked as if someone had hit him. Repeatedly. Not hard enough to break the skin but enough to hurt."

I paused. "How long ago was that?"

"Exactly what I wanted to know. 'Had Leo hurt him?' But Karen said no. Ike had the bruises and pain a couple of months ago."

"Before Leo came to Haven Harbor." Trixi rubbed herself against me because I wasn't paying any attention to her. I reached and stroked her back.

"Exactly. But it may be important that when Ike was stabbed, it wasn't the first time someone had hurt him."

"Did Karen report the abuse? Isn't that what doctors are supposed to do?"

"I thought so too. But she said Ike kept saying no one had hurt him. No one had hit him."

"If he used the word *hit*, then he was covering for someone."

"Whoever it was probably threatened him. Told him not to tell anyone."

"Has Karen told the police now?"

"She said she did, but no one seemed to think it was important. That maybe Ike had fallen and didn't want anyone to know because Ed Campbell and the Chamber of Commerce folks would use that as an excuse to put him in an institution. It would prove he couldn't take care of himself."

"Rubbish. If someone was hurting Ike—even if it was only one time—then it was very important."

"That's why Karen told me. She knew you and I were involved in this case."

"Ike talked a lot. That's one thing everyone seems to agree on. Could he really have kept quiet about someone hurting him?"

"A good question. But that's why I wanted you to know tonight, before we see Leo in the morning. Maybe Ike told Leo what happened. He might have thought Leo could be trusted because he didn't know anyone in town."

"I agree. Leo may very well have the clue to everything. He just doesn't know it."

"Or thinks he'll get in trouble if he tells something Ike made him promise to keep quiet about."

"What time will you pick me up in the morning?"

"Pete said Leo would be released about eight-thirty. We'll be by your place a little after that."

"I'll be ready," I said. "In the meantime I'll be thinking of questions to ask."

"We can't overwhelm him, or pressure him," Dave said. "Remember, he's just a scared kid."

"He'll be more scared if he has to spend another night in jail," I reminded him. "He needs to help us find one or more people who had reasons to kill Ike. And now we know at least one person hurt him this spring, maybe as a warning."

Chapter Twenty-nine

Mary let virtues charms be thine
Charms that will increase and shine
They will cheer thy winters gloom
They will shine beyond thy tomb
 —Mary Davis, age seventeen, Canterbury,
  New Hampshire, 1826. Her sampler in-
  cludes a wide border of flowers and birds.

Trixi zoomed off somewhere, probably looking for another mouse to kill, as I tried to get back to sleep. Who in quiet Haven Harbor could have had a reason to hurt Ike?

No one I'd talked to so far had said anything really negative about him.

He'd grown up in Haven Harbor. He'd tried to live in his home after it had been damaged, and he was upset when the town condemned it. Then he moved into the garage his father had set up as a workshop. He had a little heat. (Not enough for a Maine February, but some.) He had water. He knew where the food bank was, and the shelter when weather got fierce. He was (someone had said) on Medicare disability. He asked for medical help when he needed it. He might not have close friends to confide in, but Ruth and Dave both gave him food or invited him in for lunch. I wouldn't be surprised if there were more Ruths and Daves in town. Henri and Nicole Thibodeau gave him unsold bread or pastries from their patisserie. Pax drove him to the redemption center every Saturday so he could get cash for the bottles and cans he collected around town. He'd invited a homeless boy to share his home.

What negatives had I heard about him? He was a little different from other people in town. As he picked up bottles, he also picked up gossip and then spread it. The one thing everyone agreed on was that Ike talked a lot.

Ruth had given me some examples of what he'd talked about. Ike had an imagination, and I suspected Ruth, who made her living writing stories, enjoyed his take on Haven Harbor and its citizens.

But someone had hurt him, maybe two months ago. And someone had killed him last Sunday.

Could he have been killed for the stories he saw—or imagined seeing—around town?

I lay in bed, now wide awake, wondering.

What could Ike have seen or said that so enraged someone?

Trixi rejoined me. Her hunt must have been unsuccessful. She stretched out on top of the pillow next to mine and sighed.

"That's right, lady," I said. "I don't have any answers either."

By the time I'd fallen asleep, it was almost morning.

*   *   *

Dave and Leo arrived on schedule, a little after eight-thirty. "We thought we'd get started right away," said Dave. "We stopped at the patisserie for coffee and cinnamon rolls we can eat in the car."

"That place is awesome," said Leo. "Better than Dunkin' Donuts. Ike went to the back door and sometimes they'd give him bread. But we never got any cinnamon rolls."

Dave had gotten a box full. His car smelled of cinnamon and sugar and coffee and chocolate. "Yum," I said as I bit down into the sticky sweetness. "And are you drinking hot chocolate, Leo?"

He nodded, his mouth full of pastry. "I'm old enough to drink coffee, but I like chocolate better."

"The Thibodeaus make terrific hot chocolate," I agreed.

We sat for a few minutes as I decided where we should go first. But the Thibodeaus had already been mentioned. "Did you and Ike go to the patisserie often?" I asked.

"Pretty much. A couple of times a week," said Leo, licking his lips and fingers.

Dave handed him one of those little moist wipes people more organized than I am keep in their cars.

"We stopped at the stores downtown twice a week. Some of them had a lot of soda cans and water bottles. We stopped at the patisserie last, so we could put any bread they gave us on top of the bottles."

"Makes sense," I agreed. "Did Ike ever tell you anything about them? The Thibodeaus?"

"This is what you want me to help with, right?" said Leo, almost too eagerly. "What Ike said about people?"

"Right," said Dave.

"He talked a lot," Leo confirmed.

His night in jail had loosened Leo's tongue. Or maybe he'd realized that cooperating might keep him from another overnight stay at the police station.

"I've heard that," I said. "So do your best to remember what he said."

"He liked the patisserie people. He told me they came from Canada, where they spoke French. That's why they called their bakery a patisserie."

"Right," said Dave, encouraging him. "Anything else?"

"Ike said Henri's mother was sick. She has that Alzheimer's, so she couldn't remember a lot. She doesn't speak English. I asked her a question once, and Cindy, who takes care of her, said she wouldn't even remember the answer if I'd asked her in French."

"Were Cindy and Madame Thibodeau down at the patisserie when you talked to them?" I asked.

"Nah. They were at home. Cindy takes care of Madame Thibodeau when Henri and Nicole are working. We stopped to see if they had any bottles. Madame Thibodeau and Cindy were both there, but that Cindy was nasty. She called Ike a bad name." Leo looked from Dave to me as though wondering whether to repeat it. "A bad name, and said she'd take the bottles to redemption herself and keep the money. That she didn't have anything for us."

"What did Ike say about that?"

"He told Cindy she took more than bottles and he knew it. She told him to keep his mouth closed and called him the bad word again."

"What did Ike mean?"

"Ike said Henri Thibodeau told him his mother, the old lady, was upset because she was losing things, like her jewelry or silver spoons. Henri never knew whether she'd really lost her things or whether she'd imagined them or had them a long time ago. So Ike watched their house. Once he saw Cindy hiding something in her pocketbook. Another time he saw her trying to sell things down at the antiques shop near the bookstore."

Sarah's shop. Had Cindy been stealing Madame Thibodeau's small treasures? Sarah would remember what Cindy had brought in.

"So Ike thought Cindy was a thief."

"She was wicked nasty, for sure. Maybe she stole too. I never saw that, but Ike talked about it a lot. He didn't like anyone who stole from old people."

"Stealing from anyone's not good," Dave put in dryly. "But let's get going. I'm going to drive to Ike's garage. You tell me what streets you and Ike took when he went downtown. You said he did that a couple of times a week."

"Almost every day we went to the restaurant," said Leo. "That Haunts place. They always had bottles because of the bar."

Ike's garage was padlocked and circled by yellow crime scene tape.

"Ike never locked the door," Leo said, staring at it. "Never. He said locks were to keep people in, not people out."

I glanced at Dave. That was an odd way of looking at it. But Ike had his own way of looking at everything.

"So, you'd both leave here with Ike's shopping cart," said Dave. "Point out your route."

"Straight ahead," said Leo, "until you get to the Green, then turn left. When we were going to the stores we didn't stop at any houses."

"Okay," Dave agreed, following Leo's directions. "Where downtown did you start?"

"At the wharf," said Leo, pointing at a side street. "The bins for recyclables are there, and we'd clean them out."

A few puddles left after yesterday's rain sparkled in the sun. At the town wharf, Rob Trask was bailing the skiff he and Arwin Fraser used to get to Arwin's lobster boat, moored farther out in the harbor. Usually lobstermen went out at first light; Arwin must have decided not to go out today, or to delay his trap run.

A lobster boat surrounded by herring gulls hoping for discarded bait was working farther out, near one of the Three Sisters islands that helped protect our harbor from the ocean's power. A hurricane or strong nor'easter hitting at high tide could drive waves over the wharf, but most days boats tied there were safe.

This morning the waterfront was quiet.

"All the boats in the harbor are facing the same direction," Leo said, staring out at the lobster boats, motor boats, skiffs, and sailboats at anchor. "How do people make them do that?"

I tried not to laugh, and ex-sailor Dave grinned. "People don't do that. Tides do. The boats head toward land when the tide is coming in, and head out when the tide turns."

Of course. Leo had never seen the ocean until he came to Haven Harbor. Facts of coastal life we took for granted were new to him.

"How do you like the ocean?" I asked.

"It's pretty," he said innocently. "But scary too. At that Blessing of the Fleet they listed a lot of people who'd died."

"True," said Dave. "Deep waters are like other scary things. You need to learn the rules of the road to navigate them and feel safe. And even then, you have to be ready to expect the unexpected."

He wasn't just talking about the ocean.

"I guess," said Leo. "Sometime I'd like to go out on a boat. Not in a storm or anything dangerous, but just to see how it feels."

"Maybe this summer I could teach you to row," Dave suggested.

Dave was beginning to make plans for the summer. I crossed my fingers that Leo would still be with him then.

"A motor looks like more fun," Leo said, looking out at the harbor. "Faster. And less work. Do you have a boat?"

"No. But I have a couple of friends I can borrow one from," said Dave. "Did anyone talk to you and Ike when you collected bottles down here?"

Leo shook his head. "Not really. Ike talked all the time, but mostly to me. He said a lot more bottles and cans are in the big bins in the summer. That I'd see, then."

Dave drove slowly along the waterfront.

Leo pointed at the empty restaurant where I'd worked summers when I was in high school. It catered to people from away who wanted to eat lobsters, clams, and oysters on picnic tables with a view of the working waterfront, surrounded by the smells of saltwater and steaming lobsters and clams. "Ike said that place has a lot of bottles when it's open, but the guy who runs it didn't like him picking through the recyclables Dumpsters. Inside restaurants that put their trash and recyclables in back, outside, were better. Customers didn't see us picking up the empties."

"Places like the Harbor Haunts?" I asked, as we turned up the street toward Haven Harbor's only year-round restaurant.

"Right. Like that place," Leo agreed. "We stopped there almost every day. Sometimes we got so many bottles we had to take them back to the garage and go back for more," he reminisced. "Those were good days."

I wanted to find out more about Ike and about what Dr. Karen Mercer had told Dave the night before. "You told us a few days ago that Ike's back was sore."

"It hurt when he bent over. That was why he liked having me along. I could reach deep into the barrels and trash cans, and help him carry bottles that wouldn't fit in our cart."

"Did he ever say how his back was hurt?"

"He said he was getting old." Leo thought a minute. "One time I saw his back. It had marks all over it. I asked him how he'd gotten the marks, and he said he'd promised not to say. That some things were private." Leo was quiet for a minute. "Another time he told me he'd slipped on the ice and hurt himself."

I glanced at Dave, who'd raised his eyebrows. "Why do you think the bruises were private, Leo?"

"I figured he just didn't want to talk about what happened. His back looked like Mom's, when Dad had hit her. She didn't want to talk about her marks either. She wouldn't say anything, or she'd say she slipped and fell, like Ike did."

"So you think someone hit Ike, the way your dad hit your mom?"

"I figured. But, like I said, he wouldn't talk about it." Leo looked out the car window. "He used to talk about that place a lot."

He was pointing at Gus Gleason's Book Nook.

"What did he say?"

"It's kind of embarrassing," said Leo. "It was about sex. He used to talk in a really loud voice when he was near there. He didn't usually do that. But he said the man who owned the bookstore was bad, and people should know it. That he always had girls working for him, and he bothered the girls." Leo grinned slyly. "Ike said the guy who owned the store didn't spend enough time with his wife."

"Did you pick up bottles there?" Dave asked.

"Ike said he used to get bottles there, but not anymore. The bookstore guy yelled and told him not to come back anymore."

"Really?"

Leo nodded. "Ike didn't like that guy. He told me never to work there, and to tell girls at school not to work there either. But I didn't go to school, so I didn't know any of the girls to talk to. He said he was going to tell the guy's wife no matter what anyone said."

"Had he done that, do you know?" I asked. "Had he told the owner's wife?"

"I don't know. He said he saw her at the hospital. He went there once when I was at his place, but I didn't go with him. I don't know who he saw."

Gus Gleason moved higher up on my list of possible suspects. Would Gus have hit Ike? Or killed him? Had Ike told Nancy Gleason her husband was annoying the girls who worked in the bookstore? Nancy worked at the hospital, and Karen Mercer had said he went there regularly.

"Anything else he talked about on this street?" Dave was asking.

"He liked the lady in the antiques store but said she talked funny, and sometimes he couldn't understand her. She sold old things she bought from people like Cindy Bouchard, who'd stolen from Madame Thibodeau. He told me I shouldn't ever steal, and Cindy would be caught. The police were checking on the antiques place. They hung around there a lot."

That would fit with what he'd told Ruth about Sarah and the police. I needed to check with Sarah about Cindy Bouchard. I wouldn't tell Sarah her Australian accent was sometimes hard for Ike to understand. I suspected his Maine accent wasn't always easy for her, either.

"We picked up bottles over there, at the gift shop, and at Hubbel Clothing," said Leo, pointing down Main Street. "Ike said the Hubbel people sometimes gave him clothes that people returned and they couldn't sell again. They never had many bottles or cans, though. And when they had cans, they were all Moxie."

Moxie. Maine's soft drink. Someone who worked at Hubbel's must be a fan.

"Nothing else downtown," said Leo. "We stopped at a couple of houses on the Green, but most of the time no one was home. People left their empties in their garage or barn for Ike to pick up."

As Dave drove around the Green, Leo commented. "None here. None here." (That was my house. I cringed a little.) "We'd go to the church here and the one over there." He pointed left. "On Mondays. They'd put out bottles for us then. There's a soup kitchen at the Baptist church, so we'd collect there on Wednesdays, too, so we could have lunch." He pointed at Ruth's house. "An old lady there gave us sandwiches, so we stopped there at lunchtime on Thursdays. She was funny. She always asked Ike to tell her the latest news. And your house isn't far away, Dave. The yellow house. That's how I was able to find you." Leo looked slyly at Dave. "Ike said you were a really good cook, for a man. Think it's time for lunch yet?"

Dave grinned. "You're right. It's a good time for a break. Angie, want to join us?"

"Why don't you drive me home?" I suggested. I wanted to talk with Sarah. "If you go out again this afternoon, let me know. Leo, you've been a big help."

On the way to my house he pointed out the Thibodeaus' house. "That's where that Cindy Bouchard works, taking care of Madame Thibodeau. Ike said she only got Madame cleaned up before the Thibodeaus came home. He said she got that job because she could talk French, but the Thibodeaus should get someone else."

We came to the street that led to Ike's garage. "I don't like those people," Leo said, pointing at the house where Sandra and Jim Lewis lived.

"Why didn't you like those people?" I asked, surprised, as Dave pulled his car into my driveway.

"Ike used to wave at the man in the wheelchair who lives there, and visit him." Leo pointed. "He sits where flowers are on the windowsill. Ike said the man was his friend, but now he didn't talk much." Leo shook his head. "It was weird, going into a house and talking to someone who said only a few words. I went once, but not again. Ike kept saying that someday the man, Jim, would talk and have a lot of stories to tell, and he would help his friend remember them."

"What about Jim's wife? Did she mind Ike visiting her husband?"

Leo shrugged. "Ike didn't visit when the man's wife was home, except some days when she was busy with another man."

Chapter Thirty

Virtue's the chiefest beauty of the mind
The noblest ornament of human kind
Virtue's our safeguard and our guiding star
That stirs up reason when our senses err.

—Martha Mortimer Starr, Middletown, Connecticut, 1791. Martha stitched a very elaborate scene of a large building next to a line of trees, with water in front of it, and a skiff, horse, and cow on the other side. She bordered it with an elaborate weaving of birds, flowers, and ribbons among branches rooted in pots at the bottom of the sampler. Martha was born in 1777, married John Lawrence Lewis in 1799, and later was divorced.

I stepped into my house, my head full of possibilities. I was glad Dave and Leo had gone home for lunch. Leo had told us a lot that morning, and I needed to write some of it down before I forgot it. Some small thing he might have mentioned could be the clue to Ike's murderer.

And we hadn't followed all of Ike's route yet. There could be more stories to come.

One thing was clear: Ike had done more than spread his stories around town. He'd threatened to tell Gus Gleason's wife about his behavior with girls who worked in the bookstore. He'd accused Cindy Bouchard of stealing from Madame Thibodeau. He'd thought Sarah bought those stolen goods.

And yet, for all of his talking, he hadn't told Leo or his doctor how he'd gotten the bruises on his back. Ike could keep a secret when he needed to. Why did he need to?

I kept remembering that he told people he was afraid of the "Chambers." So far I hadn't heard any reason Ed Campbell, or anyone else on the Chamber of Commerce, would have hurt Ike. But some people on the Chamber had wanted Ike to get out of town. He'd been an embarrassment; his life wasn't "the way life should be," as the advertising slogan promised that attracted tourists (and new residents) to Maine.

I pulled a pad of yellow legal paper out of my desk drawer and made a list of all the people I remembered Leo mentioning this morning and what he'd said about them. Or, more correctly, what he reported Ike had said about them.

Nothing said "this is the murderer," but despite all the people who'd said Ike was a nice man who collected bottles and never bothered anyone, clearly he *had* bothered some people. As Gram might say, he'd put his nose in places it shouldn't be.

Where should Dave and I go from here? Or, more correctly, where should I go? Dave had Leo and his students. His schedule was full. On the other hand, Mainely Needlepoint was running smoothly, and I didn't expect any major new orders to come in until summer. Pete and Ethan were probably talking to some of the same people and places that I was, but we had different goals. They wanted to find the person who'd killed Ike. I wanted to do that, too, but I also wanted to get Leo Blackwell off the suspect list, both for his sake and, I had to admit, for Dave's.

Dave had gone out of his way to help Leo. Would I have been as quick to do that—to volunteer to help change someone's life? I hoped so, but I wasn't sure. I *was* sure I wanted to support my friend who hadn't hesitated to step up when he was needed.

I sat at my desk, looking out at the Haven Harbor Green. Other captains' homes like mine ringed the Green. In the early nineteenth century, folks in town grazed their sheep on the Green. In the eighteenth century, sheep and other domestic animals had been kept on the Three Sisters islands, where they couldn't escape and didn't need to be fenced in. But during the Revolution, English naval forces stole most of the cows and sheep and pigs on Maine islands to feed English sailors. After that, Mainers stopped using islands as natural pens for their animals.

Through the years Mainers who lived by the coast had learned to live with the challenges of their natural world. Snow, frigid temperatures, nor'easters, occasional hurricanes, years of drought, years of fog, and rocky soil that wouldn't support farming were accepted, and ways were found to survive despite the difficulties. Today's Mainers were dealing with the effects of warming waters on the fish and lobsters they depended on for a living and tried to balance making their world inviting to tourists, but not so inviting that towns were gentrified, taxes went up, and working waterfronts disappeared. Some families that had lived here for generations, like mine, could no longer afford to pay taxes on their homes and had to sell. The crafters and back-to-the-land folks moved farther north and inland, and the twenty-first century put satellite dishes on remote homes and solar panels on old barns.

As I mused, I heard sirens, and an ambulance and police car passed. I watched for a few seconds to make sure they didn't stop at the rectory. We were lucky to have good emergency services and a hospital here in town.

I focused on the list I'd made. Some of what Ike had said about Sarah wasn't true; she wasn't in trouble with the police, unless the trouble was that she didn't see Pete often enough. Had she bought anything from Cindy Bouchard? And if so, had it been stolen? Sarah had once told me antiques dealers kept records of whom they'd bought items from and the "provenance," or history, of the items. Sarah had also showed me lists of stolen items in antiques journals, warning dealers not to buy them.

I had to talk to her. She answered after two rings.

"Angie? Hi! I was just thinking of you! I'm unpacking some embroidered pockets."

"What? Pockets?" Had I understood her correctly?

"Pockets! Yes. Come on down to the shop. I'll show you and feed you. I bought too many cold cuts the other day."

"I assume you're not overrun by customers today?" I asked.

"You and I both wish," Sarah said.

"Okay. Actually, I want to ask you about a couple of things, and I'd like to see your pockets." (What were antique pockets?)

"Then, come on down! See you soon."

Sarah's phone clicked off.

I never minded having an excuse to see Sarah, so I pulled on a sweatshirt, gave Trixi a parting stroke or two, and headed out.

Today the air smelled like the sea. Low tide and the sun on rockweed along the shore did that, especially in the summer. I even loved the smell of mudflats, although we didn't have a lot in Haven Harbor. Earlier years in Haven Harbor, the air would have been filled with smoke from fireplaces or from stoves for heating or cooking. Those smells added to the salt air and the smells from the Green when it housed animals would have been very different from today. As I passed the patisserie I inhaled the wonderful aroma of freshly made bread. That smell wouldn't have changed over the years.

The hundred-year-old cowbell Sarah hung where it would ring when her shop door was opened clanged as I walked in.

"You made it quickly," she said from behind the counter. "I just finished making grilled ham and cheese sandwiches for us." I took the plate she handed me.

"Yum," I said. "I guess I was hungrier than I thought." I popped one of the salty chips she'd added to our plates into my mouth. "Thanks for doing this."

As I started eating I noticed a framed doll hanging on the back wall of her shop.

"New? I don't remember that doll."

"Isn't she beautiful?" Sarah said, reaching up and putting her on the counter so I could see her.

"She's made of wood."

"Exactly. A primitive, with a painted face. I keep wondering who made that for a lucky little girl about 1840."

"1840! Wow."

"She must have been treasured, she's in such good condition. Her dress is from later in the century. Maybe her owner grew up and made the dress when she was an adult, to replace one that had worn out earlier."

"Why is she framed?"

"I did that to protect her. I had a nineteenth-century shadow box just the right size." Sarah looked at her work. "She looked lonely in the frame, so I added this title page from an 1859 issue of *Godey's Lady's Book* in back of her. The magazine was a breaker."

"A breaker?"

"It was bound with other issues, but the binding had broken, and some of the articles and engravings had already been removed. It wasn't worth much except as a curiosity."

"It looks great," I said. I'd already finished half of my ham and cheese sandwich. "Now, what are the 'pockets' you were talking about on the phone?"

"Remember the nursery rhyme, 'Lucy Locket lost her pocket, going to the fair, Kitty Fisher found it. Not a penny was there in it, Only ribbon round it'?"

"Vaguely." I remembered Gram reading nursery rhymes to me, but I hadn't paid much attention, although I did remember the simple ones, like "Jack and Jill" and "Three Blind Mice."

"Well, in the seventeenth and eighteenth centuries, women didn't have pockets sewn into their skirts or dresses," Sarah explained.

"I wish we had more, actually," I said. "Then we wouldn't have to carry pocketbooks or backpacks."

Sarah nodded. "In the past, before pockets were sewn into seams, they were separate little flat bags worn around a woman's waist so she could reach through a slit hidden in a pleat in her skirt to get something out. Pockets were often tied with a ribbon or cord at the top, like Lucy Locket's. Most women had very simple pockets, made of scraps of cloth. But of course, elegant women had to have elegant pockets. Some that have survived through the years were very elaborately embroidered." She handed me a flat box. "I bought these three in an online auction, and I love them."

The top pocket was embroidered with pink and green and tan flowers on cream-colored linen. The second one, more than a foot long but not as elaborate, was made of embroidered cotton. The third pocket was faded and covered with once-yellow flowers on a tan background.

I bent down to look closer. The stitching was delicate. "What did women carry in them?"

"Likely sewing scissors and thimbles, maybe a few coins, a handkerchief, hairpins—the same sorts of things we carry today."

"Fascinating," I had to admit. "And beautiful embroidery. What are you going to do with them?"

"I'll frame them, as I did the doll. They won't need as deep a shadow box frame, but if they're protected in sun-resistant glass, they'll survive another few generations and make for interesting home decorations, or talking points."

"They're definitely curiosities," I agreed. "I'm glad you showed them to me. I can't imagine how they've lasted this long."

"Keep in mind, these pockets were probably the property of well-to-do women who had different pockets to go with different dresses. Pockets are rarely seen today because most were worn by people like us—

women living their daily lives. Their pockets wore out."

"The embroidered flowers are so carefully done. It's interesting, isn't it, that so much antique embroidery is of flowers."

" 'This bauble was preferred of bees, by butterflies admired at heavenly hopeless distances, was justified of bird.' "

"Birds, too," I agreed. "An Emily quotation?"

"Of course." Sarah smiled. "She has words for everything."

"I wish I did," I put in.

"You were the one who called. You wanted to ask me about something?" Sarah put our now-empty plates on the stairs to her apartment, where they'd be hidden from any customers. "Are you still trying to find out who killed Ike Hamilton?"

"Yes. And yes," I answered. "This morning Dave and I drove around town with Leo Blackwell, trying to find out if Leo knew anything he—or the police—hadn't connected to Ike's death. Ike talked a lot, so we wondered if something he'd said had been so upsetting to someone that they'd kill him."

"Did Leo come up with anything? Other than that the police have an eye on my shop?"

Sarah smiled, shaking her head. "I still can't get over that."

"Actually, yes. Have you bought anything in the past few months from Cindy Bouchard, the home health aide who takes care of Madame Thibodeau?"

Sarah frowned. "I have. Yes. It isn't unusual for someone to walk into an antiques shop and ask for an appraisal on something. I don't have the accreditation to do that officially, for, say, insurance purposes, but I can sometimes give a customer a ballpark answer. Occasionally someone asks if I'd like to buy something from them. Too often what they believe is a family treasure, or a find they bought at a yard sale, isn't even old enough to be considered an antique. Or it's a reproduction. You wouldn't believe the number of people who bring in Currier and Ives prints—some framed!—that they inherited. Almost all of them come from insurance company calendars that reprinted the originals and aren't worth anything. Just because Grandma loved it doesn't mean it's valuable. I hate to disappoint people who have hopes of making a fortune on vintage clothing, or a Victorian ring with a glass sapphire. Sometimes they get angry when they hear their treasure has little or no value. When that happens I suggest they go to another dealer, or to one of the auction houses that have free appraisal days, to get a second opinion."

Sarah sometimes got carried away when she talked about antiques. I'd learned a lot from her, but I needed to get back to my question. "So, Cindy Bouchard brought something in for you to see?"

"She did. Several times, in fact. I was surprised at what she'd inherited. Usually when someone dies, pieces like that are left to individuals who will value them because a beloved relative did."

"What did she show you?"

"Several souvenir spoons from Canadian provinces and New England states. Some spoons like that are sterling, and they're worth a little as collectibles. But the spoons Cindy showed me weren't silver. They had no value except to the person who bought them,

probably for sentimental reasons, to remember a trip.
Cindy was disappointed to hear that. Her aunt was
very attached to her collection, so Cindy assumed the
spoons were valuable. You can't put a retail value on
memories, but you can on precious metals."

"So you didn't buy the spoons. What else did she
bring you?"

"She asked me if I bought old jewelry. I told her I
sometimes stock good, vintage costume jewelry. She
brought me several pieces of rhinestone jewelry and
a bracelet she thought was turquoise. The bracelet
wasn't real turquoise. I'm no expert, but I could tell
that. I was tempted by the rhinestone jewelry. It was
pretty, and good quality, but I wasn't sure there was a
market for rhinestones in Maine and, as I told her, I
wasn't an expert on prices. She was disappointed and
said she could probably sell them on eBay. I told her
to go ahead, then."

"So you didn't buy anything from her."

"Actually, yes. I did. I bought one piece of the
rhinestone jewelry: a V pin from World War II. Remember I told you Nancy Gleason collected patri-
otic memorabilia? I thought she might like it. And
she did—she bought it as soon as I called to tell her
about it."

"Okay. I don't get it. A V pin?" I asked.

"V for victory. A lot of items were made with large
Vs during World War II. The one Cindy had was nice
because it was sparkly but simple. Some of the patri-
otic pins were a little garish—lots of red, white, and
blue rhinestones. Cindy was so disappointed when I
told her I couldn't buy anything else she had. But I
wasn't sorry enough to buy something I wasn't sure
I could sell."

"Well, if Ike was right, you were smart," I assured her.

"Ike? What has he got to do with it?"

"Ike thought Cindy Bouchard was stealing small things from Madame Thibodeau. Henri mentioned to Ike that his mother couldn't find some of her things. Henri just figured she'd forgotten what she did with them. That happens to Alzheimer's patients. But Ike had seen Cindy leaving the Thibodeau house with small parcels."

"Hard to know, isn't it? I'd hate to accuse that young woman if she isn't guilty. But I did wonder where Cindy got the things she brought me. They didn't seem connected, and if they'd belonged to a dear aunt, as she said, I would have thought she'd tell me more about the pieces. People who inherit things often tell me long stories about their relative who died and where the item was in their house. Cindy was very matter-of-fact about just wanting to sell the objects."

"Interesting."

"If she did steal them, I'm glad I bought just one pin. I think I gave her ten dollars for it. Nothing major. I've always been afraid of buying things from people I don't know, who just walk into the store," Sarah added. "If what they're selling has been stolen, the police could arrive on the scene and return it to the owner. The dealer would lose money—and credibility. Not to speak of having encouraged a thief."

"I don't know for sure the items Cindy had were stolen. But would you mind if I asked Henri about them? He might recognize something his mother was missing."

"Go right ahead. And Nancy Gleason has that pin, if he wants it back," Sarah answered. "I'd explain what happened and reimburse her for what she paid me. I think she'd understand."

"How long ago did Cindy come to see you?"

"Maybe two or three months. It was after Christmas, because the store wasn't open regular hours then. January, or maybe early February. When are you going to talk to Henri? Would you like me to come with you?"

"You don't have to come with me. You might miss a customer. As long as you don't mind my telling him what you've told me."

"No problem here. And I'd be happy to talk to Henri, or to the police"—Sarah almost stifled a smile—"if he decides the items did belong to his mother."

"Of course, we don't know for sure. Henri should be able to tell me more. And maybe Cindy did inherit those items from an aunt. But if she stole them, she might still be stealing, and that needs to stop. Imagine, taking things that belong to an old woman who's ill and can't stop you! No wonder Ike was angry with her."

"How did she react when he confronted her?"

"Leo said she was furious. She told him not to come back to the Thibodeaus' house for bottles."

"Angry enough to kill Ike?"

"I don't know. But it's possible. Ike was killed late Sunday morning. I saw Cindy in church with Madame Thibodeau for the early service. She was probably back at the Thibodeaus' by eleven. Which meant, if she left Madame alone, she would have had time to go to Ike's garage, kill him, and be back by noon, when Henri and Nicole closed the patisserie and came home."

The old clocks hanging on Sarah's wall, all wound and working, chimed two. It was time to check back with Dave and Leo.

But first I wanted to talk with Henri.

Chapter Thirty-one

*As the rose breatheth sweetness from Its own nature,
so the benevolent heart produceth good works.*
  —Ruth Huntington (1776–1798), age
    eleven, Norwich, Connecticut, 1787. Ruth
    stitched her sampler on dark linen with a
    wide border of flowers and three alpha-
    bets at her Norwich school. She died in
    Lansingburgh, New York, "occasioned by
    a fall from a sleigh," when she was twenty-
    one. Ruth's fifth great-grandmother, Mary
    Wentworth, had come to the New World
    on the *Mayflower.*

"I went downtown to ask Sarah about those missing
items of Madame Thibodeau's," I told Dave, talking
on my phone as I walked toward the patisserie. "I
found out what Cindy Bouchard tried to sell. Now
I'm going to see if Henri can confirm that those
things belonged to his mother."

"Call me when you get home," said Dave. "Right
now Leo is doing homework."

"Right." I heard Leo's unconvinced voice in the
background.

"And I'm grading papers," Dave continued. "We don't have to go out again today."

"Just give me half an hour," I said. "I'll check in as soon as I'm home."

Gram had left a message. What would I like other than lobster bisque and daffodil cake for my birthday dinner?

I was almost to the patisserie, but I called her back.

"Gram? You called."

"I did. But I can't talk right now, Angie. Tom just got a call that Jim Lewis died. Sandra is hysterical. We're both going to the hospital to try to help her."

"Died? I just saw Jim Sunday, at church. I didn't know he was that ill."

"He's been ill for years. But, no. His death was unexpected. I have to go, Angie. We can talk later." Gram hung up.

Jim Lewis had died. Strange. Even when you know someone has been ill for a long time, it's still a shock when they die. I shivered. Life could end so quickly. Ike, and now Jim.

I pushed open the door to the patisserie and was overwhelmed by the fragrant odors of rising breads, vanilla, and chocolate. Two people were in line at the pastry counter, where a young woman was putting selected eclairs, Napoleons, cookies, and cakes into white bakery boxes. No cinnamon rolls—like the ones Dave had bought for our breakfast—were left, but those eclairs called to me.

I refocused. I was here to tell Cindy Bouchard's employer that she might be a thief. I hoped she wasn't, that she was a hardworking young woman saving for tuition and a future in nursing. But I'd gotten this far.

Henri was in back of the counter, writing something on a pad.

"Henri?" I said. "Henri, could I talk with you a minute?"

He looked up. The little hair he had was shaved, and his scalp shone with perspiration. With a sigh, but a smile, he came over to me. "What can I help you with, Angie?" He'd been working since very early morning, and the patisserie would be open until five today. In summer it stayed open until six. Long, exhausting, hours. And then he'd return home to take care of his disabled mother. It wasn't an easy life, and what I was going to say wouldn't make it easier. He glanced at the case of desserts. "We still have a few of those eclairs you like."

"I may not be able to resist those," I said. "But could we talk for a few minutes first?" I glanced around. "Somewhere private?"

"Private? I guess so." He gestured that I should come around the counter. "No one's in the kitchen just now. Baking's finished for the day."

The kitchen in back of the shop was smaller than I'd imagined. A series of deep ovens, a stove, a three-compartment sink, and a dishwasher lined one wall. Two racks of baking pans of every conceivable size were next to a door leading to a small rear parking lot. On the other side of the door, a rack held plates and platters and molds. Shelves on the inside wall were filled with flours, sugars, spices, nuts, and ingredients I'd never heard of. Around the top of the room, reachable by a ladder in the corner, were cake stands and tiers used for weddings and other celebratory occasions. Four large industrial mixers sat on the wide table that filled the center of the room. The fourth wall held a large freezer, a refrigerator, and a rack of aprons, pot holders, knives, cooking spoons, and a wide assortment of whisks.

The room's smell reminded me of Gram's kitchen when she was immersed in Christmas baking. I couldn't resist sniffing a few times. "You should bottle this scent, Henri," I said. "It's warm and calming and welcoming."

"Not always so welcoming to me, I assure you," said Henri dryly. "And warm? Yes. Especially in July. Now, what's so private we have to talk in here?" He leaned toward me. "A surprise party for someone special, perhaps? A baby shower?" He glanced at my naked left hand. "Perhaps an engagement party?"

"No, no, nothing like that," I assured him quickly. "It's about Ike Hamilton. And Cindy Bouchard."

He looked puzzled. "Ike and Cindy? But Ike is dead, sadly. And what has he to do with Cindy?"

"I think you met Leo Blackwell. He was living with Ike, and now he's staying with Dave Percy."

"The skinny boy who was here with Mr. Percy this morning? He's like a skeleton. He needs more hearty breads to fill him out."

Henri was a good baker. His ample front, covered with his white apron, suggested he'd never been called a "skeleton."

"He's had a hard time. Dave's looking out for him."

"Good. I gave Ike and the boy extras of my bread at the end of the day when they stopped in to collect bottles. Boys that age should have plenty to eat, to grow strong."

"Ike liked to collect stories about things he saw and heard around town."

"*Certainement*, he did that," Henri agreed. "That man could talk an angel cake out of rising."

"You once told him Madame Thibodeau was upset because she couldn't find some favorite things she'd brought with her from Quebec."

Henri nodded. "*Maman* was so very upset. We looked everywhere for things she was missing. But— nothing. Poor *Maman* is losing her memory now. She thinks it is the past and I am my departed father. I suspect that the items she is missing have been gone a very long time. Why do you ask about this?"

"Because Ike Hamilton thought Cindy Bouchard was taking your mother's things and selling them."

"Cindy? But she is such a sweet girl! We feel so lucky we found someone who speaks French and is good with *Maman*. Surely she would not do such a thing. She helped us look for *Maman*'s jewelry and spoons. A wonderful, sweet, girl!"

This wasn't easy. How could I tell Henri he might not be able to trust Cindy? "I talked to Sarah Byrne today."

"Sarah from Australia?"

I nodded. "She told me that Cindy tried to sell her souvenir spoons and rhinestone jewelry. She wondered if they might have been your mother's."

Henri stopped. "Spoons? What sort of spoons?"

"I didn't see them, but small, silver colored, but not sterling. The sort that tourists buy to remember places they've visited."

"*Maman* had a collection of those. I thought perhaps they'd been lost years ago, or left in storage with some of her furniture and belongings we didn't bring here."

"And several pieces of rhinestone jewelry. A turquoise bracelet. And a rhinestone V pin."

"*Maman*'s name is Victoria. My father gave her such a broach as a birthday gift when they first met. Sarah Byrne has these things at her shop?"

"The only piece she bought from Cindy was the V pin. And she's sold it since then. But the buyer is a regular customer, and she thinks she could get it back for you. For Madame Thibodeau."

"That would be kind. *Maman* would be so happy. But Cindy . . . we trusted her. What will we do without her? How can we run the bakery and take care of *Maman*?" Henri's face contorted, from anger to sadness to, finally, despair. "Thank you for telling me all this. Do the police know?"

I shook my head. "But we should tell Sergeant Pete Lambert, because of the connection to Ike's killing."

"Connection to Ike's killing?" Henri looked confused.

"Ike saw Cindy taking one or more items from Madame and said he'd tell the police. She told him he'd regret it if he reported her and that he should never come to your home for bottles again."

"I did not know this. Nicole, I'm sure, was unaware also. Thank you for letting us know, Angie. Please, don't tell the police. I will look tonight to see what else might be missing. We trusted that young woman with our family, with our home. Maybe we can get *Maman*'s brooch back. But someone we trusted has betrayed us. Now we must find another person to help us."

Henri's eyes filled. "Perhaps having to find another job will show Cindy such behavior is not rewarded."

Chapter Thirty-two

When beauty's charms decay, as soon they must,
And all its glories humbled in the dust,
The virtuous mind, beyond the reach of time,
Shall ever blossom in a happier clime,
Whose never-fading joys no tongue can tell,
Where everlasting youth and beauty dwell;
Where pain and sorrow never more shall move,
But all is pleasure, harmony and love.
  —Mary Hibbard, age fourteen, Westtown,
   Pennsylvania, 1807. Mary stitched this
   verse with a simple line border at the
   West-Town Boarding School, Pennsylvania.

I called Sarah on my way home. "I told Henri. Those pieces of jewelry and the spoons did belong to his mother. I told him you might be able to get that V pin back—it has sentimental value for his mother. He's going to talk with you."

"I'm so sorry. I hoped Cindy did have an aunt who'd died."

"Me too," I admitted. "Ike may have gotten a few stories confused, but he had that one straight. Funny

how things work out. Dave and I thought we were trying to solve a murder, but instead we found a thief."

"Unless she was also a murderer."

"No proof. But I'll admit she had a motive—to
keep Ike from going to the police and telling them
about her. And she probably could have gotten to
Ike's garage, with or without Madame Thibodeau, on
her way back from church Sunday, or just after that."

"You think she parked Madame Thibodeau's wheelchair outside Ike's garage, went in, hit him with bottles and stabbed him with a knife, and then came out
and walked Madame home?"

Sarah sounded skeptical.

"It does sound unlikely. Cindy would have been
covered with blood, for one thing. And the Thibodeaus' house is five blocks from Ike's garage. Someone in those five blocks would have noticed her."

"I would think so."

"Oh, and I talked to Gram. Jim Lewis died unexpectedly this afternoon. She and Tom were on their
way to the hospital to help Sandra."

"Jim Lewis? He's been ill for years, hasn't he?"

"He had MS. But Gram said his death was unexpected, and Sandra wasn't dealing well."

"Very sad. And wasn't he a friend of Ike's?"

"Their houses weren't far from each other, and
Leo said Ike visited him. Maybe Jim was upset about
Ike's death, and in his weakened condition that caused
a physical reaction."

"I'm sorry about Jim. Sandra was devoted to him.
Sometimes, in warm weather, she brought him down
to the shop. She never bought anything, but she
talked about him, and fussed over him, making sure
he was comfortable."

"I'm glad Tom and Gram are with her. They're both good at staying calm and soothing people who need comfort."

"That's sort of the job of a minister, isn't it?" asked Sarah.

"And Gram's always been that way. No wonder she and Tom get along so well."

At home I picked up the pencils and pens Trixi had pushed off my desk and then scattered throughout the first floor. I crawled on the carpet, looking under chairs and behind doors. If I'd known Trixi was going to play soccer, I wouldn't have sharpened a whole box of new pencils yesterday or left them in a mug (now also on the floor).

My phone rang before I'd quite finished straightening up.

"Angie? Where are you?" Dave's voice was clear. "I've left you four texts."

"Sorry. I haven't checked my phone. I told you—I went to see Sarah and then stopped to talk to Henri Thibodeau on my way home." I didn't mention the two eclairs that had somehow found their way into the box now on my kitchen counter. "Everything took longer than I thought it would."

"What did Henri say? Was Cindy trying to sell his mother's things?"

"Yes. He's very upset. He and Nicole trusted Cindy, and now they don't."

"Well, if you want to tell Pete about that, you don't have to call him," Dave said dryly. "He's right here. Hold on."

Pete was with Dave? What was happening?

"Angie? I've heard you're talking to people around town about Cindy Bouchard."

"Relax, Pete. I was following up on something Leo

said—that Ike thought Cindy was stealing small items from the Thibodeaus' home. Henri assumed his mother had misplaced them or didn't remember where they were. Ike also told Leo that Cindy had been to Sarah's shop several times, so I asked Sarah about that."

"You got Sarah involved in this whole mess too?"

I ignored his clear exasperation. "She remembered Cindy bringing souvenir spoons and jewelry into her shop and trying to sell them."

Pete sighed. "And?"

"She didn't know Cindy had stolen them. She bought only one thing—a small pin that wasn't very valuable."

I heard Dave saying something in the background.

"Dave says you've already told Henri Thibodeau that his employee is a thief."

"I checked with him to see if the items Cindy offered to Sarah were really his mother's. Henri said he wasn't going to report the theft. So you don't have to get involved."

"You might think so. But Cindy Bouchard just called me and said you were telling lies about her and as a result she'd lost her job."

"She stole those things, Pete. And she might even have killed Ike. She would have had time."

"Angie, there's a lot going on in town this afternoon. Please, just stay out of police business."

"What else is happening, other than trying to find who killed Ike Hamilton?"

"Which is Ethan's job and mine, not yours. And we're working the case. You're complicating it by bringing in someone who may have stolen a few small pieces of costume jewelry." Pete did not sound happy.

"And souvenir spoons."

"And souvenir spoons," he added. "By the way, did you know Jim Lewis died today?"

"Gram told me."

"And did you also know that before Jim died—a man no one thought could talk or do much of anything for himself—he accused his wife of murdering Ike?"

Chapter Thirty-three

May my fond genius as I rise
Seek the fair fount where knowledge lies
On wings sublime trace heavens abode
And learn my duty to my God.
    —Mary Maury Tait, age ten, "Washington
        City" (Washington, DC), 1825. Mary
        stitched a house surrounded by trees and
        flowers and bordered by strawberry vines.

"What? Who did he tell? How?" I'd just seen Jim at the church on Sunday. I'd had the feeling he could understand me, but he hadn't communicated in any way. How could he have told anyone anything? Although I remembered Leo saying that Jim and Ike talked together.

"Seems maybe he could speak," said Pete. "He just chose not to most of the time. He talked to Nancy Gleason, the nurse who was taking care of him when his wife was conveniently out of the room. He told Nancy that Sandra didn't know he could talk. That she had killed Ike and she was trying to kill him too."

Did any of that make sense? "But he's dead now."

"He had a massive heart attack in the emergency room. No one killed him."

"Why are you over at Dave's house, Pete?"

"Because while he was talking, Jim told Nancy that Leo knew he could talk. That Leo could explain."

"And has he?"

"Not so much, so far," said Pete grimly. "We're trying to figure it all out. Ethan's talking to Nancy, and I'm with Leo and Dave."

"And where's Sandra?"

"She's with your grandmother and the reverend."

"She's not under arrest?"

"We can't make an arrest on the word of someone everyone swears couldn't talk. And there were no witnesses."

"But Nancy Gleason's a nurse!"

"Right. She should have called someone in so she wasn't the only one Jim spoke to—if he did speak. But then he had the heart attack, and it was all over."

"So, for now . . ."

"For now we have a distraught widow who's been accused of murder by her deceased husband. That's enough to cope with for today. I'm sorry Cindy Bouchard stole a few trifles from the old lady she's taking care of, and that she was fired. We'll get to her, I promise. But she isn't today's priority. So just keep out of it and let us do our jobs, Angie."

"Got it, Pete."

I put down the phone. Had what I'd done really complicated the case? Maybe not. But it brought in a whole other situation. The Haven Harbor Police Department was three people—one of whom was a clerk who worked in the office, Pete, and one other cop. Ethan was with the Maine State Troopers Homicide Division. No one had time to spare during a homicide investigation.

Could Jim really have accused Sandra of killing Ike? And—could he be right?

Medical conditions were something I knew very little about, so I did what twenty-first-century people did. I did an online search on multiple sclerosis.

A progressive disease, with improvement and then relapses. An immune system disorder affecting the nervous system. Muscle weakness. Blurred vision. Numbness. That could explain the bruise I'd seen on Jim's arm. Trouble with coordination and balance. Sandra had said Jim had fallen. Trouble swallowing was on the list. Speech problems. Confusion. Unstable moods.

Nowhere did it say those with MS totally lost the ability to speak. And only in later stages did MS patients have to rely on wheelchairs. Jim must have had the disease for years.

And, assuming he could speak and chose not to, what would have convinced him to start talking to his nurse? And if he was confused (one of the symptoms of MS), could what he said be believed?

No wonder Pete and Ethan hadn't arrested Sandra.

But whether I understood his condition or not, certainly his wife did. She spent most of her time caring for him. And the doctors and nurses at the hospital would understand.

How was Sandra now? I hesitated, and then called Gram. It took several rings, but she did pick up.

"Angie? Is everything all right?"

"Are you with Sandra Lewis now?"

Gram said softly, "She's with Tom and me at the

rectory. I'm in the kitchen, making tea. Sandra's in the living room with Tom. She's very upset. Jim is gone, and the nurse who was with him right before his heart attack said he'd accused Sandra of killing Ike. I have to believe he was delusional. It makes no sense. But now the police are involved. They haven't arrested Sandra, thank goodness. The poor woman just lost her husband. But they won't let her go back to her home tonight."

"Why not?" I asked.

"Because," Gram whispered, "it might be a crime scene. Jim had a lot of problems, but his heart was fine, so far as his medical records show. Of course, something can happen suddenly, and his body had been struggling for years with different problems. But Nancy Gleason—the nurse he talked to, if he really did speak—also said Jim accused Sandra of trying to kill him. And then he died. The police asked Sandra if they could search her house, and she agreed."

"So no warrant was necessary. They probably won't find anything, and Sandra will be cleared."

"I hope so, Angie. That woman has suffered enough, caring for Jim all these years. She's exhausted and confused, and she just keeps saying she wants to go home and sleep in her own bed. Which, of course, is the one thing she can't do right now."

"Has she said anything about Ike?"

"Ike? No. She's focused on her husband. She knew Ike, of course. He lived right down the street from her. Ike and Jim were friends. But in the past years Ike has lived his own life, and as Jim's illness got worse, Sandra's been with him almost every hour of every day. A couple of years ago she even asked the church if someone could pick up their groceries for her so she wouldn't have to leave her home to shop."

"Did someone volunteer?" I asked.

"Ed Campbell did. As I understand—Tom would know more—Sandra calls him once a week, tells him what she needs, and he does her shopping for her. She even has a joint credit card with Ed, so they don't have to quibble about bills every week."

"How kind of him," I said, admittedly surprised. "I didn't know he did volunteer work. He always seems busy with the Chamber of Commerce and his used car business."

"True enough. But the grocery isn't far from his business, and I suspect Diane, his wife, convinced him to help out. She's active in a lot of outreach programs here at the church."

"Gram, if there's anything I can do to help, let me know."

"I will. I promise, Angie. But we're fine for the moment. I'm hoping Sandra will decide to go to bed early. I fixed our guest room for her, and one of the doctors at the hospital gave her some pills to help her relax. She was pretty close to hysterical when they called Tom and asked us to come over and sit with her."

"You take care of yourself, too, Gram," I said. "This whole situation sounds very strange. Too many turns."

"It does, indeed. Like one of those mysteries people read."

"Only a lot of the possibilities seem to be heading toward dead ends," I agreed.

"Unfortunately, Ike and Jim are both dead. Jim had been sick for a long time, so maybe it was his time. Ike's death is another situation. But the police will figure it all out, and I hope Sandra can go home tomorrow and start preparing for Jim's funeral. She's too upset to think about that tonight."

I hoped Pete and Ethan would figure it out. Right now, I was just confused. All I knew for certain was that two men were dead and Cindy Bouchard had stolen some tokens from Madame Thibodeau, which probably had nothing to do with either of the deaths.

No wonder Pete had been aggravated that I'd brought that up this afternoon. My timing hadn't exactly been excellent.

Gram was making tea. That sounded like a reasonable course of action. I decided to add cognac to my cup.

And then I was going to pay another visit to Ed Campbell's car business. If he'd done weekly grocery shopping for Sandra and Jim Lewis, he might know something about them that would explain whether Jim could talk. And if he could talk, why Jim had said Sandra had killed Ike and was going to kill him.

Chapter Thirty-four

Reason's whole pleasure, all the joys of sense
Lie in three words, health, peace and competence:
But health consists with temperance alone:
And peace, O virtue: peace is all thy own.
  —Margaret A. Cassady dated her sampler
    "Oct. 3 1826" and included two couplets
    from Alexander Pope's "An Essay on
    Man." She stitched a large brick building
    on a hill, many trees, and a wide border of
    vines and flowers. Because of its similari-
    ties to the work of other girls, her sampler
    is probably one of a group stitched by
    young ladies who lived in the Washington,
    DC, Navy Yard community.

"Ed Campbell's busy right now," said the young man
who greeted me in the used car showroom. "May I
help you?"

"I need to talk with Ed. It's personal," I explained.

The young man rolled his eyes "Of course. Let me
see if he's available. Your name?"

"Angela Curtis," I said, ignoring the eye roll. He

could think whatever he wanted. "I'd like to talk with him about the Lewis family."

"Give me a minute," he said, heading toward the closed doors at the back of the showroom.

I glanced at the cars. I'd leased one after my previous car had had . . . an accident . . . in February. I hadn't had enough money to buy a new ride, so leasing seemed a reasonable, if temporary, solution. The cars here were used but spruced up to attract new owners, like dogs at the humane shelter getting a bath before an open house, or a realtor advising a homeowner to put all her junk in a storage unit before her house went on the market.

When it was time to buy another car, I might well check here. Ed's dealership wasn't far. It would be easy to take a car back if I had any complaints.

While I was focusing on cars, the young salesman came back. "He can see you for a few minutes, but he has another appointment very soon."

"Thank you," I said, following my escort to his boss's office.

The office, and Ed, smelled of Scotch. It hadn't smelled like that when I'd talked to him before.

"You've come back," said Ed. "More questions about Ike Hamilton, I'll wager. But you'll get no more information from me. I didn't kill the guy, and I don't know who did." He leaned toward me. "Or maybe you've decided to join the Chamber of Commerce?"

"I'm not here to talk about Ike," I assured him. "Or the Chamber of Commerce. I'm here to talk about Sandra and Jim Lewis."

"Good folks. We all go to the same church. Your—what is he now—your step-grandfather's church."

"I've seen you and Diane there," I agreed. "And my grandmother told me that both of you are active in charitable activities sponsored by the church."

"Diane's the one with the time to do that. She's on every committee you've ever heard of. I have work to do." Ed spread his arms out to encompass his office and knocked over a mug on his desk. The liquid seeped into a pile of papers as he tried to sop it up with tissues from a box in his desk drawer. The liquid wasn't coffee or tea. The smell of Scotch in the small space was now even stronger.

"Gram told me you've been doing grocery shopping for Sandra and Jim Lewis. That's a kind thing to do."

"Not a big deal. Sandra texts me whatever they need. Sometimes once a week. Sometimes more often. I pick up the groceries, and prescriptions for them at the pharmacy, and I drop them off. Sandra didn't like being away from her house in case Jim needed her." Ed balled up the soaked tissues and tossed them toward his wastebasket. He missed, and a small puddle of liquor started forming on the floor under the tissues. He didn't seem to notice. "Jim takes a lot of care."

"Jim died this afternoon."

Ed stared at me. "I heard that. But I'm not going to mourn. He hasn't been living a full life for years."

"Who told you about his death?" I asked curiously.

"Sandra called. She was all broken up about it, of course. But once she thinks about how her life will change, she'll be all right."

I went back to the grocery shopping. "You said Sandra texted you her list of groceries when she needed your help."

"Right. That's what I said. Glad you're listening."

"What happened when you took the groceries to her?"

"What're you saying? I gave her the groceries. She said, 'Thank you, Ed.' What else do you think happened?"

I tried to be patient. Ed Campbell was clearly not at his best. Was this a normal after-lunch condition? Or was he upset about something? If he was upset, it didn't appear to be about Jim's death. "Did Sandra ever invite you in? Offer you a drink, or a snack? Chat with you?"

"Sometimes, I guess. She was a lonely woman. Stuck in that house with an invalid."

"So you and Sandra were friends."

"Sure. Friends. There's nothing wrong with being friends, is there?"

Ed's reactions were a little overblown. Was there a reason he was being defensive? Was I asking questions he'd rather not answer? Sandra must have called him right after Jim died. That sounded as though they were good friends. Close friends? More than friends?

"Not at all," I assured him. "Everyone should have friends. Do you know who Sandra's other friends were?"

"No clue. People from the church, probably. She never mentioned anyone special. Course, she couldn't exactly meet friends for lunch or go shopping with them, like my wife does."

"Of course not. She must have been very grateful for all your help."

"I suppose so. Why're you really here, Angie? You can't care that much about what groceries I delivered."

"Maybe you hadn't heard. Just before he died, Jim spoke to one of the nurses at the hospital. He said Sandra had killed Ike Hamilton and was trying to kill him."

"That's impossible! Jim couldn't talk!"

"So you never heard him speaking."

"A couple of years ago, sure. He used to talk. But not for a while now."

"And you saw him, at his home."

Ed hesitated. "Not often. He was usually in bed, I guess, or in his chair near the kitchen window where he could watch the birds. I'd put her groceries on the counter, and she'd put away anything frozen. Then she'd pour a cup of tea or some wine, and we'd sit and chat in the living room. I didn't pay much attention to Jim."

"So he might have been able to talk."

"Why would Sandra lie about something like that? She had to live with the man. He'd lost a lot of his senses, and he couldn't speak. If anyone says otherwise, they're lying."

"So you don't think Sandra killed Ike Hamilton or that she wanted to kill her husband?"

"Angie, between you and me I can understand why Sandra Lewis might have wanted Jim to die. He was destroying her world. But no way do I think she killed him. And why in the world would she kill Ike Hamilton?" Ed sat back in his black padded executive chair. "Whoever that nurse is, she's wrong. Dead wrong."

Chapter Thirty-five

This work perhaps my friends may have
When I am in my silent grave
And which when e'er they chance to see
May kind remembrance picture me
While on the glowing canvas stands
The labour of my youthful hands.

  —Mary Ann Baily, Pennsylvania, 1842. Mary
    Ann's sampler includes a mansion house,
    a tenant house, a flock of sheep, a cow, a
    dog, and a variety of trees, all worked in
    Berlin wool. Three sides of the sampler
    are bordered in flowers, and a green rib-
    bon with a rosette is embroidered in each
    corner.

I drove slowly back to Haven Harbor. Ed's business
was out on Route 1. Technically, yes, it was in Haven
Harbor, but I never thought of Route 1 as being anything other than Route 1.

Someone once told me it went all the way down
the East Coast from Fort Kent, Maine, to Key West,
Florida. In Maine most of it was scenic. Was it scenic
all the way to Florida? Maybe someday I'd find out.

Today I wanted to find out if Jim could talk. If he couldn't, why would Nancy Gleason say he had?

It made no sense.

I drove by Dave's house. Pete's car wasn't there, so I took a chance and stopped.

"Angie. I didn't expect you this afternoon." Dave looked exhausted. He opened his front door farther and gestured that I should come in.

"Is Leo here?"

"In his room. Pete just left a few minutes ago. Glad you stopped, actually. Tea? Beer?"

I thought about Ed Campbell. "Tea, I think."

"Com'on back, then." He led the way to his kitchen, filled a mug with water, and stuck it in his microwave. "Hope you won't mind if I have a beer."

"No problem," I agreed, sitting at his kitchen table as he opened a cold beer.

"Black, green, or herbal?" he asked, opening a cabinet and pointing to a shelf of tea.

"Black," I said. "This afternoon I need the caffeine. I'm tired too."

Dave nodded and handed me the mug of hot water and the tea bag as he sat across from me. "Rough day for sure. Rough week, actually."

"How'd it go with Pete?"

"Not sure if he got all the information he'd hoped for. He thought Leo would have heard Jim speak. But Leo said he'd met Jim only once. Jim had whispered some sounds that Ike seemed to understand, but Leo didn't. He said Ike visited Jim often, though, and waved to him if he was sitting in the window as they walked by.

"I talked with Ed Campbell again today, after I found out he did grocery shopping for Sandra and Jim."

"Ed Campbell did that?"

"Gram told me."

"Had Ed heard Jim talk?"

I shook my head. "He and Sandra would go into the living room to chat after the groceries were put away. He said Jim talked a few years ago but hadn't recently. Sandra had told him Jim couldn't. Ed wasn't surprised at Jim's death. He seemed happy that Sandra would be free of caring for him."

"Sandra's life was taking care of Jim. With him gone—what is she going to do?" Dave thought out loud.

"No idea. But do you think she killed Ike—or Jim?"

"Doesn't make sense why she would. Jim, maybe, sort of a mercy killing, maybe mercy for both of them. But why would she have been so angry at Ike that she'd stab him with bottles and a knife?"

"No motive," I agreed. "And yet, who *has* a motive?"

"From what you said, Cindy Bouchard may have lost her job today because Ike saw her stealing, and you followed up with Sarah and Henri."

"True. And Cindy was angry at Ike. But kill him? Other people were angry at Ike too: Ed Campbell, since he thought Ike embarrassed the town. Gus Gleason, because Ike threatened to tell Nancy about how he acted with his young female employees. So that's at least three people. There may be more." Who could the others be?

"The police keep mentioning that Leo took Ike's money," Dave pointed out. "Leo's still on their radar."

"But such a little amount of money!"

"When you haven't got any money, thirty-two dollars might seem like a lot."

"Murder investigations focus on suspects who have MOMs: motives, opportunities, and methods. No one needed to bring a murder weapon to Ike's garage. The bottles and the knife were already there. So the murder probably wasn't premeditated. Someone went to see Ike, got angry, and picked up whatever was close at hand."

"Several people were angry at Ike. In most cases, he'd threatened to tell someone something the suspect would rather have kept quiet."

I had to agree. "Ike saw things through a slightly different lens than others in town, but he had a strong sense of morality. He picked up on things like betrayals of various sorts. He wanted to make them right. He didn't want anyone getting away with something he knew was wrong."

"What about the 'O' in your acronym? Where were all those people when Ike was killed?" Dave asked. "Leo was at the gym. Pete said his story held up. People remembered him showering there."

"Cindy was with Madame Thibodeau at church earlier. But they left at about ten forty-five, before the second service, and they could have gone to Ike's garage instead of going directly home. Leo would have been at the gym then."

"What about Gus?"

"He and Nancy were in church too. As they left I noticed they'd taken different cars. Maybe Nancy had to go to work." I hadn't checked that.

"So Gus could have driven to the garage too."

"I guess so." I sighed. "And now we have to add Sandra's name to our suspect list, with lots of question marks around it. She was at the church, with Jim. She could have driven home, gotten Jim set up in his window, and walked down to Ike's."

"If she'd done that," said Dave, "Jim could have seen her. According to Leo, Jim could see not only the birds he loved but also the street to Ike's, and part of the garage."

"So Jim might have witnessed the killer entering Ike's garage."

"And now he's dead," Dave pointed out. "So what good is a dead witness?"

"Or a witness who talked, when everyone who knew him said he couldn't talk."

I wondered.

Chapter Thirty-six

No longer I follow a sound
No longer a dream I pursue
O happiness not to be found
Unattainable treasure Adieu.
> —Mary Coles, Ellisburg School near
> Philadelphia, Pennsylvania, 1818. Mary's
> sampler included a floral border, a house
> with trees and small animals, and separate
> designs of flowers, baskets, and birds.

Dave and I weren't getting anywhere, and he had to get dinner for himself and Leo and prepare to go back to school the next day.

I headed home, puzzled by everything that had happened. At first it had seemed so simple: Find out who had killed Ike. Now we had several suspects but no proof of guilt, or even a major motive. Although killers' motives were slippery. Someone could kill because someone else cut them off on the highway, or had stolen their girlfriend years before. Some slights evoked an immediate response; some festered and exploded years later.

I fed Trixi, checked my messages (nothing important), and decided soup (and those two eclairs I'd left on my counter) would be dinner. I didn't even make the soup. Gram would be disappointed in me. Instead, I opened a can of my childhood favorite, chicken noodle. What I needed today was comfort food.

I wanted to call Gram, but with newly widowed (and accused) Sandra Lewis staying in her house, calling to chat didn't seem like a good idea. But living alone sometimes left me needing someone to talk with. Trixi listened but didn't talk back.

Sarah? I'd spent time with her today, and I didn't want to talk about Cindy Bouchard and the missing jewelry and spoons anymore. I seemed to have reached a dead end there.

But I hadn't spoken with Patrick in a couple of days. Had he gone to Portland to have dinner with Linda Zaharee? Had she agreed to show in his gallery?

And, most important: Why hadn't he called me?

I felt a bit like a petulant child. Truthfully, there was no reason Patrick should call me every day. And my days had been very full this week. But still.

I called him. His phone rang four times. Usually he picked up by then. I glanced at the clock: He should be home from the gallery by now.

"Angie! I was just about to call you." He sounded out of breath.

"What are you doing?"

"I finished setting up the new exhibit for the opening next week, and when I was in Portland this week I bought a new easel and a small taboret to hold art supplies here at the gallery."

"I remember. You were thinking of setting up a

space where you could paint while you were waiting for customers."

"Exactly. Well, that's what I'm doing. I had to move some furniture around and rearrange a few paintings I'd already hung. If I'm going to paint here, I need decent natural light. I've finally got it all set up the way I like it, though. You should come down and see!"

"You're at the gallery now?"

"Have been all day, moving stuff around and checking to make sure a work area won't distract from the art for sale and will still be usable for me. On the other hand, I don't want the gallery to look as though I'm doing a live demonstration, like shearing a sheep at Old Sturbridge Village."

I smiled. I'd never been to historical Sturbridge Village, but I could imagine.

"So—want to join me? We could go down to Harbor Haunts and have dinner."

I hesitated. Dinner with Patrick would be fun, and I did want to see his gallery. The can of soup was open, but I hadn't heated it yet. The eclairs would be here when I got home. Or they'd make a wicked good breakfast. "I'd love to see what you've done to the gallery," I decided.

"It won't be as elegant a dinner as I'd thought we'd have this week, but right now I just want to stay in Haven Harbor. I suspect you've had a busy week too. Solved Ike's murder yet?"

Patrick was teasing, I knew, but it wasn't the right time for teasing. "Not yet. I'll tell you when I see you," I answered. "Let me put on a jacket and some lipstick. I'll be there in fifteen minutes."

Soup can in the refrigerator. Lipstick on, and a comb through my hair. (I should really get a trim.

Tonight my long brown hair looked as disorganized as I felt.) I pulled a decent jacket out of the downstairs closet and decided to wear leather gloves. The sun was still out, but temperatures were falling. My gloves were in the small bureau in the hall where I also kept my Glock. I wouldn't need that tonight, but it reminded me to get some more ammo. I'd been a Girl Scout once. The badges had long since fallen off my sash, but the "be prepared" had stuck.

Trixi complained loudly when I headed for the front door, and jumped up, holding the brass doorknob with her paws. Some days she did not appreciate the wisdom of being an indoor cat.

"I won't be out late," I assured her. "I'm just going to see Patrick. You like Patrick." She did not look reassured.

Every time I visited Patrick's gallery something had changed. He still displayed what he called the "bread and butter" paintings popular for summer cottages or to take home as souvenirs: ocean surf, harbor scenes, and lighthouses. But he'd also added more modern art, large and small. Triptychs that a decorator could hang above a couch. Large paintings for over mantels. Narrow pieces for hallways. He had sculptures, too: Space limitations didn't permit too many pieces, but he'd managed to squeeze some in.

One definite: He insisted on displaying art only from Maine artists. "Maine is so rich with artists, galleries should show their work with pride. Artists shouldn't have to send their work to New York or Boston or Santa Fe to make a living," he'd said.

So far he hadn't included any of his own work in the gallery. I assumed it was partially because he hadn't painted much in the past year. Last June his hands had been badly burned, and he hadn't even attempted to paint again until December. Before he'd moved to Maine his work had been large, modernist designs and textures. Recently he'd been working on some smaller, more realistic scenes.

I loved all his work.

I walked into his gallery and into his arms. "Close your eyes," he whispered, turning me around. "Now— look!" No wonder he'd been out of breath earlier. He'd moved the large mahogany desk that had always been in the center of the gallery and put it on one side. In the front right corner, near the window, he'd set up a large pine easel on oil cloth flooring and added a taboret filled with paints, brushes, cloths, and an assortment of other painting tools and liquids. "It looks like its own little room," I said, walking toward it. "But that oil cloth is going to be covered with paint in weeks. Maybe days."

"Part of the plan," he grinned, clearly pleased with what he'd done. "It will lend atmosphere, and I'll only use acrylics in the gallery. They'll be easier to clean up than oils, and dry faster." He pointed at a long white shirt hung on the wall in back of the taboret. "My smock will be covered with paint soon enough too." He put his arm around my shoulder. "Think I got the atmosphere right?"

"Absolutely," I agreed. It was wonderful to share his excitement and joy. Sometimes when I got involved in trying to solve a murder, I forgot that the rest of the world went on in its own relatively sane way.

"So. Hungry? I'm starving," Patrick said as he pulled on a sweater and held the door open for me. "I've been thinking about salmon. . . ."

Harbor Haunts was comfortably full, but no one was waiting. In another six weeks we'd have to make a reservation, or be prepared to spend time at the bar before eating. Today we found a comfortable table for two in the far corner. From my seat I could see everyone in the café, and several people waved to me.

"I think I'll go with the haddock stuffed with crabmeat," I decided. "And a glass of white wine. You decide on the wine, since you're having fish too." Patrick was an expert on wines. I drank almost anything and always enjoyed his choices.

Food and drink ordered, he said, "All right. How has your week gone? Are you still trying to figure out who killed Ike Hamilton?"

I nodded. "It all started because that young man we saw with Ike was suspected of his murder. But now I'm confused. Dave and I've found several other people who could have gotten to Ike's garage at the time he was killed, and who had some reason to want him dead."

"For Leo's sake, I'd guess more suspects are better. Right?"

"True. I hadn't thought of it that way. But I'd feel better if we knew what really happened. Right now I'm just confused. And, on top of that, Jim Lewis died today. Did you know him?"

"Was he the guy in the wheelchair? His wife is always—I guess *was* always—with him."

"Right. Well, before he died, Jim told Nancy Gleason, one of the nurses in the emergency room, that his wife had killed Ike and wanted to kill him too."

"Wait!" Patrick held up his hand. "I may be thinking of a different person. The man I remember couldn't talk."

"And that's just the first puzzle," I agreed. Quickly I filled him in on all the people I'd talked to this week.

Patrick was a good listener. "So, you have several people who'd been angry with Ike at some time, most of them because he'd threatened to tell someone else, potentially the police, or their wife, about what was going on. And a man who no one thought could talk blamed his wife for killing Ike, and trying to kill him."

"Right," I agreed. "I wish someone else would testify that Jim could talk. Not just mumble, but talk. Because, if not . . . But why would his nurse lie?"

I'd been talking so much I'd hardly touched my meal. Patrick, who'd been listening, had already finished eating.

"Okay," he said. "You stop talking and eat. Even amateur detectives need food."

"The haddock and crabmeat are delicious," I agreed.

"Hush," Patrick said gently but firmly. "Eat. Nod if you need to answer."

I almost giggled, but nodded, taking a bite of the haddock.

"It's like a giant jigsaw puzzle," Patrick mused. "Mom used to give them to me for Christmas. I never finished them. We had a whole bookcase full at our place in the mountains. So, let's look at the pieces."

I nodded and kept chewing.

"I assume everyone in town knew Ike, or at least knew who he was."

I nodded again. This could be an interesting game.

"Do all the people you've been talking about know one another? At least to say hello?"

Another nod.

Patrick sat for a minute. His forehead creased, and he put up his finger. He had an idea. "Do all these people go to Reverend Tom's Congregational church?"

I nodded. I hadn't thought of that connection, but, yes, they did.

"Do they all shop at the patisserie? Oh, forget that. Of course they do. How about the bookstore? Do they all shop at Gus's bookstore?"

Another nod.

"I'm going to assume that your young friend Leo is innocent, okay?"

I nodded emphatically. Earlier in the week I'd wondered about Leo, but now I was convinced he was innocent.

Patrick reached over to an unoccupied table and took a paper napkin. Then he pulled out a pen. I kept eating, enjoying both my meal and the show he was putting on. He might think of some connection, some motivation, I hadn't come up with. Ike had been killed Sunday. This was Thursday. I felt as though I'd been talking to people about Ike and his murder . . . and his stories . . . for months. Most of what I'd learned was new to Patrick.

"Okay. Let's start with Gus Gleason, who harasses girls who work for him and threatened to kill Ike if he told anyone. Cos Curran, Gus's current target, or at least the only one we know of, is coping. I don't think she'd have any reason to kill Ike. Who else would Gus's behavior affect? His wife, Nancy, who probably at least suspects what he's doing, and isn't happy about it. She also happens to be the one who says Jim told her his wife killed Ike." He glanced at me to confirm what he'd said was true. I nodded.

"Okay. Motive. Gus likes pretty young women. Maybe Nancy killed Ike to protect her husband's reputation."

I wasn't convinced. "An interesting idea."

"Okay. Try this one. Cindy Bouchard is attractive."

I frowned at Patrick and then grinned.

He laughed. "Okay. She's not gorgeous but she's not bad looking. She shops at the bookstore, so Gus knew her. Maybe they were having an affair."

I shrugged. I supposed it could be. But I couldn't figure out where this was going.

"What if Nancy knew her husband had threatened Ike? Maybe she killed Ike so no one would know Gus betrayed her. It was a matter of pride."

Maybe. I let Patrick continue.

"Or maybe Nancy thought Gus killed Ike. She lied about Jim's dying words to try to get her husband off the hook."

I gave a half nod. Possible. I hadn't thought of that angle, but, yes, that made sense.

"Okay. On to someone else. Henri and Nicole now know Madame Thibodeau's home health aide stole a few trifles and tried to sell them to Sarah. They fired Cindy?"

I nodded.

"I think that's a dead end so far as Ike is concerned. Henri and Nicole wouldn't have killed him. They didn't know what was happening. And Cindy's young, and planning her future. I can't see her risking all that for a few trinkets." Patrick was staring at the piece of paper where he'd listed all the possible suspects, with circles to show their interrelationships. "Now, if she'd stolen hundreds of thousands of dollars, that would be a different story. But she didn't. I think we can rule out Cindy Bouchard." He put a big X over Cindy's name, matching the one he'd put over Leo's.

I watched as new eyes looked at the mystery I'd been trying to solve.

"Ed Campbell is on the list because he and Ike had crossed swords in the past. He wasn't happy that Ike was living in that garage, scrounging for bottles in the town he wanted to present as the perfect Maine village. Ike knew that. He told people the 'Chambers' were after him."

Another nod.

"But despite his not being thrilled with Ike or his lifestyle, Ed's a prince of a guy. His wife does all sorts of good deeds, and even Ed takes time from running both the Chamber of Commerce and his own car dealership to get groceries for the Lewis family. Why would he kill Ike? Heads of the Chamber of Commerce don't want their town to get a reputation for murders." Patrick looked at me almost mischievously. "Although if the past year is any model, murders seem to happen around here without Ed's being at all involved."

I pointedly rolled my eyes.

"That brings us to the devoted wife, Sandra Lewis, and her disabled husband, Jim, who probably but not definitely couldn't talk." Patrick thought about that for a few minutes. "Jim was Ike's friend. He'd probably heard all Ike's stories. After all, Jim was pretty much confined to his house. He would have encouraged Ike to talk to him, and Sandra probably appreciated someone else sitting with Jim occasionally."

I nodded. That made sense, but was it relevant to Ike's murder?

"Jim often sat at a window where he could watch the birds but could also see the entrance to the garage where Ike lived. If he and Sandra had gotten home from church by then, it's possible he was watching when whoever killed Ike entered the garage. But, we're back to, how could he tell anyone if he couldn't speak or—I assume—also couldn't write. You did say he was very uncoordinated, right?"

I nodded.

"But just for now, let's assume he could speak. Maybe he chose not to, for some reason. Why would he say his devoted wife had killed Ike? Why would he think she was trying to kill him?"

I shrugged my shoulders. Patrick was following the same lines of thought I had. Lines that led nowhere.

Then, suddenly, he put down his pencil. "Okay, my lady. You're the one who's been solving crimes around here. But I'm pretty sure I know who killed Ike."

"What?" I said, breaking my silence. "Who?"

Chapter Thirty-seven

Mrs. Whitby, from London, now living at Daniel Hoots, next door to Robert's Coffee House, teaches all sorts of Embroidery in Gold, Silver, Silk or Worsted, Bazel or small work. Also to pickle, preserve, and make fine Paste; likewise dry'd Gravies for the Sea.
   —Advertisement in Pennsylvania Journal,
      August 17, 1749.

"If you know who killed Ike, then tell me!" I said.

Patrick grinned and sat back in his chair. "Before I came to Haven Harbor last June, I lived a quiet life."

"Totally boring," I agreed, raising my eyebrows. "Just Hollywood parties and trips on yachts and attending the Oscars and wild parties in your studio by the Pacific."

"Exactly. But in the time I've known you I've seen you solve murders and figure out who set fires and blackmailed people, and generally make life exciting and interesting." He reached over and took my hand. "You've cued me in to a couple of situations you've been in. You even solved one crime when the police were watching to make sure you wouldn't leave my carriage house."

"They were protecting me, for my own good," I protested.

"I agree. Otherwise, what possible excuse would I have had to be the host to a beautiful woman who just happens to be the love of my life?"

I gulped. And blushed. Patrick had never said anything like that to me before. Neither of us had ever said the "L" word, even in jest.

Here we were, sitting in the Harbor Haunts, enjoying a good dinner and trying to solve a crime. Just your everyday evening. And he'd said . . . But maybe he was kidding. I decided to ignore any distractions for the moment and get back to what we'd been talking about. "Okay. So what is the point of all this?"

He hesitated. Maybe I'd misunderstood him? Maybe he hadn't meant to say that? "The point is that maybe I can help this time. So, let me, okay?"

"But who do you think murdered Ike?" I protested.

"I don't know for sure, you understand," he said.

"But you think you know."

"I have an idea," Patrick said. "That's all. Just an idea. But I want to test it out. So, bear with me? To see if my idea is at least leading in the right direction, we need to talk to Sandra Lewis."

I shook my head. "Maybe sometime. But right now she's very upset, understandably. Her husband just died, and because of what he might have said before he died, the police asked to search her home for evidence, and she agreed. That probably made sense to her at the time, but now she can't even go home and mourn quietly."

"So where is she?"

"She's staying with Gram and Tom tonight. Gram told me she was hysterical, so one of the doctors at the hospital gave her some anti-anxiety pills, or something to help her sleep. Gram hoped she'd go to bed early."

"Then I guess we should pay the good reverend and your grandmother a visit," said Patrick, calling for the check. "Before the newly widowed Mrs. Lewis retires for the night."

"Patrick, I really don't think this is a good idea," I said as we headed for the rectory in Patrick's BMW. "That poor woman has been through so much. She's spent her life caring for her husband, and then right before he dies he accuses her of murder, and maybe attempted murder."

"Do we know whether Jim died of natural causes?" Patrick asked.

"It was a massive heart attack."

"Will they do an autopsy?"

Patrick was really getting into this crime-solving thing. "Probably not. Autopsies are done only when someone dies of unknown causes, or dies a violent death. Jim was under a doctor's care, and he died in the emergency room of a hospital. They tried to revive him, but he didn't make it. I doubt anyone is going to request an autopsy."

"Maybe they should," Patrick suggested, pulling into the rectory's driveway. "Why was Jim in the emergency room today, anyway, if he was there before he had the heart attack?"

"I don't know," I said. "He's sick a lot."

"Agreed. But doesn't it sound funny that he died of a massive heart attack just after he said his wife was a murderer?"

"I think it's stranger that a man who didn't talk for years said anything at all," I answered.

Patrick came around to my side of the car and opened the door for me.

"Remember," I said, getting out. "Sandra has had possibly the worst day in her entire life. And Tom and Gram are there too. They won't let you—or us—quiz her on details of what happened today. And rightfully so."

"I'll be good," said Patrick. "You trust me, don't you?"

I glanced at him sidewise as he reached for my hand. "I hope so."

Chapter Thirty-eight

The Record of
Elizabeth Hill, born Nov 6 1745
And died Feb 12 1833
Our days alas our mortal days
Are short and wretched too
Evil and few the patriarch says
And well the patriarch knew
    —"Wrought by Jerusia S. Hill," age fifteen,
    Wells, Maine, June 17, 1834, in honor of
    her grandmother.

Gram answered the door. She looked from me to Patrick and then back to me again. "We didn't expect you this evening," she said quietly.

"We just stopped for a brief visit," I said, glancing at Patrick so he'd confirm what I said. "We wanted to let Sandra know how sorry we were about Jim's death."

Gram hesitated. "I'm not sure that's a good idea. She's just beginning to settle down. She's had a very rough day."

"Who's at the door, Charlotte?" called a weak voice from the living room.

"It's Angie and Patrick West. They stopped in to give you their condolences," Gram answered.

"Is Tom here?" I asked.

"He was, but he had to go over to the church for an hour to chair the Outreach Committee." Gram looked drained. "The spring fair is coming up, and they wanted him to help make decisions. He'll be back soon."

"Tell them to come in," called Sandra. "Don't leave those young people in the doorway."

Gram shook her head, but whispered, "You might as well both go in. But a very short visit, please."

I glanced at Patrick to make sure he'd gotten the message. Questioning someone about a murder was hard under any circumstances, but talking to a newly bereaved widow was nothing I would have done on my own.

Sandra was sitting on the end of the couch. A box of tissues was on the table next to her, and her lap was full of crumpled, used tissues. Her face was puffy, and her eyes red. "Thank you for coming," she said. Her voice was much flatter than it had been at church last week. She'd probably taken one or more of those pills the doctor had given her.

"We're so sorry about Jim," I said. "You've taken such good care of him for years."

"I can't believe he's gone," said Sandra. "You're right. I took care of him. That's all I've done for the past nineteen years. And then the bastard had the nerve to tell the world I was a murderer."

Gram looked at me meaningfully. "Sandra's not herself right now, you understand."

"Sandra, caring for Jim all those years, almost never leaving your house, or him, you must have been very lonely. No one to talk to except a man who wouldn't talk," said Patrick, sympathetically.

"Jim and I used to talk all the time. We talked about everything. We spent all our time together, especially when he had relapses. I wasn't lonely. Jim and I had each other then."

"Then what changed?"

"He had trouble swallowing, and his speech was a little garbled. But I understood him, even when the doctors didn't. But then, one day, he just stopped trying. He didn't speak to me, or to anyone else, so far as I knew. But that wasn't the worst. The worst was that he shut down. Jim wouldn't look at me directly. The life, and love, in his eyes was gone. That was when I really lost Jim. Today was a nightmare, but it was also a relief. Jim left me two years ago."

"I'm so sorry, Sandra," I said, sitting next to her and briefly touching her hand. "Those years must have been awful. You were so alone."

She nodded, and the tears started again. She dabbed at her nose and eyes with the tissues.

"Didn't anyone come to see you during those years?" asked Patrick quietly. He'd sat on a chair across from her and leaned toward her as he spoke.

"A few came. Charlotte came." She looked up at Gram, who was still standing near the door, ready to shoo Patrick and me out if necessary. "And the dear reverend. And Ike Hamilton. He used to come and sit with my Jim and talk to him. Sometimes they'd sit there for hours. I don't know what Ike had to say, but Jim looked relaxed when he was there. He and Ike had known each other since they were kids. I never understood what those two saw in each other." She looked at Gram. "I told you that, didn't I, Charlotte? It's strange that the two of them died the same week."

"But you had other visitors sometimes, didn't you? Didn't Ed Campbell bring you groceries once or twice a week?" Patrick asked.

For the first time since we'd been there, Sandra smiled, just a little. "He did. Ed did errands for me when I couldn't leave Jim alone. He brought groceries and things we needed from the pharmacy."

"And did he sit and talk to Jim, too, the way Ike did?"

"No! Ed hardly knew Jim. He came to see me. He talked to me." Sandra shook her head, and her voice faded again. "Sometimes he even brought me flowers. He knew how lonely I was, except when he was there." She looked down. I could hardly hear her as she said, "Sometimes I asked Ed to bring things to the house just because I wanted to see him."

Gram interrupted. "I think we've talked enough. Patrick, Angie, I think Sandra needs to get some rest."

Sandra nodded. "I'm very tired."

Patrick and I stood. "We're very sorry about Jim. We wanted you to know," I said, as Gram ushered us both out into the hallway.

"Why'd you let her go on like that? Don't take all of what she said as gospel, you two. The woman's taken three or four of those pills the doctor gave her. She's exhausted and grieving, and she doesn't know what she's saying."

"It's all right, Gram," I said. "She explained a couple of things we wanted to know."

"You and your crime solving," Gram said, shaking her head and opening the door for us to leave.

"Sometimes it's better to leave things as they are and let the Lord take charge." She held the door open for us. "I'll see the two of you here for dinner tomorrow night, remember!"

As the door closed in back of us, Patrick added, "'Let the Lord take charge.' I'd rather depend on the police department. Sandra Lewis had a horrible life. She was self-sacrificing, but it must have been a nightmare to almost never leave that house and take care of someone who was closed off emotionally. He should have been in a hospital, or a nursing home, or had home health aides like Cindy Bouchard come in to help out so Sandra could leave her house sometimes."

"Maybe she wanted to care for Jim herself," I pointed out. "Maybe she loved him. Or maybe she didn't have the money to hire someone to help." We got back in his car. "Now, tell me why we had to put that poor woman through that," I asked. "She looked devastated. Did you find out whatever you wanted to know?"

"Not totally," said Patrick. "But I got some answers."

"So, what next, detective?" I asked. Questioning Sandra had been exhausting. "Do you still think you know who killed Ike?"

"I'll admit, I wondered if it were Sandra," Patrick said. "But looking at her tonight, I don't think so. She's a strong woman in many ways, but I don't think she could kill someone. Even if that someone was destroying her life."

"So?"

"I think someone did it for her."

Chapter Thirty-nine

Learn Your Manners Before you grow old
For Learning is better than silver or gold
That may vanish away but
Once you get Learning it will never decay.
—Elizabeth Karch (born in 1806 in
Lebanon County, Pennsylvania) stitched
this in silk with painted decorations in
1822. She embroidered the bodies of a
young couple but painted their heads directly on the linen. Perhaps they were
people she knew? She also included a
house, with a tree towering over it, and
added a silk ribbon border. Elizabeth married David Shirk in 1826.

"Actually, I don't want to know anything more. Not tonight, anyway. I'm exhausted, Patrick. Why don't you just take me home." Too much had happened today. I needed time to process it all.

"Sure you don't want to come back to my place? We could have a nightcap, and you could stay if you'd like."

"Tempting. But not tonight," I demurred. "I want to go home, check Trixi, and just sleep. We'll see each other tomorrow night. By then the police should have finished going through Sandra's house, so she can go home."

"I'll call you in the morning," he promised. "The gallery's set up for the opening next week, and no customers are clamoring at the door, so I think I'll take the day off. Maybe we can do something special. After all, it will be your birthday."

My birthday. I'd forgotten that until Gram had reminded us of dinner tomorrow night. "Let's talk in the morning," I agreed. "Maybe everything will make more sense then."

Patrick kissed me lightly and held me for a few moments outside my door. "Sleep well, Angie. A new year starts for you tomorrow."

It was only ten-thirty, but I checked Trixi's food and water; somehow found the energy to clean out her litter, which I'd forgotten that morning; and crawled into bed.

I didn't hear anything else until my phone rang the next morning.

"Happy Birthday to You!" A musical greeting.

I groaned and swung my legs over the side of the bed. My foot landed on something . . . furry.

Trixi had given me my first birthday present. A dead mouse.

I sighed and put my foot back in the bed. "Good morning, Sarah," I said, looking at my clock. "Seven in the morning?"

"I wanted to be the first to wish you a happy birthday!"

"Well, you did it," I grumbled as I swung my legs over the side of the bed again. Carefully. "How did you know it was my birthday, anyway?"

"Last summer we were talking about horoscopes, and you told me. I wrote it down on my calendar."

"You're much more organized than I am. When is *your* birthday?"

"Not telling."

"It's too early in the morning to argue." I yawned.

"Pete told me Cindy Bouchard was fired."

"I told Henri. I thought he should know," I said.

"You're right. I just wish it hadn't been Cindy. She seems so young, and she's trying hard."

"Stealing from your employer isn't trying hard," I pointed out.

"True. Pete said she was going back to Madawaska to live with her family until she found another job. Henri isn't pressing charges," Sarah said.

"I'm glad. She made a mistake. Even a misdemeanor on her record could keep her from finding another job."

"So, on a topic that's more fun, what are you doing for your birthday?" Sarah asked.

"I *was* going to sleep in a little," I answered petulantly. "No special plans, except that Gram and Tom invited Patrick and me to their place for dinner tonight. She's even making the birthday cake she made for me when I was a little girl."

"That's sweet!" said Sarah. "I admit, I envy your relationship with Charlotte."

Sarah had been close to her grandmother, too, before her grandmother died. "I am lucky," I admitted. "I didn't appreciate her as much as I should have when I was growing up, but now I understand how much she did for me. I'm glad to be able to tell her that. And I'm happy that she found Tom. They seem really happy together."

"I agree. I think they are," said Sarah. "We should only be as lucky to find the right person."

"Maybe we already have," I said. "Pete and Patrick are both good guys."

"True," Sarah admitted. "But, at least for me, it's too early to tell whether the relationship is for the long haul."

"It's hard to know, isn't it?" I said, thinking of what Patrick had said the night before. "I'm not ready to jump off a cliff with anyone yet."

"Well, if Patrick asks you to do that, then I'd back off, too!" Sarah laughed.

"You're right. I did use a pretty dramatic example, didn't I." I smiled. "Hey, Sarah, Trixi is kneading my arm like crazy and reminding me that it's time for her breakfast." Of course, Trixi was ready for breakfast, lunch, or dinner at any time of the day. She didn't discriminate.

"Okay. Just wanted to check in. Hope you have a great day, no matter what you do. And how old are you now?"

"I could say sixteen," I answered.

"But you'd be lying, and Patrick wouldn't be dating you."

"Twenty-eight," I admitted. "Born right here in town at Haven Harbor Hospital. Too many people know to be able to hide the truth."

"You're still a youngster," Sarah advised. "Wait until you get over the big 3-0 bump, like I have. Twenty-eight will seem very young."

I hoped so. Right now I felt as though the world was on my shoulders. A fast shower woke me up more, and then I disposed of the dead mouse and shared the kitchen as Trixi ate her breakfast and I sipped coffee and treated myself (after all, it was my birthday) to the eclairs I'd bought yesterday.

Gram was the next person to call. "Happy birthday, Angel!" She and Mama had always called me that. Now Gram was the only one who did. "How does it feel to be twenty-eight?"

"About the same as twenty-seven felt yesterday," I answered. "Sorry if Patrick and I upset you or Sandra last night."

"Don't worry. Right after you left she went to bed. She just went home to see what condition her house is in after the police searched it."

"What were they looking for?"

"I'm not sure. Something to prove her either innocent or guilty of killing Ike, I assume. And maybe of hurting Jim."

"Do you think she did either of those things?"

Gram hesitated. "I can't see her killing Ike. But honestly, there've been times in the past years that I've wondered about how she treated Jim. I've only known one other person who had MS, and she was my mother's age, so that was a long while ago. Treatments must have changed over the years. But as I remember she had months, maybe even years, when she was all right. A little unsteady on her feet sometimes, but she lived a pretty normal life. Married, had two children. I remember Mom saying Florence—that was her name—couldn't read because her eyes tired easily. But she was almost sixty then. She had relapses when she had to use a wheelchair, but she was never as weak as Jim. He got sick about twenty years ago and was never well again. Several times he seemed to be getting better, and then he'd have a bad fall and break his leg or wrist. Or he'd get pneumonia and end up in the hospital. Sandra was always very sympathetic and caring, but sometimes when she asked for prayers at the church she seemed to be asking them for herself more than for Jim."

"They probably both could have used prayers. It must be hard to care for someone full time, for so many years."

"Certainly, yes, I agree. And Sandra's been caring for people all her life. She took care of her father for years, after he had a stroke. A couple of years after her dad died she married Jim, and he was diagnosed within a year. There was just something funny about the way Sandra dealt with it. Last night she never said she'd miss Jim. And she'd talked about how lonely she'd been."

"Except when Ed Campbell came to visit."

"Yes. I noticed that. I knew Ed delivered her groceries. His wife, Diane, volunteered him for that job as I remember."

"Do you think there was anything other than groceries between Ed and Sandra?"

"I wouldn't have thought so, but I'll admit, last night I wondered."

"I also thought it was interesting that Ike and Jim were such good friends."

"That I knew. They'd been friends since they were boys. Ike was always a little . . . different . . . a little slow, as people said, and he didn't attend school with other students. His mother kept him home. In those days I don't know if it was officially 'homeschooling' or whether she just said he wasn't ready for a classroom. And maybe he wasn't. But the two boys lived close to each other—the house Sandra and Jim live in was Jim's family home, where he grew up. Ike's family lived on the next block. The boys spent a lot of time together."

"Do you think Jim could talk?"

"I have no idea. But if he talked to anyone other than Sandra, it would have been Ike."

"What time do you want Patrick and me to be at your house for dinner?" I asked, changing the subject.

"Six o'clock sounds good," she said. "Do you have any special plans for today?"

"Patrick said something about taking the day off from the gallery, so he may have something in mind."

"No crime solving, then."

"I don't plan any," I told her. Not unless the opportunity or idea came up. I still didn't know who'd killed Ike.

"Good. You and Patrick should take some time for yourselves. He's been working long hours at the gallery, and you keep finding new crimes to solve. Sometimes I think you should have gone ahead and applied for your private detective's license."

I shook my head. "That requires a lot more hours than I worked for Wally in Arizona. Besides, you started Mainely Needlepoint, and now it fills my hours." Although I still seemed to have time to do a little investigating, I admitted to myself. Sometimes that annoyed Patrick, and worried him, but last night he seemed to find trying to identify a killer a sort of parlor game.

I didn't have anything planned until dinner at six.

That is, I didn't have anything planned until Dave called.

Chapter Forty

Now in the opening spring of life
Let every flowret bloom
The budding virtues in thy breath
Shall yield the best perfume.
  —Charlotte Clubb, age twelve, Washington
    City (Washington, DC), July 20, 1813.
    Charlotte composed her large sampler of
    a bell tower on a large brick house with a
    garden, enclosed in a geometric floral
    border.

"Angie?"

"Dave? Aren't you at school today?"

"I'm between classes. So could you follow up on something for me? It has to do with Jim Lewis's death. And maybe Ike's."

"Of course," I assured him. "Is Leo with you in school today?"

"He'd better be. He came with me this morning. But I don't see him every minute, since he has his own classes to attend."

"So what can I check for you?"

"You know that before Jim died he talked to Nancy Gleason, right?"

"She was his nurse in the emergency room."

"Right. Well, Karen Mercer, who was also on duty yesterday afternoon, called me this morning to ask about poisons. Seems she and Nancy were comparing notes. They didn't want to call the police until they were sure what happened. They didn't want Pete or Ethan to think they were crazy, but they're wondering if Jim was poisoned. Could you go and talk with them? Karen's been at my house and seen my poison garden. We've talked about poisons before. I told her you'd know what to do. What questions to ask."

"Me? I don't know poisons the way you do."

"Students are coming in. I have to start my class. Just find out why they suspect poison, and what symptoms they observed. Then call—no, text me back. I'll let you know what I think." Dave's voice disappeared.

I might have been born at the Haven Harbor Hospital, but I hadn't planned to visit it on my birthday.

Dr. Karen Mercer was a friend of Dave's. I didn't know Gus Gleason's wife, Nancy, as well, but we waved at each other in town. They were both serious professionals. If they had doubts about Jim's death, Dave was right. We needed to follow up.

"Trixi, you take care of the house," I told her. "I'll be home as soon as I can."

She meowed and followed me to the door. After all, I hadn't appreciated her birthday gift. I'd thrown it in the garbage.

"I'm Angie Curtis. I'm here to see Nancy Gleason or Karen Mercer," I explained to the emergency room receptionist at Haven Harbor Hospital. Except in July or August, it was a quiet place.

She looked at me. "What seems to be the matter?" she asked, looking up my record on her computer.

"I'm fine. I'm here for . . . a consult," I told her. "Karen and Nancy asked me to come."

"Are you a doctor?" she asked.

"No. But please check with Nancy or Karen. Tell them Angie's here. I'll wait here."

The receptionist looked doubtful, but, luckily, no patients were bleeding out in the reception area. She left and went into the ER.

In a minute or two she was back. "Dr. Mercer will see you. She's in her office." She buzzed me in.

I'd talked to Karen before, but usually outside the hospital or in an exam room. She waved at me from an office door across the floor.

"Angie. Thank you so much for coming. Dave couldn't talk this morning, but he said you could help." She gestured at Nancy, who was at the nurses' station in the center of the room entering something in her computer. "Come in, so we can have some privacy. I want Nancy here too."

"Karen, just so you know, I'm not an expert on poisons. That's Dave, for sure. He asked me to come, ask questions, and get back to him."

"What happens then?"

"I'm sure he'll get back to us quickly. And to anyone else who needs to know."

Nancy joined us and stood near the office door.

"Nancy, would you close the door? I don't want anyone listening in. If one of us is needed, they'll knock or buzz us."

Nancy nodded, shut the door, and smiled at me. She was a striking brunette, her long dark hair braided

and circling her head. Was her husband being un-
faithful to her? I hoped not. Gus was one of Dave's
and my possible suspects in Ike's death, but we hadn't
thought much about him in the past couple of days.
Patrick had even suspected Nancy. Could he have
been right? If he was, it didn't make sense that I was
meeting with Nancy and Karen about poisons now.
But I was certainly going to listen carefully to whatever they said. In a murder investigation, I kept all
options open.

"Morning, Angie. Thanks for coming so quickly."

"No problem," I said. "It sounds as though you two
have serious concerns."

"We do," Karen said, taking over. "First of all, we
can't give you any specific information about Jim
Lewis's medical history. But his symptoms have varied over the years, and they weren't all typical of patients with MS. Although in later stages MS patients
can be awkward, and have balance problems—even-
tually, they can't walk—Jim has had a pattern of broken bones and bruises and burns over a period of
years."

"Was he abused?" I asked, cutting immediately to a
serious question.

"We wondered"—Karen glanced at Nancy—"but
we had no proof. When Jim was still talking, he never
said anything implying that. But it's possible."

"What made you think he might have been poisoned?" I asked.

"Nancy, you saw him when he was first admitted.
Tell Angie Jim's symptoms," Karen instructed.

I realized the two were trying hard not to give me
detailed information on Jim's diagnosis. Patient privacy was important. But if he'd been poisoned? Murdered?

"First, despite all his problems over the years, Jim's heart has always been fine. When Sandra brought him in, he was alternately vomiting and drooling. His pupils were dilated, and he had bradycardia—his heart rate was unusually slow. And he had a horrible headache."

"Excuse me. But if he didn't talk, how did you know about the headache?" I asked.

"He's been here often enough that we understood his sign language. He pointed to his head and then to the pain chart. I moved my hand on the chart, and he nodded when I got to ten."

"That's extremely severe pain," Karen put in.

"Okay," I agreed. "So I'm guessing you cleaned him up and put in an IV and gave him some anti-nausea medicine and something for pain."

"Exactly," said Karen. "At first everything was by the book. We didn't know what was wrong. It could have been anything from a bad case of the flu to food poisoning."

"Was Sandra with him the whole time?"

"Most of the time, yes. Then she went out to the nurses' station to verify his insurance information." Nancy's lips tightened. "That's when Jim talked to me. His words weren't totally clear. But he was definitely talking, and I could understand him. He said Sandra had killed Ike and was trying to kill him."

"Did you believe him?" I asked the nurse. "He wasn't hallucinating or fantasizing or looking for someone to blame for the way he felt?"

"People with MS can sometimes get confused. But Jim was very clear."

"I tried to ask him about what he was saying, but as soon as Sandra came back into the room he stopped talking. I excused myself a minute and came to Dr. Mercer."

"Unfortunately," Karen put in, "Nancy was still explaining the situation to me when Sandra Lewis started yelling. Jim was having a massive heart attack. I ran, we called a Code Blue and got Sandra out of the exam room, but it was too late. He'd been sick for so many years, his body just couldn't take any more. We tried to resuscitate him, but . . ."

"He died and wasn't able to tell you anything else." I finished her sentence.

"Right. But after it was all over, Nancy and I talked. We put his medical history together with what Jim had said. Jim's symptoms didn't scream 'poison'! But we decided to quietly do a little investigating on our own." Karen smiled at me. "You've been known to do a little of that too. Dave's helped out before when we needed some information on poisons, and I knew he was already trying to figure out who killed Ike Hamilton. He told me when he brought Leo in here a day or two ago so I could check him over. The boy hadn't had a physical exam in years."

"How was Leo?"

"A little undernourished, but Dave's taking care of that," answered Karen. I suspected she'd been the beneficiary of some of Dave's cooking. "But the boy was very nervous. He was afraid he'd be blamed for Ike's death."

"So that gave you another motivation to call Dave when you heard what Jim had said."

"Exactly."

"Okay. Did Jim or Sandra mention any food or drink Jim had before he got here?"

Nancy shook her head. "All his wife said was that she'd given him a cup of tea. She brought him to the

ER because his nausea was getting worse, and he was burning up one minute and then cold the next. Plus, the intense headache. She thought he had the flu. She brought him here because she was afraid she was going to get it too."

"But she was fine?"

"Physically, yes. She got hysterical when Jim died. But that's not an unusual reaction from the wife of a patient."

"You said his pupils were dilated. Is that usual with the flu?"

Nancy shook her head. "No. But we didn't have time to check out a lot of possibilities before his heart failed."

"Okay," I said. "I'm going to check with Dave. He'll get back to you as soon as possible—I hope later today." I stood, planning to leave. "Before I go, two more questions. I'm guessing there wasn't an autopsy. Right? Or could one still be done?"

"No autopsy that I know of. Jim had been ill so long . . . and Sandra said something about cremation, to save space in the world."

"You're right," Nancy added. "She said she was going to put Jim's ashes in her garden. That Jim loved flowers."

"And Jim didn't say Ike was poisoned?"

"Only that Sandra had killed him. He didn't say how."

"Dave or I will get back to both of you. Thank you. You've been a big help."

Back in my car I went through what they'd said about Jim's symptoms. It wasn't a lot. Maybe the details would mean something to Dave. They didn't to me.

Last Sunday morning, when Ike had been killed,

I'd seen Jim and Sandra in church. He'd been in his chair, and Sandra had said she was going to wheel him home. Would she have wheeled him home and then left him; gone to stab Ike, which would probably have covered her with blood; and then gone home and cleaned up? If there had been blood, the police should have found it when they searched her house, right?

It wouldn't have been impossible for her to leave her house, kill Ike, and then get home quickly. But although I could imagine Sandra poisoning someone, or maybe even abusing her husband (if his coordination was poor, how would he have burned his arm? He wouldn't have been cooking or carrying a candle, or . . .), would Sandra have stabbed someone?

Last night, when I'd been too tired to question his ideas, Patrick had suggested that someone might have helped Sandra.

As soon as I got home I texted Dave with what Nancy and Karen had said.

Then I called Patrick.

Chapter Forty-one

On Earth let my example shine
And when I leave this state
May heaven receive this soul of mine
To bliss divinely great.
    —Sally Martin Bowen, born in 1789 in
      Marblehead, Massachusetts, stitched her
      sampler in light silk threads on dark
      linen, surrounding flowers and animals
      on three sides by a floral border. She'd
      dated her sampler but, not unusually, at
      some point she removed the date, per-
      haps to conceal her age. (It was probably
      done about 1800.) Sally married Isaac
      Story Jr. in 1813 and had at least twelve
      children.

"Patrick?"

"Happy Birthday to You," he sang, dreadfully off-key. The second time today someone had sung to me. Laughing, I put down the phone and applauded.

He was still singing when I picked the phone up again. "Good thing you decided to be an artist, not a singer," I pointed out. "That was awful!"

"But from the heart," he answered. "So you're awake. You looked so tired last night I decided to let you sleep in."

I glanced at the time. Ten o'clock. I felt as though I'd been up for hours. "Been a busy morning," I admitted.

"No doubt racing to the door every few minutes to accept all your birthday packages," Patrick teased.

I laughed again. "Not exactly."

As if on cue, my doorbell rang. "Just a minute. Someone's at my door."

"What did I say?" Patrick asked.

He was right. The woman at the door was holding a huge bouquet of red roses. "Angie Curtis?"

I nodded.

"These are for you!"

The bouquet was gorgeous. Two dozen long-stemmed red roses. Before I picked up my phone I searched for the card.

"Because of who you are, and how lucky I am to have you in my life. Happy Birthday. Your Patrick."

"Wow," I said, back on the phone. "Someone named Patrick just sent me an incredible bouquet of roses."

"He must be a good guy," said Patrick.

"Not bad," I admitted. "But what a pain. Now I have to find an enormous vase and put them in water."

"Always something to do. I know we're going to the rectory for your official birthday dinner tonight, but how about you and I having a special lunch before that?"

"Do you have anywhere particular in mind?"

"I have a couple of ideas. Pick you up around noon?"

Time for me to change out of my jeans and sweatshirt and maybe even break down and put on some lipstick. "That sounds fine. And—thank you. The roses are spectacular."

"For a spectacular lady."

Ouch. That was a little over the top. But, still. Nice.

"See you at noon."

Those roses *were* pretty spectacular. I sniffed them, but they didn't smell like the roses in Gram's garden. Had I read somewhere that hothouse roses didn't smell? Wherever these had come from, they were gorgeous. No one had ever sent me flowers before. Certainly not roses.

I found a large mason jar under the sink. Gram had canned a lot of tomatoes one year.

Not elegant, but as long as there was water, I didn't think the roses would mind. Trixi watched closely as I cut the stems a little and arranged them in the jar. Then she reached out to nibble a leaf.

Were roses poisonous to cats?

I picked up Trixi and went to my computer to check. Several clicks later I'd learned a lot. First, roses weren't dangerous for cats, although thorns and cats didn't go well together. No problem there. Trixi was an indoor cat, and these roses didn't have thorns. But the daffodils I loved were poisonous to cats, as were tulips and azaleas and lilies of the valley, among other flowers. In the future, before I decorated my house with flowers I'd better check online for their compatibility with cats. I printed out the list of plants poisonous to cats and then returned to the kitchen, just in time to catch the jar of roses before Trixi pushed it off the table. "Those are my flowers," I scolded her. "My birthday present." I tucked the card that came with them under a magnet on the refrigerator.

Nice. I'd wondered what Patrick would give me for my birthday, and roses were just fine. Not permanent, but a statement. Now, where could I put them so Trixi wouldn't push my improvised vase onto the floor while I was out for the day? Lunch with Patrick, dinner at the rectory . . .

But still no solution to Ike's murder. And maybe Jim Lewis's too?

I checked my phone. Dave had received my text but said the symptoms Nancy and Karen had told me about were pretty general. He'd check his books on poisons when he got home. So, no answer yet.

What had Patrick planned for lunch? I had no idea, but I put on newer jeans than the ones I'd been wearing and a yellow sweater that seemed springlike. It would even match tonight's daffodil cake, since I had a feeling that if I spent the afternoon with Patrick we'd go directly to the rectory.

But what about my roses? I could leave food for Trixi and she'd be fine. But *I* wouldn't be fine if in my absence she decided to push my flowers off the edge of a table or counter.

I hoped Patrick wouldn't ask where they were. Just for the afternoon, I put them on the floor of the downstairs bathroom and closed the door. They'd be safe in there, although I suspected of all the rooms in the house where he might think I'd put his gift, the bathroom wouldn't have been his first choice or guess.

Promptly at noon Patrick drove into my driveway and, to avoid questions about rose placement, I met him in my front yard.

"Starving?" he asked, hugging me.

"Always," I answered. "I can't believe it's really my

birthday. Your roses are incredible. I've never been given roses before."

"Then it's about time," he said, kissing my forehead.

I looked around my yard. "When I was a little girl I didn't have birthday parties. But I always felt spring had arrived just for me."

Daffodils were still blooming in corners, but the snowdrops Gram had planted under trees to be the first blooms of spring had already disappeared, replaced by lilies of the valley.

My lawn was beginning to green. In a couple of weeks I'd be getting out the old hand mower in the barn, oiling it, and mowing. I loved the smell of freshly cut grass, but I hadn't missed the chore of mowing when I'd been in Arizona.

"Why didn't you have a birthday party when you were young?" Patrick asked as he held his car's door open for me. "Every child should have a birthday party!"

"Oh, I had a family party," I explained. "Mama and Gram always gave me a gift or two, and Gram made the daffodil cake she's making for tonight. I didn't have a party for friends. Not many families in town wanted to send their impressionable little girls into a house with a mother who drank and slept around."

Patrick grimaced and patted my leg. "Those days are over. You have lots of friends now, and I've even seen them at your house."

"True," I said. "I shouldn't even have mentioned the past. It's over. What did you do on your birthday when you were little? Have pony rides?"

Patrick shrugged, almost embarrassed. "Well, yeah. Sometimes. Or magicians or clowns. Once Mom rented an amusement park for all my friends and their families."

"What? An entire amusement park?"

"It was a small amusement park," he backtracked. "Usually we just had pool parties at our house."

"Catered, I assume?" I rolled my eyes.

"Always," he confirmed, laughing. "Tease me all you want, Angie. It was another world. Not a better world. Just another one."

"Pool parties . . ." I thought. "I don't know when your birthday is, Patrick. How did I miss that?"

"I wasn't here for my birthday last year. I was in the rehab hospital in Boston."

Last June Patrick had been badly burned. He'd been gone for most of the summer. He and I hadn't become friends until fall. "So, what's the date? I have to put it on my calendar," I teased.

"July 20," he said. "If you must know. And . . . Mom will be here by then."

"She's flying in from L.A. for your birthday?"

He frowned. "I haven't said anything, because it wasn't definite. But she's been talking to that Ed Campbell—the Chamber of Commerce guy?"

"Yes . . . ?"

"It looks pretty certain that she'll be making a movie here this summer."

"What?" My heart sank. "I thought she didn't want to do that. That she wanted to keep her private life and her work life separate." I liked Skye. But if she and her whole entourage were here in Haven Harbor, the summer wouldn't be mine and Patrick's.

"I guess she changed her mind after being here at Christmas."

"And the director and screenwriters who were here with her?"

"They'll be here this summer too. But it won't be announced for another week or two, so please don't say anything. Of course, Ed knows. But Mom and the director are still lining up investors, so they didn't want to say anything before it was definite."

Really, really mess up the summer. Patrick didn't look thrilled about it either.

"So, where are we going for lunch?" I asked.

"A little place I found when I was driving around a couple of weeks ago looking for places to paint. It's called Kindred Spirits, on Quarry Island, and it's run by two sisters. They do a nice job, a little different than a lot of places, and I thought we'd enjoy the drive."

"Sounds good to me," I said. "I don't think I've ever been to Quarry Island."

"You're kidding. A place in Maine I've been to and you haven't?"

"It is possible," I said, as we drove down one of Maine's peninsulas and waited for a sailboat to pass before the drawbridge opened that led to the island.

The café was on the waterfront near the drawbridge, which meant a continuing view of lobster boats, fishing boats, skiffs, and sailboats moving between the island and the mainland. The small dining room was bright, filled with tables and mismatched chairs painted in vivid enameled colors, with two quilts and a wildly colorful abstract painting on the wall. Not traditional Maine. But I loved it, and I could see why Patrick did too.

He'd ordered in advance. I'd never had cheese fondue, but as we indulged in the melted cheeses liberally flavored with kirsch and white wine, using long forks to dunk chunks of baguette in the mixture, swirl them, and then savor them, I promised myself

I'd learn to make it. It was fun to eat and delicious, and the wine and kirsch made it seem slightly decadent. A great way to celebrate a birthday.

"I'd planned to have champagne, since it's your birthday, but fondue is cooked with wine, so it's better with wine than with champagne," said Patrick, apologizing when there was no need.

"I can cope with that," I said, spearing another piece of bread and turning it in the warm, thick cheese. "This is fantastic." My next chunk of bread fell into the cheese and was lost.

"Fondue is an après-ski dish in Switzerland. The tradition there is, if you lose your bread in the cheese, the person next to you can claim a kiss," Patrick said seriously, but with a wink.

I reached over and kissed his cheek. "You don't have to claim a kiss. I'll grant you one, even if I don't lose my bread."

We sat sipping and dunking and enjoying the day, far from Haven Harbor's secrets.

We'd almost finished when I asked, "Last night you said you thought Sandra Lewis had killed Jim and Ike, as Jim told Nancy. But that Sandra had help. Who did you think helped her?"

"You're the sleuth," Patrick said, both of us feeling mellow with wine and cheese. "Sandra cared for Jim for years. He hadn't even spoken—at least to her—for the past two years. She seldom left her house, especially in winter, when Jim's wheelchair was hard to manipulate over snow and ice. Ike was Jim's friend, and we've heard they used to sit together, with Ike doing most of the talking, but Jim listening. But who did Sandra talk to?"

I hesitated.

"Who visited her once or twice a week? Who stayed

for a cup of tea or a glass of something stronger? Who came if she needed help?"

"Ed Campbell."

"And who didn't want Ike in town?"

"Ed Campbell."

"In fact, when Ike told your young friend Leo that he was scared of one person, who was that?"

"The 'Chambers,' as he told Leo. Ed Campbell."

"Maybe Ed and Sandra were having an affair. Or one of them wanted them to have an affair. I don't know. But Ed would have been strong enough to kill Ike."

"Yes. But that still doesn't explain Jim." I hadn't told Patrick about my morning. "Nancy Gleason and Karen Mercer think maybe Jim was poisoned. Dave's going to check some of his reference materials to see whether Jim's symptoms matched the effects of any poison."

"Maybe Ed and Sandra worked together?"

"I don't know," I said. "Your idea makes sense in some ways. But poisoning and stabbing are very different ways of killing. Most killers have a method they're comfortable with, and stick to it."

"You're the expert on murders," Patrick said. "But two Haven Harbor men are dead now who were alive last week, and so far I haven't heard an explanation."

"Today is my birthday," I said. The wine was making my head swirl comfortably. "I don't want to think about murders anymore."

"I promise," said Patrick. "Why don't we drive around the island and then take the slow way home. We're not due at the rectory until six, right?"

"Right," I said. "But I've already had a wonderful birthday. Roses, and fondue and wine. More than I ever imagined."

"And your birthday isn't over yet." Patrick smiled, handing our waitress a generous tip. "You still have that daffodil cake ahead of you."

"Daffodils are poisonous to cats," I said, a bit out of context.

"Then I think we'd better eat all that cake ourselves."

Chapter Forty-two

*Sarah Osborne, Schoolmistress in Newport, proposes
to keep a Boarding School. Any person desirous of
sending Children may be accommodated, and have
them instructed in Reading, Writing, Plain Work,
Embroidering, Tent Stitch, Samplers, &c. on reasonable terms.*

    —*Newport Mercury* advertisement, Newport,
       Rhode Island, December 19 and 26, 1758,
       and January 2, 1759. Sarah Osborne
       (1714–1796) taught in Newport for more
       than forty years. In May 1759, Sarah had
       ten young lady boarders and more than
       sixty day scholars.

After a leisurely, slightly alcoholic, and definitely ro-
mantic lunch, Patrick and I drove slowly along the
Maine coast, seeing some towns I'd never visited and
many Patrick didn't know. We didn't talk much, but
when we did it was to make plans to revisit intriguing
spots we wanted to see when beaches were warmer,
or historic houses were open for the summer, or
when we felt like trying a new restaurant. Patrick
noted that he hadn't visited the Farnsworth Art Mu-

seum or galleries in Rockland, and I wrote down the names of several gift shops focused on Maine-made crafts that might be interested in needlepointed items.

But for most of the drive we just relaxed. Patrick's gallery was set to open a new exhibit next week, and he'd be able to paint there between customers. I'd spent the past week talking to people about Ike Hamilton, helping Dave with Leo, and trying to solve a murder.

We were both tired, and an afternoon enjoying sunshine and sea breezes and being together was just what both of us needed. True, in another month midcoast Maine's trees and grass would be green. Purple, yellow, and pink lupines would be blooming, and tourist shops and cafés and attractions would be open. But we didn't need any of those today.

It was my birthday, and I quietly told myself that my twenty-eighth might be my best year yet. It certainly had started that way.

My only regret was that I'd agreed that Patrick and I would go to the rectory for dinner with Gram and Tom. I knew it meant a lot to Gram, but I would just as soon have curled up with Patrick and Trixi and had a quiet evening.

But we couldn't disappoint Gram. It meant a lot to her that I had come home to Haven Harbor, and now it felt as though I was going to stay.

"Looks as though you've timed the afternoon perfectly," I commented as Patrick drove into the center of Haven Harbor at a few minutes before six. "Gram will be pleased, and I just hope I can eat some of the lobster bisque she was planning to make. I'm still full from lunch."

"I think I could always find space for your grand-

mother's lobster bisque," Patrick said as we pulled
into the rectory driveway. "She's a terrific cook. Do
you think she'd mind if I asked for some of her
recipes?"

"She'd be flattered," I said as he opened the car
door for me. "I'd like some of her recipes too. I don't
want them to be lost." Patrick was a better cook than
I was, but I was catching up. Food was more interesting when it was shared, and wasn't just to fill my
empty stomach. One of the things I'd most valued
about being home in Maine was being able to eat the
seafood, molasses cookies, and maple-flavored cakes
and pies that I'd loved when I was growing up. In Arizona I'd learn to appreciate southwestern and Mexi-
can specialties, but Maine food tasted like home.

I rang the bell. I had my own key to the rectory,
but Gram was married. I didn't feel comfortable
walking in without warning.

Gram answered, looking happy and a bit dressed
up in a coral sweater and tan slacks. Like me, she
usually wore jeans. "Happy birthday, Angie," she said,
giving me a hug. "You're right on time. And how are
you, Patrick?"

"We've had a lovely day," I told her as we walked
toward her living room. "Patrick sent me roses and
then . . ."

My story was interrupted by a chorus of "SUR-
PRISE!"

How had Gram managed this? Although a glance
at Patrick said maybe he'd been in on the plan. All
the Mainely Needlepointers were there—Captain Ob
and Anna, and Sarah, and Ruth. Dave Percy was
there with Leo, and even Pete Lambert and Ethan
Trask were in the living room. Maybe Dave had invited Dr. Karen Mercer, who waved at me. Nancy and

Gus Gleason were in one corner. I couldn't believe how full the room was. Even Sandra Lewis was there, looking much more pulled together than she'd been yesterday, despite her husband's death. And Ed and Diane Campbell were standing by the fireplace.

I was speechless as they clapped and I looked at the balloons and Happy Birthday sign strung along the top of the front windows.

Tom handed me a glass of champagne, and I realized everyone else already had a drink. "Happy birthday to my special granddaughter," said Tom. "Haven Harbor's lucky to celebrate her birthday, almost a year since she came back to us."

Another cheer, and everyone raised their glasses to me. I was overwhelmed. I didn't drink to myself. I felt like hiding on Gram's or Patrick's shoulder. How had Gram managed this? I hadn't had a hint of what she'd planned. No cars were nearby.

"Wow" was all I said, to general laughter. "Gram, how long have you planned this?"

"A couple of weeks, dear," she said, smiling even more than usual. "And it looks as though we all kept it a real surprise."

"I had no clue," I said, thankful I hadn't tried to talk Gram out of dinner or Patrick out of coming. "But . . . where has everyone parked? Who decorated the house?" The more corners I looked into the more flowers and Happy Birthday signs I saw.

Sarah grinned. "We all parked behind the church. And brought some food to help Charlotte feed such a crowd. Pete and Leo and I came a little early to help decorate and set everything up."

"You've done a fabulous job," I said. "I'm still stunned. What am I supposed to do?"

"First, take a sip of champagne," said Tom, taking

my arm and guiding me over to the couch, where a seat had been left empty. "And then open your birthday gifts. After that we'll have dinner."

"Presents?" I said, sounding foolish to myself. I kept looking around the room.

"On the coffee table," said Tom.

"Ed and Diane Campbell are here?" I whispered to Tom as he led me to my seat.

"Saw him at the Chamber meeting the other night and he wrangled an invitation. Wants you and Patrick on the Chamber with him," Tom whispered quietly. "Something to do with Patrick's mother?"

I nodded. Skye's movie. Ed wanted Patrick and me on the Chamber so we could help plan whatever needed to be done for that movie to be produced in town. He could keep hoping.

I sat down and looked at the pile of boxes wrapped in flowered papers. "I've never had a birthday party like this," I managed to say before my tears started. "Not ever."

"Then it's about time," said Sarah, who was sitting next to me. She handed me a package. "Now, birthday girl, open your presents so we can all see them."

Tom was refilling glasses. Patrick was sitting on the arm of the couch. He reached toward a box on a nearby table and handed me a tissue.

"Blow your nose like a good girl and do as Sarah says." He smiled. "Looks to me as though a lot of people went to some trouble for you."

"Thank you all," I said again, looking around the room. "I'm in shock."

"Open the presents," called Ruth from the chair where she was perched. "This is a birthday party, so there have to be presents!"

And there were. Dave and Leo gave me a lasagna

pan, with his recipe for lasagna. Ruth gave me (what else?) a needlepointed sign that said MAINELY NEEDLE-POINT. ("To hang in your office," she pronounced.) Gram gave me a loose-leaf notebook full of all her recipes I'd loved as a child. "Just what I've been wanting to ask you for," I pronounced. Ed and Diane Campbell gave me a navy sweatshirt with HAVEN HARBOR on the front. Tom's gift was a bottle of champagne. Really good champagne. Sarah's gift was one of those wonderful embroidered pockets I'd seen at her store, framed beautifully. Ruth gave me an on-line certificate for ebooks. ("They don't even have to be mine," she whispered.) Captain Ob and Anna gave me a half-dozen jars of her fruit jams and a gift certificate so Patrick and I could go on one of his deep sea fishing trips. Pete and Ethan gave me a leather mag holder for my Glock that I could wear on a belt. Several people shook their heads at that, but I was thrilled. My law enforcement friends took my gun seriously. Gus and Nancy Gleason gave me a stack of mystery and suspense books that I could hardly wait to examine in detail. Karen Mercer, whom I'd been talking to only that morning, gave me a blue sweater. And somehow Trixi had managed to wrap a framed picture of herself for my desk.

"I'm overwhelmed," I said, probably too many times. "You all know me so well."

I'd hardly noticed that Patrick hadn't given me a wrapped package. After all, he'd given me two dozen roses and a wonderful lunch and day. When he handed me a small box, I could feel my heart palpitating.

The box was too small. I wasn't ready for anything serious. He couldn't be giving me a ring, could he? But there was no way around opening it, as the room became silent. Probably everyone there was thinking the same thing I was.

I unwrapped the box carefully. And slowly. It was the right size for . . . I felt a rush of relief. Earrings! I reached over and kissed Patrick, I was so thrilled and relieved.

"They're tourmalines, the Maine State gem. I chose blue, to match your eyes. I've always thought your eyes were the color of the ocean on a summer's day."

My heart melted. I also noticed the small diamonds above each tourmaline. "They're gorgeous," I said, looking at them, then passing them around so everyone could see. "I never thought I'd own any tourmaline jewelry. I don't know where I'll wear them, they're so spectacular."

"Leave that to me to figure out," he assured me, as Gram called us all to dinner.

It was a buffet and, as Sarah had said, others had helped Gram fill the table. Lobster bisque, as promised. Baked beans—no buffet supper in Maine was complete without homemade baked beans. Chicken, shrimp, a couple of kinds of spaghetti, biscuits, salads . . . I was overwhelmed. Dave and Leo filled a plate for Ruth, and everyone else seemed to be taking a little of everything.

"Gram, thank you," I said, hugging her again. "This is perfect."

"It doesn't make up for all those birthday parties you didn't have when you were little. But I wanted to do something special for you, after all you've done for us in the past year."

I just held her. What I had done for them? Nothing, compared to the life they'd all given me. "One question. Is Sandra still staying here?" I whispered.

"I told her she could, and when she found out

about the party she decided to stay tonight. I think she's a little nervous about going home to that big house alone, without Jim."

Without Jim. The more I thought about it, the more I wondered.

As the birthday girl, I circulated a little, speaking to everyone, thanking them for the wonderful gifts (which they were!) and generally making sure everyone was relaxed. When I got to Ethan, I pulled him aside for a moment. "I think I know what happened to Ike Hamilton," I said. "And to Jim Lewis."

"Angie, I've told you not to play detective. It's dangerous, and it could mess up an official police investigation."

"You've told me. But when you and Pete were accusing Leo, I had to see what I could find out. Do you know what happened?"

He hesitated. "No. Not really. We have some ideas. But nothing specific that we can pin on one person. And what did you mean about Jim Lewis? He died of a heart attack."

"I don't think so. There should be an autopsy."

"I don't suppose you're going to do anything about this here, in the middle of your own birthday party?"

"Wouldn't it be wonderful to solve those crimes tonight?"

Ethan sighed. "Your ideas always make me nervous, Angie. But I'll admit they usually work. What do you plan to do?"

"I'm going to get some more lobster bisque before it's all gone," I said. "And then I'm going to talk about Ike Hamilton. Hang in with me, please. If my plan doesn't work, then nothing lost."

"You're a real pain sometimes, Angie. But—all right.

Just don't go accusing someone who isn't guilty. I don't want to deal with that."

"Trust me," I promised him.

"I want to. Believe me," said Ethan, running his hand through his thinning hair. "Go get your lobster bisque. I'm not going anywhere."

Gram's lobster bisque was delicious, as always. I didn't take any more food; I was still full from Patrick's and my lunch, and I was beginning to get nervous. I hadn't planned to accuse a killer tonight.

I stopped Dave on his way to the bathroom. "Did you figure it out? The poison, I mean?"

He nodded. "I was pretty sure, but this afternoon I confirmed it. Of course, we don't have autopsy results to confirm it."

"Mind if I guess? I've learned so much from you about poisons."

I told him what I'd thought, and he grinned. "My partner in crime. You came to the same conclusion I did. Promise you won't do anything about it until I get back."

I didn't do anything until after we'd each had a slice of Gram's white and yellow daffodil cake and ice cream, and I'd blushed and laughed and then applauded as everyone sang "Happy Birthday" to me, dramatically off-key. This was not the church choir, and even the choir didn't hit every note.

But the sentiment was touching.

I looked around the room at the people who'd filled my life in the past year. Wonderful people. And . . . a murderer.

"I want to thank you all for coming. Gram, and every one of you, was amazing. I had no idea. Not a clue!"

Smiles and nods throughout the room.

"And, as most of you know, clues have been something I've focused on during the past week. To be exact, since Ike Hamilton's death last Sunday morning."

Despite the libations that had been consumed, the room was suddenly silent.

"Last week I met Leo Blackwell." I pointed to him. "And Dave Percy and I knew we had to find out what had happened to Ike, and prove Leo had nothing to do with it."

A few murmurs in the room.

"And then, suddenly, yesterday, Jim Lewis died. Ike died in his home, his garage. Jim died in the emergency room of Haven Harbor Hospital, despite the efforts of Nancy Gleason and Karen Mercer, both of whom are here tonight, as is Jim's wife, Sandra. Before Jim died, he told Nancy the name of his killer and said that person had also killed Ike."

Several people looked at each other uncomfortably. Word hadn't spread about Jim's last words.

"Ike and Jim had been friends for years. They'd played together as children, and despite their differences and the separate challenges they faced, they'd confided in each other as adults. In the past few years both Ike and Jim had been bullied and abused. Neither of them talked about it, although Ike talked about pretty much everything else that happened in Haven Harbor. Two years ago Jim stopped talking. He sat at his kitchen window, watching the birds. And watching the door to Ike's garage. And sometimes Ike would visit, and Jim would talk with him."

Several people in the room looked surprised. Several others looked uncomfortable.

"Ike had had enough. He told Jim he was going to report the person abusing them. Jim wasn't sure that was the right thing to do. He was afraid. He'd been hurt too often in the past. But Ike was determined. Ike saw the world in black and white. He didn't believe anyone should hurt anyone else."

I turned to Sandra. "Sandra, for years you took care of Jim. He had multiple sclerosis. But over the years he also had bruises from falls, and broken bones, and his arms were burned. As his disease progressed he was clumsier, and you told the doctors and nurses"—I nodded at Karen Mercer—"that Jim tried to do things he was no longer capable of doing. He slipped and fell when he tried to walk. He burned himself when he tried to cook. He lost his balance on the stairs, and fell. But through all of that, you took care of him. You seldom left him alone, unless he was sleeping, or unless his friend Ike was visiting. Ike was harmless, you thought. Ike was confused. Ike was a bit simpleminded. Ike didn't understand. He just told Jim stories about what was happening in Haven Harbor. But about six weeks ago you overheard Ike telling Jim about the person who was abusing him. Saying that he was going to tell the doctors, tell the police. Tell anyone who would listen. And you saw Jim nod his head in agreement."

Sandra stood up. "You're making all this up. I won't stand for it. I spent most of my life caring for the man I loved. I won't have you accusing me of anything else!"

"Then why, six weeks ago, did you take your spade and go to work in your beautiful garden? You waited for Ike to come home, and then you followed him and told him not to talk to the doctors or police. You threatened to tell Ed Campbell that he was a liar. You knew Ike was afraid of Ed because of the Chamber of Commerce's efforts to relocate him. When Ike stood up to you, why did you hit that man's back with your spade, over and over? Six weeks later, when he died, his back was still bruised."

"You have no proof. You're defaming me in front of half the town," Sandra said, bursting into tears. "My dear husband died yesterday, and now you're telling lies about me."

"What you didn't know was that Ike hadn't changed his mind. After you beat him he was even more determined to free himself, and his friend Jim, from your abuse. He told Leo, the young man he'd offered shelter to. And he came, more often than before, to talk to Jim. You didn't know what he was saying. You didn't trust him. You were afraid of what Ike might do or say, Sandra, because he wasn't afraid of you, the way Jim was. Jim depended on you to take care of him. He knew if he told anyone how his bones had been broken and he'd been bruised and burned, people might not believe him. After all, what loving wife would hurt her disabled husband? But Ike told Jim he was going to tell Leo. Leo had seen the bruises and knew how much Ike's back still hurt. And you couldn't allow that to happen, could you, Sandra? You wanted everyone in town to feel sorry for you, the poor wife who had to take care of her husband, the martyred woman who couldn't go shopping and lunching with other women. So last Sunday morning you took Jim to church, and then, on your way home, you stopped at Ike's garage. You wanted Jim to know what you were doing.

"You picked up a bottle from the ones Ike and Leo had collected the day before and you hit your husband's friend. You hit him so hard the bottle shattered. And then you picked up another one. Ike hardly resisted. He didn't want to hurt a woman. But his taking your abuse made you even angrier. You grabbed a knife from Ike's shelf of kitchen supplies, and you stabbed him and left him on the garage floor. Then you wheeled your husband home, letting him see that you were covered with Ike's blood.

"And Jim started talking. He told you he'd had enough, that he didn't care what happened to him, he just didn't want to be with you anymore. And you couldn't take that, could you? And the solution was right there, in that beautiful garden you take such good care of."

Sandra paled. "How did you know?"

"Because Dave Percy knows poisonous plants, and he's taught Dr. Mercer, and she and Nancy Gleason didn't think Jim's heart attack was like others they'd seen. Every morning you made tea for Jim, didn't you, Sandra? Only yesterday the water you made the tea with was water from the small vase where you'd put a few lilies of the valley the day before. And lilies of the valley are one of the most poisonous plants. You killed your husband, Sandra, because he was going to tell people what you'd been doing to him for years and what you'd done to his friend Ike."

Ethan and Pete glanced at each other and moved toward Sandra, who'd moved closer to the front door as I'd talked.

"You have no idea, any of you. You don't know what it's like to take care of someone for years. Take care of someone you don't even love. Waste all your good years pretending to be servile and sweet, when all you wanted to do was run, screaming, to anywhere else on earth! I didn't plan to hurt Jim, but he made it so easy. He took it. He didn't tell anyone. And then he even stopped talking! Can you imagine living with someone who never makes a sound? And then, to find out he could talk. He was talking to that idiot friend of his, who collected bottles for a living and lived in a drafty old garage. I couldn't take it any longer. I couldn't take either of them!"

Sandra burst into tears again as Pete and Ethan gently moved her out of the room and out the front door.

The room remained silent.

Ike Hamilton's killer had been found. Jim Lewis had finally, in his last moments, found the strength to tell someone what had happened.

To tell a nurse, Nancy Gleason, who'd believed him.

Chapter Forty-three

The Tear of Sympathy:
No radiant pearl which crested fortune wears
No gem that sparkling hangs from beauties ear
Nor the bright stars which nights blue arch adorn
Nor rising sun that gild the vernal morn
Shines with such lustre as the tear that breaks
For others woe down virtues lovely cheeks.
> —"Respectfully presented to Anthony and Elizabeth Miskey by their affectionate daughter Elizabeth Miskey done in her 12th year, Philadelphia, April 26th, 1822." Elizabeth Miskey (1811–1832) had two children before her death at the age of twenty-two. Her silk and wool sampler on linen was decorated with grapes, flowers, and a floral border.

The opening at Patrick's art gallery the following week went wonderfully. Half the town, it seemed, came, drank wine, ate cheeses and cocktail sandwiches, and exclaimed over the way he'd arranged the gallery. Two of them even bought small prints. They weren't major purchases, but they were a beginning.

I wore the new blue sweater Karen Mercer had given me for my birthday, and my new earrings. I felt elegant and competent.

"I love having all these people here, but I suspect most of them are here to gossip about what happened last week. After Jim's autopsy results came back confirming he'd been poisoned by the lilies of the valley his wife grew, and that Sandra had been abusing him for years, tongues haven't stopped wagging," Patrick pointed out.

"Domestic violence isn't just a problem for women," confirmed Nancy Gleason, who'd joined us. "You'd be surprised what we see in the emergency room. Women who're being abused are often scared to tell anyone. Abused men are too proud to admit that their wife or mother is hurting them. Maybe admitting they're being abused threatens their manhood. And if an abuser isn't stopped, the abuse gets worse."

"Last week was horrible," I agreed. "Too many secrets, too much pain. But one good thing came out of it." I nodded across the room to where Leo and Dave were standing together in front of a painting of a nude. "Leo has found a home and a mentor, and Dave seems thrilled to have someone depending on him."

"Everyone needs to be needed," Gram added, joining us. "Taking care of you all those years kept me going after my husband died and my daughter disappeared. I couldn't fall apart, because you depended on me."

"I'd never thought of it that way," I admitted. "We all try to be strong. But it does feel good to be needed."

"I suspect Sandra Lewis felt that way. She wanted so much to be needed that she made the man who was already dependent on her even more dependent. She needed to be needed to value herself. And she wanted other people to recognize what appeared to be her sacrifices, and tell her what a wonderful woman she was."

I shuddered. "You make it sound like an addiction."

"It was, in many ways," Nancy said.

"Does that mean depending on someone, and having them depend on you, is an addiction?" Patrick asked, putting his arm around me.

"It could be," Nancy added. "Of course, it also could be love."

Patrick bent down and kissed my forehead. "I'll accept that interpretation."

Please turn the page
to enjoy recipes!

DAVE'S LASAGNA

For the Sauce

1 pound Italian sweet sausage
1 Tablespoon olive oil
1 large yellow onion, diced
¾ Tablespoon salt
½ teaspoon pepper
6 cloves minced garlic
2 Tablespoons tomato paste
2 (28-ounce) cans Italian whole tomatoes (if possible, San Marzano)
2 teaspoons dried oregano
½ Tablespoon red pepper flakes

For the Lasagna

2 (10-ounce) packages frozen spinach
1 pound mozzarella cheese
2 large eggs
30 ounces ricotta cheese
1 cup fresh basil leaves, packed
½ cup fresh parsley leaves, packed
1 cup grated Parmesan cheese
1 box "no boil" lasagna noodles (9 ounces—rectangular pasta)

To make the sauce, remove the sausage from its casing, cut into small pieces, and brown in a skillet; drain. Put the sausage pieces and other sauce ingredients in a large pan, bring to a boil, and simmer for about an hour, stirring frequently. Taste, and add more salt or pepper if needed.

While the sauce is cooking:

Preheat the oven to 375°F.

Defrost the spinach (in a microwave, if necessary) and squeeze out the water with paper towels. Set aside.

Lightly oil a lasagna pan (about 13 × 9 inches).

Grate the mozzarella cheese and set aside.

Beat the eggs in a large bowl and then add the ricotta cheese, basil and parsley snipped into small pieces, and Parmesan.

Put a light layer of sauce in the lasagna pan. Cover with a layer of noodles, then a layer of the ricotta mixture, a layer of spinach, and a layer of mozzarella. Repeat (probably three times), ending with a sauce layer. Sprinkle any remaining mozzarella on top.

Bake in the oven until bubbling, about 45 to 50 minutes.

Dave prefers his lasagna the second day, so he makes and bakes it one day, and the next day he reheats it for about 30 minutes just before serving.

Serves 10 to 12

ANGIE'S BIRTHDAY DAFFODIL CAKE

For the Cake

1 cup egg whites (6 or 7 eggs)
1 teaspoon salt
1 teaspoon cream of tartar
1 cup plus 2 Tablespoons sugar
6 or 7 egg yolks, beaten
⅔ cup plus ½ cup flour
1 teaspoon orange extract
1 drop yellow food coloring
½ teaspoon vanilla extract

    Angel cake pan or Bundt pan

For the Frosting

½ cup softened butter
4 cups confectioners' sugar
1 teaspoon vanilla extract
½ to 1 cup heavy cream
Yellow food coloring, if desired

For the cake, beat the egg whites until foamy. Add the salt and cream of tartar and beat until stiff but not dry. Fold in the sugar carefully.

Divide the mixture in half and place in separate bowls. To one half, fold in the egg yolks, ⅔ cup flour, orange extract, and yellow food coloring. To the other half, fold in the ½ cup flour and the vanilla extract.

Place the cake mixtures in the ungreased pan by spoonfuls, alternating yellow and white batter.

Bake 60 minutes in a slow oven (325°F).

Remove the pan and invert it until cool.

The cake may be served as it is, or perhaps with ice cream or frosted.

For the frosting, combine the softened butter, confectioners' sugar, and vanilla extract, and cream well. Then add heavy cream until a preferred consistency is reached. If desired, add yellow food coloring. Frost the top of the cake, letting the frosting drip down the sides.

Serves 8-10

KINDRED SPIRITS CHEESE FONDUE

This fondue may be served as a main course (the way Patrick and Angie ordered it) or as an appetizer. As a main course, this serves two people. It may be doubled.

Ingredients

2 baguettes, or Italian bread
1 Tablespoon cornstarch
3 to 4 Tablespoons kirsch (Swiss cherry brandy)
1 clove peeled fresh garlic
1 plus ½ cup dry white wine (e.g., Chablis) (also have extra wine to serve with recipe, and to add if fondue thickens)
1 Tablespoon lemon juice
½ pound freshly shredded Switzerland Swiss cheese
½ pound freshly shredded Gruyère cheese
Pepper

1 fondue pot, preferably ceramic, and as many fondue forks as those dining

Cut the bread into 1-inch cubes with crust on one side. In a small bowl, mix the cornstarch with the kirsch and stir. Put aside.

Cut the garlic clove in half and rub both a cooking pan and the fondue pot with the inside of the clove. Add the wine to the pan and heat. When the wine is hot but not boiling, add the lemon juice. Add the shredded cheese by handfuls, stirring constantly with a wooden spoon or fork until the cheese is melted and blended. Bring the fondue mixture to bubbling, briefly. Add pepper to taste, stirring until well blended. Add the cornstarch mixture to the fondue and allow this to boil for another 15 to 30 seconds.

Pour the mixture into the fondue pot and keep it warm with a votive candle. Spear the bread cubes through the soft side of the bread and into the crust, then dunk and swirl in the fondue. Stir the fondue frequently. If it starts to thicken too much, add additional wine as needed and to taste.

Serve with a dry white wine—preferably the wine used in the recipe.

Leftover cheese fondue may be melted and served on toast.

Acknowledgments

With great thanks to my agent, John Talbot; my editor, John Scognamiglio; and to Claire Hill, my publicist at Kensington, who makes sure people know about my books.

To my "kitchen cabinet" (or, more correctly, "writing cabinet"), the Maine Crime Writers (www.Maine crimewriters.com), especially Barbara Ross, Kate Flora, and Kathy Lynn Emerson (aka Kaitlyn Dunnett), who've listened to my questions and frustrations too often and always provided inspiration, hope, and support.

To Nancy Cantwell, sister extraordinaire, who is fighting her own health battles but is still my first reader, along with Dee Berger, who kindly volunteered for the job this time around.

To my neighbors, Barbara and JD Neeson, who were always there when Bob or I needed help—and who understood when I had to hang out in my study instead of enjoying salt air (and a glass of wine or beer) with them. JD, you even supplied the beer!

To all the adoptive and foster single parents, men and women, who chose to reach out to an older child or teenager with a helping hand that wouldn't be withdrawn when the child was eighteen.

To Henry Lyons, who nagged me just often enough and kept my website up-to-date.

To the independent booksellers, librarians, and needlecraft shops who recommend my books; and to the readers who have made regular visits to Haven Harbor. To the museums who value and display the needlework of earlier generations, encouraging and inspiring crafters of today. Without all of you, there would be no books.

Please, if you've enjoyed *Thread on Arrival*, write a brief review on an online site, "like" my Lea Wait/ Cornelia Kidd page on Facebook, write to me at leawait@roadrunner.com to be on my mailing list, and check out my website, www.leawait.com, for prequels and news about my books and appearances.

And remember. Shared stories make our world smaller . . . and life is the real mystery!

Books by Lea Wait

Mainely Needlepoint Series:
1—*Twisted Threads*
2—*Threads of Evidence*
3—*Thread and Gone*
4—*Dangling by a Thread*
5—*Tightening the Threads*
6—*Thread the Halls*
7—*Thread Herrings*
8—*Thread on Arrival*

Shadows Antique Print Mystery Series:
1—*Shadows at the Fair*
2—*Shadows on the Coast of Maine*
3—*Shadows on the Ivy*
4—*Shadows at the Spring Show*
5—*Shadows of a Down East Summer*
6—*Shadows on a Cape Cod Wedding*
7—*Shadows on a Maine Christmas*
8—*Shadows on a Morning in Maine*

Maine Murder Series (written as Cornelia Kidd):
Death and a Pot of Chowder

Books for Young People:
Stopping to Home
Seaward Born
Wintering Well
Finest Kind
Uncertain Glory
Pizza to Die For
For Freedom Alone
Contrary Winds

Nonfiction:
Living and Writing on the Coast of Maine

Connect with Us

Visit us online at
KensingtonBooks.com
to read more from your favorite authors, see books
by series, view reading group guides, and more.

Join us on social media

for sneak peeks, chances to win books and prize packs,
and to share your thoughts with other readers.

facebook.com/kensingtonpublishing
twitter.com/kensingtonbooks

Tell us what you think!

To share your thoughts, submit a review,
or sign up for our eNewsletters, please visit:
KensingtonBooks.com/TellUs.

Grab These Cozy Mysteries
from
Kensington Books